PRAISE FOR MICHELLE MC

'A gripping whodunnit and an engaging, emotional read ...
I can't wait to read more from this author!'
Jeanine Cummins, author of *American Dirt*

'McDonagh skilfully weaves a web of intrigue. This
perfectly paced slice of rural noir is extremely addictive'
Business Post

'Smart, compelling, and nothing if not topical and timely'
Sunday Independent

'I flew through it. A page turner with a scenario at
its core which feels terrifyingly possible'
Andrea Carter

'A compelling page-turner with well-drawn characters who
have secrets to keep. It will keep you guessing till the end'
Sheila O'Flanagan

'Cleverly plotted and unpredictable with a fantastic
cast of characters'
Rachael English

'A superbly crafted mystery, an original tale highlighting
the volatility of family relationships and the invisible
ties that hold them together'
Swirl and Thread

'Pacy and highly enjoyable ... with a very sharp edge'
Woman's Way

Michelle McDonagh is an Irish journalist with over twenty-five years' experience, including twelve years as a staff reporter at the *Connacht Tribune*. She now works freelance, writing features and health pieces for numerous Irish papers, including *The Irish Times*.

She is married with three children and lives in Cork.

She is the author of two novels: *There's Something I Have to Tell You* and *Somebody Knows*.

MICHELLE MCDONAGH

SOMEBODY KNOWS

HACHETTE
BOOKS
IRELAND

First published in Ireland in 2024 by Hachette Books Ireland

1

Cataloguing in Publication Data is available from the British Library

Trade paperback ISBN 9781399716482
Ebook ISBN 9781399716499

Typeset in Cambria by Bookends Publishing Services, Dublin

Printed and bound in Great Britain by Clays Ltd, Elcograf S.p.A.

Excerpt from 'The Statue of the Virgin at Granard Speaks'
by Paula Meehan from *As If By Magic: Selected Poems* (Dedalus
Press, 2020) is reproduced by kind permission of the publisher.

Hachette Books Ireland policy is to use papers that are natural, renewable and
recyclable products and made from wood grown in sustainable forests. The logging
and manufacturing processes are expected to conform to the environmental
regulations of the country of origin.

Hachette Books Ireland
8 Castlecourt Centre
Castleknock
Dublin 15, Ireland

A division of Hachette UK Ltd
Carmelite House, 50 Victoria Embankment, London EC4Y 0DZ

www.hachettebooksireland.ie

For my father, Seamus

I did not move,
I didn't lift a finger to help her,
I didn't intercede with heaven,
nor whisper the charmed word in God's ear.

From 'The Statue of the Virgin at Granard Speaks'
by Paula Meehan

Gardaí 'extremely concerned' for safety of missing Galway woman Lucia Casey (22) last seen leaving Galway Regional Hospital on Sunday

Irish Independent
Tuesday, 10 December 1990

Gardaí are appealing to the public for help in tracing the whereabouts of 22-year-old Lucia Casey, who has been missing from Galway city since Sunday.

Lucia was last seen leaving Galway Regional Hospital at Newcastle Road, where she works as a nurse's aide, after her shift finished on Sunday at around 4.30 p.m.

The missing woman is described as 5'2" in height with a slight build, mousy-brown hair and blue eyes. She was wearing a brown suede jacket, stonewashed denim jeans and black ankle boots.

Gardaí and her family are extremely concerned for her safety. Anyone with information is asked to contact Galway garda station, any garda station or the Garda Confidential line.

PROLOGUE

1992
Toombeola, Connemara

It was the bike that caught his eye first, the rusted frame of an old Raleigh Chopper, just like the one that had stood propped against the side of the house at home for years. When he came across it, he had been cursing Máirtín Ó Conghaile under his breath for naming him in his will, leaving him a hopper of turf that Josie had been foolish enough to go footing himself on such a hot, dry day.

There had been no need at all for the old man to do that – sure Josie had only done what any good neighbour would do. Giving Máirtín the odd lift into town after he was put off the road that time, dropping in a bottle of whiskey and a tin of sweets at Christmas, letting Nuala use the phone to ring her sister in Dublin on a Sunday night before they got their own line in. And, of course, helping Tadhg out of that spot of bother he'd got himself into last year, that unfortunate business in the public toilets in Clifden. All Josie had done was throw a quick word into the ear of his cousin Seamus, the sergeant-in-charge in town that night, explaining that Tadhg wasn't the full bob, that there was a bit of a want in the lad, but no badness. Tadhg

3

had been given a stiff talking-to (yes, himself and Seamus had chuckled over that), and had kept his nose and everything else clean since.

He shouldn't have been cursing Máirtín. 'Twasn't the dead man's fault that Josie had been too impatient to wait for his own lads to come out and give him a hand. Or that his back was now half broke after hours of cutting turf with an old *sleán* he had borrowed. He had driven the narrow spade with its right-angled wing into the peat over and over and over, carving out the wet, heavy bricks before flinging them to his right to land on the bog. Then he stood the sods upright, five or six of them, leaning against each other wet side out, the way his grandfather had taught him, for the sun and wind to dry. Bending and straightening, bending and straightening. The tight, burning band that marched across his lower back a warning that he'd be in trouble tomorrow.

It was sweltering now. His throat was dry as a cat's tongue, and there wasn't a drop left in the two-litre bottle of water he had brought with him. The cloudless sky looked as if it had been coloured in by a child, the bluest of blues with a bright yellow ball of a sun. A day for the beach for sure. He could feel his face burning. Could picture the *told you so* look on Bernie's face when he arrived in home this evening. The only time in his life he had ever used sun cream was when they had gone to Tenerife on their honeymoon. He had still been on his best behaviour then. The heat of that place had nearly killed him altogether. Thank God he had taken her advice on the cap today at least, his bald patch protected from the sun's beating rays.

As the sweat beaded on his forehead and above his top lip, the idea of the roaring peat fire that would be the payoff for all his hard labour, come the winter, wasn't one bit appealing. Another twenty minutes, he promised himself, and he'd head across to Tigh Nora's for a nice cold pint of Special to quench his thirst. Smithwick's, with a creamy Guinness head. His mouth couldn't even muster enough saliva to water at the thought of it.

It took him a minute or so to realise what he was looking at: that the pile of manky old rags lying in the boghole under the rusted bike frame wasn't just a pile of manky old rags. He stood there like a gombeen, staring into the ditch, scratching his chin with his peat-encrusted fingernails, thinking that surely his eyes must be playing tricks on him. That he wasn't seeing what he thought he was seeing. In what was basically a giant sponge in the arsehole of nowhere where he wouldn't be standing right now if it wasn't for Tadhg Ó Conghaile pulling his mickey out in public and his father remembering Josie in his will.

Had it not been for this series of events, the body could have lain there for decades, for ever maybe, without detection.

1

It all started the day before her mother died. Well, it started long before that, of course, but she had been totally in the dark until then.

The country was basking in a heatwave that broke Irish temperature records. The weather was all anybody could talk about, the national obsession having gone into overdrive. Met Éireann had issued a status yellow high temperature warning and the country was split firmly into two camps: those mopping their brows and exclaiming, 'I can't stick this feckin' heat,' and those descending en masse on the beaches along the coast.

Cara loved the heat, and God knew they saw little enough of it in this part of the world, but it felt wrong for the sun to be blazing outside when her mother was inside, dying in a darkened room.

She had been glad to get out of her car and into the relative coolness of the hospice after her drive from the far side of the city, stuck in traffic most of the way. The only time Cara had ever set foot in the place before was about seven years ago when she had been sent out to cover the opening of a new extension, never imagining for one moment that her own mother would end up living out the last days of her life there.

It wasn't as depressing a place as one might imagine, given all the dying that went on within its walls, its ethos being to help people to die well. To deliver them out of this world as peacefully as possible. Like a reverse labour ward, if you thought about it. For her mother, like many of the other patients, cancer had brought her here.

The vast dormer bungalow was sunny and welcoming, its walls hung with paintings by local artists. There was a play room for children and a little chapel where patients and family members could go to say a prayer or weep in private.

Cara wandered down the hall towards her mother's room, nodding as she passed the wife of a man dying two doors down. Only in his late thirties with two small children, Dad had told her. Life could be so bloody cruel.

Her mother's name was on her door: Katherine Joyce. Nobody called her Katherine, though. She was Kitty. Their favourite nurse, Mary C, was just coming out of her room.

'She's not in great humour today,' she said. 'Didn't have a great night. She's dozing now.'

'Thanks, Mary. Is Dad in with her?'

'I think he's gone to light a candle, love. He's not far anyway. Helena was here again – she's not long gone.'

Aunty Helena, her mother's younger sister, had been as devastated as they were by the diagnosis.

Cara stuck her head around the door of the room.

Christ.

You'd think she'd be used to it by now, but no. It was so hard to comprehend that her poor mother, who seemed to have spent most of her life on a diet, had somehow shrivelled into this tiny, gaunt figure propped up against her pillows, like a child in the bed.

Cara decided to leave her to sleep and see where her father had got to.

As she turned down the corridor towards the chapel, the sweet smell of melting wax drifted towards her. She heard her father's voice, low and urgent coming from inside, the door left ajar to allow air in. She was about to enter when she heard a second voice, hushed too. Aunty Helena.

She would never know what made her stop in her tracks at that moment, to step away from the door and linger outside. A feeling that she was intruding on something, perhaps. She hovered outside for a few seconds, debating whether to go in or turn back to her mother's room. She would curse herself afterwards for not walking away. For moving closer to the door instead.

'Sure she's off her head on drugs, Helena. She doesn't mean it. Not really.' Her father sounded upset.

'I know, I know. She worked herself up into a right state, though. Going on about Lucia and wondering did ye do the right thing. Whether ye should have told her.'

'God Almighty. I hope she doesn't say anything like that in front of Cara.'

'That's why I wanted to say it to you, Billy. To warn you, just in case.'

Cara backed away from the door, and went up the corridor.

Who was Lucia?

And what did her mother think they should have told whom?

2

Paul was sitting at her mother's bedside when she got back to the room.

'How'ya? I just went home for a shower and a change of clothes,' he said, a false brightness in his tone. 'Everything OK?'

'Grand, yeah.' As grand as she could be when her mother was hours away from death. Two days at most, according to Dr Jennings, the palliative-care consultant. 'I just needed a bit of fresh air. She was asleep a few minutes ago when I looked in.'

'Where's the aul' man?' Her brother looked behind her. 'Ah, speak of an ass. How'ya, Dad? Lighting more candles? You'll be broke.'

Her father gave a pinched smile. Their mother had been a lifelong believer in the power of a lit candle and a prayer to good old St Jude. The shock of being given only months to live had knocked her mother's faith, though, a cause too hopeless even for the patron saint of lost causes. So her father, who used to roll his eyes at his wife's perpetual candle-lighting, had taken over and was now the one imploring St Jude, and anybody else who might be listening, to intercede on her behalf. Not to cure her, that would have taken nothing short of a miracle, but to give her as good a death as possible under the circumstances.

He looked drained. The weeks of driving back and forth through traffic from the far side of town to watch the woman he had spent the best part of his life with waste away in front of him were taking their toll.

'Why don't you go out for some fresh air, Dad? Take a break for a while. Or go home and have a shower. I'll stay with Mum,' Paul said.

'No, I'm fine. I went out earlier while Helena sat with her. She's just after heading off there. I'm happier staying here.'

He didn't have to spell it out. Mum didn't have long left and he didn't want to miss a single precious second. He was trying to hold it together for her mother, for all of them, but his eyes betrayed him. Dulled by the pain of nursing his wife of over 50 years through terminal cancer. Only five months since her secondary diagnosis, the dire prognosis, so little time to get their heads around it before she got sick.

Maisie had been only a few months old when her granny Kitty had initially been diagnosed. Ironically, Cara had been waiting for the right time to tell them she had decided to search for her birth-mother, but that had been pushed into the background by her mother's illness. Breast cancer. The surgery and chemo had been a success and she was put on Tamoxifen to prevent a recurrence of her disease. The oncologist had outlined the risks involved, the increased risk of endometrial cancer, but recommended that she take it.

They had no way of knowing whether the drug had caused the secondary tumours in Kitty's womb two and a half years after her primary diagnosis or if that would have happened anyway. What they were told, though, was that it was an aggressive cancer of the womb lining, and that even after an emergency hysterectomy, she had only months to live. Too late for treatment.

Cara would never forget the shock of that news, herself, her father and Paul sitting in the consultant's office staring blankly at him. He had been wearing a navy polka dot tie and the spots had begun to jump around in front of her eyes.

Her mother had still looked perfectly healthy, her only complaints a bloated belly and some slight spotting that she hadn't mentioned to anyone. She had never smoked, and two half-pints of Guinness was a bender for her. Cancer was a lottery, though. You could have every risk factor on the list and swerve it or not a single one and succumb to it after a short battle.

She had harboured a secret hope that her mother would be one of those miracle stories you heard of, one of those people given six months to live and still walking around hale and hearty twenty years later. Sadly it wasn't to be.

The symptoms had hit her thick and fast. Nausea, exhaustion and pain. As if the disease had been waiting for the diagnosis to be confirmed before it attacked in full force, running rampant through her body. The weight slid from her bones as if she had undergone some drastic form of liposuction. In just a few months, she went from a healthy-ish seventy-four-year-old carrying an excess stone or so to the skeletal figure in the bed before them who looked years older. The worst part was watching her try to hide her suffering as the tumours grew and spread, pressing on the nerves in her abdomen.

Despite her pain, her mum always managed to muster up a big smile for Cara, still the same, just set now in a different face.

Until today. There was no smile for her today. Instead, her mother's eyes, clouded by sickness and opioids, welled up as Cara moved towards her bed. She hadn't slept for long.

'Hi, Mum.' She bent down and brushed a light kiss off her frail forehead.

To her dismay, her mother's eyes overflowed. Cara's nose tingled, her own tears threatening. She swallowed hard.

'It's OK, Mum, you're OK,' she soothed, wiping the warm tears from her mother's cheeks with her thumbs. As she would for Maisie. Of course Mum wasn't OK. She never would be again.

Fucking cancer!

But what else could she say?

It's shite, Mum, absolutely shite, and we're all in bits, trying to hold it together in front of you.

Her mother let out an agonised moan and thrashed beneath her covers, trying to kick them off, to get out of the bed, but she was thwarted in her efforts by the safety rails on either side.

She grabbed Cara's hand, her grip still surprisingly strong.

'Stop now, Kitty love, you'll hurt yourself.' Her father put a gentle hand on her mother's shoulder.

'The baby! Where is she?' Her mother tightened her grip on Cara's hand, pinching her skin. 'Help me, Billy. Oh, God Almighty, she's going to take her.'

She was thrashing harder now, banging against the railing. Her eyes were wide with fear.

'Relax, Mum. It's just Cara.' Paul stood beside her father on the far side of the bed. 'Maybe we should give one of the nurses a shout,' he murmured. 'Where's the bell yoke?'

Jesus, this was horrific. Every time they thought things couldn't get any worse, they did. Seeing her mother so agitated, so frightened, was even worse than seeing her in physical pain. It was so fucking unfair. She didn't deserve any of this.

As Cara rooted around under the bed covers looking for the call bell, her mother shot straight up in the bed, as if she had been electrocuted, and leaned over the safety rail towards her, still clinging to her hand.

Oh God! She was going to fall out if she leaned any further.

'No, NOOO, stop her, she's trying to take the child. Oh, Lord, help us, please. Somebody do something ...'

Cara's fingers finally made contact with the bell, but her mother's wailing had already summoned Mary to the room.

'Now Kitty, my love, what's all the commotion about, hmm? You're making an awful racket altogether.'

The nurse plumped up the pillows behind her, and guided her gently against them. Cara envied her calm, comforting composure. It was as if not even an earthquake would rock her. Her mother dropped Cara's hand, and grabbed for Mary instead. Then she let out another distressed moan, more of a whimper now, and her hand fell heavily onto the covers as if somebody had unplugged her.

She continued to mutter strings of gibberish that made no sense, as Mary tidied the covers around her, tucking her in neatly.

'You're alright, Kitty my love. I'll give you something to help relax you a bit now, OK?'

Cara had to leave the room, to get away from her poor mother, who was still moaning quietly and plucking at the bed covers with her skinny fingers. She stood outside in the corridor wanting to run as far away from this hell as she could but not wanting to leave her mother at the same time. Terrified that Mum would die if she left, of not being with her at the end. She wanted the nightmare to be over, but the only way it could happen was for her mother's life to be over, and she couldn't face that either.

Her bowel contorted in a painful spasm. The stress of her mother's illness was playing havoc with her IBS, causing the nerves along the wall of her gastrointestinal tract to become hyper-sensitised to normal gut movements. Like a smoke alarm shrieking furiously when there was no fire.

It was torture having to watch her mum, who had been good and kind her whole life, end it this way. Cara had never been in any doubt that her parents had adored her, had never felt any less loved than Paul. More, if anything – she had been so spoiled by them all.

And there was surely never a prouder grandmother than Kitty Joyce. Parading Maisie down the Prom, like a chubby little empress, in her pram, stopping every two minutes to talk to somebody she knew, any opportunity to show off her grandchild. How could it be fair that she was spending the last days of her life like this?

She felt a hand touch her shoulder. Mary C.

'She's grand now, love. She'll sleep for a while. Why don't you go and sit somewhere quiet for a bit?'

She didn't know how Mary and her colleagues did this job

day in, day out, managing to keep so positive and upbeat in front of the patients and their families.

'I'm fine, Mary. I'll go back in a minute.'

Her father emerged from the room, Paul close on his heels. Paul had been eighteen when Kitty and Billy adopted Cara, but despite the age difference they had always been close. The four of them had. Things would never be the same again after her mother, the heart of the family, was gone.

Paul looked shook. He had stayed there last night with her father and was insisting on staying again tonight with Cara. She had tried to talk him into going home and getting a proper night's sleep, but he wouldn't entertain the idea. He, too, would never forgive himself if he wasn't there when his mother took her last breath.

'She's settled again now, thank God,' her father said.

'Why was she so upset? What was she on about? A baby being taken? Do you think she was talking about Maisie?'

Cara had been plagued with dreams of harming or losing her baby in the first year after her birth. Of going to take the baby seat out of the car only to find it empty. Or looking into the pram to see a stranger's child looking up at her. Of dropping her on her head so that it smashed into smithereens, like a piece of fine bone china. She knew they were pure anxiety dreams, that she wasn't the first new mother to have them, but that didn't make it any easier when she woke at night, heart pounding, unable to get back to sleep until she had checked that her baby was still breathing.

'That's only the medication talking, love. It's no wonder her poor brain is mithered, the amount of stuff she's on.'

'Dad's right, Car. It's probably the morphine,' Paul said. 'Making her see things that aren't there.'

There was every possibility they were right, of course. That the opioids were causing her mother to act so strangely. Or perhaps it was a sign that the disease had spread to her brain. Still, Cara was left feeling distinctly unsettled by the whole thing.

And rightly so as it turned out.

3

Her mother died the following evening at twenty-four minutes to eight. They were all gathered around her bedside, aware that death was imminent. She had fallen asleep the night before around eleven and hadn't regained consciousness. Her breathing had changed, grown so shallow it had been barely perceptible and then she had taken one deep gurgling breath in.

There was no breath out.

'I think she's gone,' her father said.

'No,' Mary C said softly. 'I think she has one more breath left.'

And, incredibly, she was right.

Her mother took one last gasp and that really was it. They stood staring at her, waiting for another breath, but there were no more. The palliative nurse, with her years of experience of guiding patients out of this world, had been able to gauge it right down to a last single breath.

She was gone.

4

The conversation she had overheard between her father and Helena had been flickering in the back of her mind, but she had been too caught up in the flurry of the funeral arrangements to give it attention. The church in Salthill was packed, the crowd spilling outside as neighbours, friends, her father's former pupils and their parents – some of whom were also former pupils – turned out in their droves to pay their respects.

It was a cruel day for a burial. A band of low pressure had pushed in, bringing with it thunderstorms and heavy showers. As they stood at Kitty's graveside in Rahoon, biblical sheets of rain bucketed from the heavens, drowning the mourners, and causing flash floods around the country. As she watched her mother's coffin swallowed by the earth, Cara had felt the soggy ground swaying beneath her feet, as if she were standing on a pontoon, her mother drifting away from her out to sea in a row boat with no oars.

The days after the funeral were a blur. She functioned on auto-pilot, dropping and collecting Maisie to and from crèche, trying to work from home, mentally and physically drained after the last weeks and days of her mother's illness.

Kian had gone back to work the day after the funeral, a Saturday. He had fought hard for the contract he was currently working on, a new school build in Oranmore, and couldn't afford to take any more time off. Sometimes she wondered if the decision for him to go out on his own had been right for their family. He had always wanted to work for himself, and drove his Connolly Electrical van with pride. There were benefits, not least the autonomy it gave him, but being the boss also brought plenty of headaches. Getting the school contract had been a major coup, but she hoped Kian hadn't bitten off more than he could chew. He had a great reputation as an electrician but, these days, he spent most of his time managing the lads on the job as well as the budget, areas in which he had no experience.

She was due back to work tomorrow. It was probably for the best, although it felt all wrong for the world to be turning as normal without her mother in it. For her to be mindlessly pushing a trolley around Dunnes now while everybody else went about their daily business around her.

At least she had work to distract her. As did Paul. She didn't know how her dad would cope, though. Her parents had lived in each other's pockets although her father at least had maintained a bit of independence. He had worried about being bored after he retired as principal of Scoil Bhríde, the boys' national school within walking distance of their home in Bayview Crescent, but he had thrived. Seven mornings a week, he pounded the pavements of the Prom before adjourning to Ground & Co. beside the aquarium to meet some friend or other for coffee and a chat. That had all changed with her mother's diagnosis, of course.

Kitty had always been happiest at home, fluttering around her little nest with no real interest in hobbies or a social life outside her family. She was close to Helena, the pair of them very different from their other sister, the glamorous Maryanne, who had never looked back after she left her first husband. She had enjoyed a succession of suitors before she eventually settled down with her second husband in their swanky mansion on Taylor's Hill. Maryanne was always on the go between tennis, swimming, power-walking the Prom and meeting friends for lunch. It was hard to believe the three women were sisters. Helena had married a Claddagh lad and moved into the house where he lived with his widowed father, only a stone's throw from where they'd grown up on Grattan Road.

Cara couldn't face sitting in the empty house for the afternoon. She hadn't wanted to drop Maisie to crèche that morning, had wanted to keep her at home, but she knew Kian was right. It had taken her so long to settle there that they would be making it harder for her by not sending her in. She would never forget those first days and weeks after her maternity leave had ended and she had gone back to work. Her baby's confused eyes had tracked her as she walked away, abandoning her in that strange place for hours.

She had left her for one hour the first day and gradually increased it but Maisie had quickly cottoned on to what was happening and begun to cling to her and whimper as soon as they approached the door of Little Tots.

It didn't matter how many people told her it was *good for Maisie to socialise with other children*, Cara had known that all her baby wanted was to be with her. And all Cara had wanted was to be with Maisie during those guilt-filled early days back at work. For the first year or two, she hadn't been able to tell where she ended and Maisie started, as if they had remained physically connected even after her birth. Joined by an invisible umbilical cord. She was aware this probably wasn't normal. Or healthy.

Things had definitely become easier. Maisie had eventually settled. She was three now and seemed happy enough going into crèche most days, but Cara still felt torn.

It wasn't until she had held her baby in her arms for the first time that it had hit her. The shocking recognition that this perfect miniature being was the first blood relative she had ever met.

The midwife had laid her slimy naked daughter on her chest, their hearts beating together for the first time outside her body. She had cradled her baby's fragile skull in her hand, felt the blood pulse through the soft spot on top where the bones had not yet come together. Those soft spots of which there were two, she had learned, one at the front and one at the back, made it possible for the bony plates of the skull to compress and overlap as the head passed through the narrow birth canal. One of many clever design features.

She had expected to feel love for her child, of course, had felt the bond between them strengthen as her baby developed from the size of a poppy seed into a fully formed being inside her, but the sheer ferocity of that love had taken her by surprise. It was a feeling she had never experienced before, not even for

Kian. Powerful enough to bust through a wall, to lift a bus, to die for.

She had leaned down and inhaled the sweet cheesiness of her newborn, who was rooting and snuffling into her chest, oblivious to Kian leaning over them, and to the nurses bustling around at the end of the bed. Oblivious to anything but the little creature who had lived inside her for the past forty weeks and was now, miraculously, outside her.

And then, the euphoric rush of love had been swamped by a suffocating swell of terror as the reality struck of how momentous a responsibility now lay on her shoulders. That she was going to have to keep this vulnerable human being safe in the crazy world she had brought her into. A Joan Didion quote came into her head: *Once she was born, I was never not afraid.*

She had started to cry then, no tears, just wretched contractions of grief that erupted from somewhere deep within her belly.

Kian had been alarmed: she wasn't a crier. He moved to take the baby from her, but she shook her head, held her closer.

'Don't worry, love. That's just the baby blues,' the midwife assured her. 'Your hormones will probably be all over the place for a couple of days, but they'll settle down.'

This wasn't hormonal, though. She could sense that this went deeper, far, far deeper. Primal. A memory imprint from a time before conscious memory. It was as if, with her child, she had delivered the long-buried trauma of being separated within days of her own birth from the mother *she* had grown inside. The shock and pain of being severed from her mother's heartbeat, her smell, the bond that no other human could replicate.

Growing up, she had always known she was adopted, but she had never thought too much about it. She had been reared by loving, caring parents, who had provided her with everything a child could ask for and more. She had never felt different, never felt like an outsider in her family, secure in the knowledge that she was loved beyond measure. She had never harboured any real interest in finding her birth-mother, or considered that her lack of interest might have been born of an innate protective instinct. That she had somehow sensed she was better off not knowing.

But lying skin to skin with her firstborn baby, she had wondered if she had lain like that on her birth-mother's chest, soothed by the familiar pulse of her heartbeat. An unbearable sadness had weighed down on her as she imagined having to hand over her child, already so precious to her, to strangers to be reared. Never to hold her again.

The tears came then.

That day, and in the weeks and months that followed, Cara thought more and more about the mother who had given her life, about the trauma they had endured in being wrenched from each other so soon after her birth. How, she wondered, had her mother coped with living in a world apart from her? What were the circumstances in her life that had meant she couldn't keep her?

After she put the shopping away, she got back into the car and drove down the Prom. She needed to breathe the sea air, felt the urge to be near the water. She parked as close to Blackrock as she could, and walked back towards her mother's favourite spot on the top row of the curved tier of stone seating, like a half-amphitheatre facing out to the sea, Galway Bay the permanent residency act. The Clare hills looked close enough today for her to touch.

The concrete felt cool and solid beneath her thighs. How many times had she sat in this exact spot over the years with her mother, somehow assuming she would always be there? How would she ever grasp that she was gone for good? That she would never see her dear face again, or hear her voice? She was grateful for the numb haze that was keeping her grief at bay, as if her feelings were suspended in aspic, enabling her to keep functioning.

The tide was coming in now, an endless row of flamenco dancers kicking up their frothy white petticoats. The salty Atlantic breeze whipped her hair into her eyes. Over at the diving tower, young people were flinging themselves into the sea. Jumping, diving, belly-flopping. Shrieking. She felt the urge to join them, to push to the front of the queue of goose-pimpled bodies and launch herself head first into the icy depths of the water even though she hadn't dived off the tower since she was a teenager.

Her mind returned again to the conversation she had overheard in the hospice the day before her mother had died. It had been niggling away at her. Something about the tone of their voices, her father and Helena. The mention of a Lucia.

She got slowly to her feet and headed back down the Prom,

hoping she wouldn't bump into anybody she knew. She was worn out from all the sympathising. The same conversation over and over.

'Sorry for your loss.'

'She got no time, God bless her.'

'At least her suffering is over now.'

The place was thronged, the fine weather bringing people out to Salthill in their droves. Mothers pushing buggies and prams, with little ones on buggy boards and scooters. Teenage girls in skimpy thong bikinis, the cheeks of their arses on show. Older people taking the sea air.

Holidaymakers lined the benches along the Prom, their dogs on leads flopped out in the shade, flattened by the heat. Mobile-home owners spread out their picnics in the grass beside the road. A sharp stench of ammonia wafted from the direction of the public toilets, biting through the salty air.

Cara stopped on the path above Ladies Beach where she had spent so many hours with her mother as a child, drinking warm MiWadi and building endless sandcastles, painstakingly digging out and filling moats with buckets of seawater. The tide swished lazily in and out, stealthily coming further up the sand each time, like a teenage boy moving his hand up a girl's thigh.

Children ran in and out of the freezing water, squealing, gulls soared and squawked overhead, and dance music from the amusements in Leisureland drifted across the road. A pack of clouds had gathered ominously over the bay, blocking out the sun every now and then, teasing the sunbathers splayed on the sand below.

As she walked on, the name Lucia popped back into her mind. It was an unusual name. The only Lucia she knew of was Lucia Casey, the young woman whose body had been found in a bog in Connemara after she had gone missing back in the nineties.

And who had been distantly related to Cara's mother through marriage.

5

When Lucia Casey went missing, Cara had been too young to understand what was going on, but years later, after she had started working as a reporter, she had read a feature in one of the Sunday papers about the Vanishing Triangle, an area in the east of the country where a number of high-profile disappearances of Irish women had taken place in the nineties. The women, who had ranged in age from late teens to late thirties, disappeared suddenly and inexplicably and were never seen again. The popular hypothesis was that a serial killer, or killers, might have been active in the area during this period given the similarities between the cases.

The article had included a side panel on other, unrelated, unsolved murders involving women. There was a small paragraph on the unsolved case of Lucia Casey. Cara had asked her parents about it but they had told her they didn't know much beyond what had been printed in the papers at the time. It had been very distressing for the family, they said, and to that day, nobody knew what had happened to her. Indeed, they still didn't know.

Lucia was the daughter of Marcus Casey, an older brother of Aunt Maryanne's first husband, Luke. The Caseys owned the five-star Kylemore Manor hotel near Letterfrack, close to Kylemore Abbey, which had been a prestigious boarding-school for girls up until 2010. One of the wealthiest and best-connected families in the west, the Caseys' power and influence spread well beyond Connemara and County Galway.

Marcus, the eldest of the Casey brothers, had to be well into his eighties by now, but was still involved in running the hotel. The *Champion* had published a photo of him recently accepting yet another hospitality award. One of his brothers, Simon, was a retired district court judge. Maryanne's ex, Luke, was a retired consultant obstetrician and Joseph, who had died some years back, had been a Fianna Fáil TD and former junior minister. Many of the Casey offspring had also been very successful in their various ventures – property development, hospitality, the law and medicine.

She was still mulling over whether it could have been Lucia Casey they had been talking about when she passed Salthill Park on the far side of the road. A group of young lads were kicking a ball around and a pack of foreign students lined the cast-iron railings of the old bandstand.

What was it Helena had said again? Something about Lucia and whether they should have told *her*? Was Cara the *her* they had been referring to? Why had her father been concerned about her mother saying anything in front of her? And why had Helena felt the need to warn her father?

It was, of course, entirely possible that she had been mistaken, her ears playing tricks on her. Her father and aunt had been speaking quietly. More than likely she had simply misinterpreted what she had heard.

6

She stood staring across two lines of traffic.

Stopped in her tracks.

Coco's. Her mother's favourite coffee haunt.

Was this what her life would be like from now on? Would she be hit with a fresh lash of grief every time she passed somewhere she associated with her mum? There were so many places.

A solitary figure was sitting at her mother's usual table outside the café, wearing sunglasses and a hat. She was waving in Cara's direction.

Was that ...? Ah, God, it was.

Aunty Helena. Sitting there on her own without her partner in crime. As if Cara had somehow conjured her up just by thinking about her.

She waved back and stepped out onto the edge of the road, waiting for a break in the traffic.

Helena stood up as she got to the far side and opened her arms. 'Cara, pet, how are you?'

They hugged tightly. She had always been close to her mother's sister, but crisis had brought her family even closer to Helena. She hadn't missed a single day of visiting her sister in hospital or when she was moved to the hospice on the far side of the city. Close friends as well as sisters all their lives. Others had visited too, but towards the end, her mother hadn't wanted to see anybody other than her husband, her children and Helena. It must be so tough on her aunt to lose the sister who had been in her life since she was born, Kitty two years older.

'*Ara*, you know yourself. Hanging in there.'

'Have you time for a coffee?'

'Well, I should be working, but I'm in no mood for it.'

'Sit yourself down there so.'

Helena insisted on going in to order her drink and Cara settled herself in her mother's usual seat facing out onto the bay and wondered again how they were expected to carry on living around the chasm their mother had left as if it was no big deal.

She stayed with Helena for nearly three-quarters of an hour swapping anecdotes, snort-laughing about the time her mother had marched into the school and nearly taken the head off Sister Monica for falsely accusing Cara of stealing Rachel Kelly's rubber when she had been taking back the rubber Rachel had stolen from her pencil case the day before. A fierce mother hen altogether, nowadays her mum would probably be accused of helicopter parenting, but it was understandable after what she'd gone through.

Cara had experienced severe separation anxiety when she started school, had had to be prised, wailing, off her mother's leg for months before she settled. And then, of course, she had gone through the same thing with Maisie in crèche. She often wondered if Maisie had picked up on her own anxiety, and how much of her distress as a child had been transmitted from *her* mother.

Her yearning to trace her biological mother had grown alongside her baby, as she celebrated every milestone that the woman who had given birth to her had missed out on. The first smile, the first steps, the first heart-stopping *Mama*. Kitty's illness had forced her to put it on the back burner, but it had welled up stronger than ever in the days following her death.

Her parents had told her, as a small child, how she had come to live with them. 'Our precious miracle.' Her mother had made up a story about a mama bear, a dada bear and a little-boy bear, who wished and wished for a little baby-girl bear, until one day, another mama bear gave them a beautiful baby bear called Cara. She had loved that story, begged to hear it every night before she went to sleep. In the story, the other mama had gone off and 'lived happily ever after'.

In her teens, when her friends had suggested she search for her birth-mother, Cara had tentatively broached the subject with her parents. They had told her they'd support her in whatever she decided to do, assuring her they wouldn't be one bit upset or offended if she wanted to make contact with the woman who had given birth to her. But Cara somehow knew they were only saying what they knew she wanted to hear. The following morning, after her father went to work, her mother had brought up the topic again. That was when she had told Cara about Susan Fallon's daughter, how she had been rejected by her birth-mother, and was devastated by the experience.

'Just remember that whatever happens, love, there isn't another mother in this world who could love you as much as I do,' she had said. 'We'll help you if you want to trace your birth-mother, but we'd hate to see you hurt like Lisa Fallon.'

And Cara had understood then. It wasn't that her parents didn't want her to find her birth-mother: they were just trying to protect her, as they had always done. In case she didn't like what she found. And that wasn't a chance she wanted to take, not when she was perfectly happy with the family she had. So she had packed away the idea of searching for her mother like a memory stick in the back of a drawer, and there it had remained gathering dust, until Maisie was born.

She rarely thought about her birth-father. He didn't interest her in the way her mother did.

'I've been thinking ...' she said now to Helena. She had always been able to talk to her aunt. 'I'd been thinking about it for a while, but with Mum getting sick, I had to put it on hold for a while. I want to trace my birth-mother.'

The look of shock on her aunt's face took her aback. Surely it wasn't that startling an idea. And if Helena had taken it so badly, how would her father react? She had hoped they would understand, especially now.

Her aunt forced a tight smile to her lips, and reached across the table for Cara's hand. 'Look, Cara, I can see why you'd feel this way after losing your mum ... but this is such a huge decision, love. Do you not think you should give yourself a bit of time before you take such a big step? After everything you've just been through?'

'It's not just because of Mum, though. I've been feeling like this since I had Maisie. I was going to talk to Mum and

Dad about it but then, well, we found out she was sick again and ...'

'I'm sure it's probably normal enough to feel like that after you've had your own baby, but I just think it's a bit too soon. For you and ... well, for your father too. Maybe take some time to think about it before you do anything.'

She knew her aunt was right. This was probably not the time to cause any more upheaval in their lives, but she had already put it off for so long, and it might take months, even years to find her mother once she started the search. There was no guarantee, of course, that her mother would want to see her. She could be married with a family of her own who knew nothing of Cara's existence.

She hadn't planned to bring it up, it was one of those spur-of-the-moment impulses.

'Aunty Helena, before I go ... I wasn't spying on you or anything,' she smiled, 'but, well, I overheard you and Dad talking in the hospice on Tuesday ... in the chapel.'

The colour drained from her aunt's face.

'Something to do with Lucia and Mum and hoping she didn't say anything in front of me ... It wasn't Lucia Casey you were talking about, was it?'

The look of pure horror on Helena's face answered that question.

7

By the time she got back to the car, her T-shirt was sticking to her back and a band of sweat had formed along her hairline. The clouds had moved away and the sun was a hot ball beating directly into her windscreen.

She had booted it up the Prom, wanting to put as much distance between herself and Helena as she could. There was no distancing herself from her own mind, though, from the thoughts that were rushing around in a blind panic inside her head, like sheep being chased by marauding dogs.

It had been hovering around the edges of her consciousness ever since that day in the hospice, a flimsy mote of suspicion drifting closer and closer. The eighteen-month period of Lucia Casey's disappearance had been such a strange time. Cara would have been six or seven. She could still remember the grown-ups talking about the missing girl. The hushed tones that faded into awkward silence any time she entered a room. She had been listening, though, the top of the stairs her preferred eavesdropping perch. Wondering why her family were so concerned about this stranger who was missing.

It wasn't until she saw the look on Helena's face that the notion broke through the surface.

Was there any way ...? No, of course not. Crazy thought.
But what if ...?
'Oh, my God! Was she my mother?'
Her aunt had stared back at her out of wide, panicked eyes.
'Jesus Christ! She was, wasn't she?'
'No, I didn't say ... God Almighty, Cara ... You need to talk to your father. I'm sorry but it's not my place.'
Cara had got to her feet, shoved her chair back and walked away from her aunt. She had stepped off the edge of the footpath onto the road, barely checking that it was safe to cross. Barely able to hear above the whooshing of her pulse.
Her aunt called for her to wait.
'No.' Cara had put up her hand, and Helena had stopped on the far side of the road. 'Please, no.'
She was finding it hard to catch her breath, her chest tight with shock. She turned the engine on, the air-conditioning as high as it could go.
What the actual fuck?
She was so confused. How could this be? How could Lucia Casey have been her mother?
She began to root in her bag for her phone. She had to talk to her mother.
Thwack! It hit her like a punch in the solar plexus.
She couldn't talk to her mother. About this or anything else. Ever again.
And then another realisation hit her, a second gut punch that almost took the breath from her. If this was true, and judging by Aunty Helena's reaction surely it had to be, it meant the hope of a fairytale reunion with her birth-mother was gone. Just like that. *Pfft.* A bubble popping.

Two mothers gone in the space of a week.

It was too much to take in. A young couple walked by, hand in hand, licking ice-cream cones, as if they hadn't a care in the world.

This couldn't be happening to her.

She rang Kian. No answer. On the site, he probably couldn't hear her. She sent him a message: *RING ME PLEASE!* He would call as soon as he saw it, knew she wouldn't send a message like that if it wasn't important.

She needed to talk to her father. Not on the phone. Her parents' house was only five minutes up the steep hill of Threadneedle Road. She couldn't move. Her limbs felt weighted down, her body stuck to the seat.

She wondered if Paul knew. And who else? Maryanne, of course, and Luke. Was Cara the only one in the family who didn't?

Her parents had been open with her from a young age about the matter of her adoption. How could they have neglected to mention that she had been adopted from within her mother's extended family?

During the strange period after Lucia had gone missing, Cara had known somehow not to question her parents about why everyone was so worried about the girl with the pretty name who they were talking about on the telly and the radio. She had sensed it was another of those subjects that was not to be brought up. Like the blood on that girl's towel in the changing room at Leisureland, or the time Rambo from next door had developed his obsession with humping her mother's leg.

She remembered feeling that something really bad had happened to this Lucia, though.

And then her body had turned up and there had been even more whispering and head-shaking and pursed lips. Cara had heard it on the nine o'clock news when she was supposed to be in bed. They'd had the sound turned down low so she'd had to creep halfway down the stairs to listen. Buried in a bog in Connemara. She had felt so sorry for the poor girl, left out in the cold and the dark, all alone for so long. She didn't understand that by the time she had been dumped in the bog the girl would no longer have been able to feel cold or wet or fear.

8

She tried Kian again, but there was still no answer. It was at times like this that she missed Alison so much it hurt. Her best friend since secondary school had moved to New Zealand five years ago and married a Kiwi. The eleven-hour time difference made it hard to keep in touch. They communicated mainly via voice notes and email, these days. What she would have given to have her friend beside her just then. To hold her hand and spill everything out to somebody who knew her nearly as well as she knew herself.

Her mother had always warned her that she needed to widen her friendship group, that it wasn't good to be so reliant on one person. Cara had other friends, but she had never met anybody who got her the way Alison did. She couldn't even remember the last time she had been out with the girls. Since her mother had been sick, their monthly nights out had fallen by the wayside and her current relationship with her friends was largely reduced to rushed calls, constantly interrupted by one of their kids.

Cold air blasted from the vents and now she was shivering and sweating at the same time, as if she had a fever. She looked at the phone in her hand. Who could she call? Paul.

Her brother was one of the first people she would call if she was in trouble – he always had her back. But what if he was in on it too?

She opened the Safari browser, her thumb hovering over the keypad for a few moments before she started typing into the search bar.

Lucia Casey.

Could there be a simple explanation behind all this? Some other reason for her mother to have been talking about Lucia, for her father to hope she didn't say anything in front of Cara?

But that look on Aunty Helena's face.

She scrolled down until she came across a tabloid article about a review of the case that had been published on the twentieth anniversary of the discovery of Lucia's body, ten years ago. She zoomed in on the photo of the dead woman and smacked a hand over her mouth.

Oh my God!

A big perm dwarfed a small heart-shaped face. That shy smile, the neat snub nose, the sprinkle of tiny freckles across her cheeks. So achingly familiar. Cara had the same chin, and the same colour eyes, although her nose was longer and more defined, but it was like looking at an age-progressed picture of Maisie. One of those heartbreaking photos they used for children who had gone missing years ago to show what they'd look like today.

She couldn't take her eyes off it. Her daughter was the image of the woman staring out from her phone. The last time Cara had seen a picture of Lucia Casey, Maisie hadn't been born. Her parents must surely have noticed the resemblance. You'd have to be blind not to. How could they have kept this from her?

Surely they must have known there was a chance of her finding out for herself.

She began to read the article, a rehash of the details of Lucia's disappearance and the discovery of her body in a remote bog in the townland of Toombeola, between Clifden and Recess. It mentioned that, while two men had been questioned after the remains were found, nobody had been charged in connection with her death. An inquest had been opened and indefinitely adjourned, pending the garda investigation. The pathologist had been unable to provide a definite cause of death given the state of decomposition of the body after eighteen months' submersion in a wet bog drain, so the cause was recorded as undetermined. The body had been identified by dental records.

There was no doubt in Cara's mind after seeing that photo.

Lucia Casey was her birth-mother.

She had never seen the similarity before but she hadn't been looking for it. People saw what they wanted to see. Just like the people who used to tell her she was the image of one of her parents or her brother, ignorant of the fact that she was adopted.

9

Lucia
Kylemore, Connemara
1984

It didn't just look like Ireland's most romantic castle, it really was. A nineteenth-century Gothic fantasy set into the face of a mountain in Connemara. Straight out of a fairytale. One in which, sadly, the beautiful prince and princess didn't get to live happily ever after.

Lucia had always been fascinated with the story behind Kylemore Abbey. A Mills & Boon type tale of romantic love and joy, of tragedy and grief. Mitchell Henry, a wealthy doctor and businessman from Manchester, had built the castle for his beautiful wife, Margaret, after they had fallen in love with the area on their honeymoon in the 1840s.

She had known the tragic story long before she'd started at the Abbey as a day pupil, and from the first time she'd set foot inside the door, she had felt the sadness in the place, seeping from the old stone walls. Underneath the giggling girls, the bustle of a prestigious boarding-school – home over the years to pupils from Japan and Mexico and even two princesses –

she sensed the lingering grief of the castle's first inhabitants. She imagined what it must have been like in happier times, when the Henry children, all nine of them, chased each other through the warren of corridors. What a magical playground it must have been. Before.

Mitchell Henry had aimed to make the property equal, if not superior, to any royal castle and in that he had succeeded, employing more than two hundred people on the estate in its heyday. Margaret had thrived as lady of the manor and was much loved by the local tenants, but sadly, only a few years after the castle was completed, she had died from dysentery during a holiday on the Nile. Mitchell was heartbroken. His wife's body was embalmed in Cairo, then returned to the castle where, according to local lore, she lay, like Snow White, in a glass coffin beneath the grand staircase.

Distraught, Mitchell commissioned a miniature cathedral in her honour beside the castle. Further tragedy struck some years later when his daughter Geraldine, said to be his favourite, was killed in a jaunting accident on the estate while out with her baby daughter and nurse. Lucia had cried when she first heard this story.

Although he remained at Kylemore, Mitchell never recovered from the loss of his wife and daughter. He was forced to sell his beloved castle and estate but Lucia took comfort from knowing that he had been reunited with his beloved Margaret in death. Their remains lay alongside each other in a mausoleum in the Kylemore woodlands.

In 1920, a group of Irish Benedictine nuns arrived at the remote castle as refugees after the First World War. They had fled Ypres in Belgium after the destruction of their home. Three years later, they opened their doors as a boarding-school to Catholic girls from near and far.

Lucia had been nervous starting at the Abbey even though she lived closer than any of the other pupils, even the other local day girls. She had always been shy, struggled to make friends, and was happiest in the company of her beautiful grey Connemara mare Misty and her family's golden retrievers. And Tommy, of course. Her first cousin and closest friend. Her only friend, really. An odd one out, just like her.

She had hoped she might make some new friends, even just one, in secondary, but although there were some very nice girls in her classes, she was never quite able to feel part of any group. Even her connection to one of the most popular girls in the school hadn't helped her. Her older cousin Victoria was a boarder in Leaving Cert, head girl, and captain of the hockey team; she who had got nine As in the Inter Cert. On top of all that, she looked like Wonder Woman with her long thick hair as black as coal, her sparkling blue eyes and tiny waist.

Despite her failure to make any friends, Lucia had settled well into the Abbey. One of the older nuns, Sister Breda, now retired from teaching, had taken Lucia under her wing in the first year when she realised that her writing and spelling were so atrocious because she couldn't make sense of the words on the page. She had been written off as lazy or *not trying hard enough* by her teachers in primary school, but Lucia had been trying her best. It was just that words and numbers became jumbled in her head. Sometimes the words came out of her mouth wrong too: *fips and chish* instead of *fish and chips*.

When she was younger, her brothers used to make her say *fish and chips* in front of their friends, who fell about laughing. She had laughed too, delighted with the rare attention, until she realised they were laughing at, not with, her.

Things had improved since Sister Breda had begun to help her, sitting with her after school and teaching her to read again from scratch using the Ann and Barry books. Lucia enjoyed the one-to-one attention, and the little nun always had a treat for her afterwards. A hot buttered scone with jam and cream, and a glass of Ribena or homemade lemonade. Or a slice of Madeira cake or some chocolate biscuits.

She loved roaming around the school in the late afternoons, when the day girls had gone home and the boarders had disappeared into the bowels of the building. She was pretty much left to her own devices. She often wandered through the walled gardens where, back in the Henrys' day, grapes, nectarines and even bananas had grown, luxuries unthinkable to the ordinary Irish people of that time. She loved hearing stories about those days. Of how the fruit and vegetables grown at Kylemore were often served at the Henrys' posh London dinner parties, how salmon caught in the lake was wrapped in cabbage leaves and posted to England. Of how guests from London and Manchester and other places were presented with a posy of violets to wear at dinner, a craze in Victorian London that was said to represent loyalty and friendship. She could picture Mitchell, his beautiful bride in his arms, dancing on the sprung oak floor in the ballroom where the talented family performed most of the music.

While most of her fellow pupils were looking forward to the summer holidays, Lucia had been dreading them. She thrived on the routine of the school day, even if she still struggled in some of her classes. That summer Sister Breda, perhaps sensing her unease, had arranged a part-time job for her in the little shop the nuns ran, selling religious items and crafts the sisters, local artists and craftspeople made. It was just a few hours every morning, but it gave her something to look forward to each day as well as spending more time with her pony.

At night in bed she dreamed of her very own Mitchell Henry, swooping in on a stallion, and falling head over heels in love at the sight of her riding Misty along a woodland bridle path.

Little did she know that this summer she would meet him.

10

When he saw Helena's message asking him to ring her, Billy assumed his sister-in-law was calling to check up on him again. To make sure he was having a proper dinner, not his current go-to comfort meal of fish fingers, beans and chips. Since Kitty's diagnosis, his diet had gone to the dogs. His wife's hearty appetite had vanished on the day the consultant had broken the news, far too abruptly in Billy's opinion. He didn't think he'd ever get over the shock, and he wasn't the one who had just been given five months to live.

Now that he had only himself to cook for, he couldn't be arsed with peeling, chopping and all that malarkey. While Kitty was in hospital and then the hospice, he had been shoving something from the freezer into the oven or microwave and eating it in front of the telly. He couldn't face sitting at the kitchen table where the two of them had chatted over so many meals through the years, staring at Kitty's empty chair. He'd have to cop on at some point, though, he knew that, but for now, it was as much as he could do to get through each day without her.

Poor Kitty, who had spent most of her life on a diet, a constant yo-yo of losing weight and putting it back on with interest, had been nothing but skin and bone at the end. She had always bemoaned her lack of height, as it meant she had nowhere to spread the extra pounds, while Cara could eat like a horse and never put on a pick. Different genes, though.

His wife had never been a fan of exercise, unlike Billy who had been a fine soccer player in his day and still pounded the Prom daily, hail or shine. Kitty used to walk down the hill with him as far as Blackrock where she loved to sit on the steps and people-watch while he went the full length of the Promenade as far as the Swamp. The trek back up the hill was exercise enough for her, she said. Ralph, their three-legged rescue Yorkie, used to do the longer walk with Billy, but he had slowed down over the past couple of years and taken to staying with Kitty. She inevitably ended up chatting to somebody – if not someone she knew, then a complete stranger – always coming home with some kind of a story. She had had a way about her, Kitty did, that drew people to her, made them pour their hearts out.

Kitty. What in the name of God was he going to do without her?

They had been like two peas in a pod. Over to Dunnes every Friday evening for the food shop, he pushing the trolley as she filled it. Into town on Saturday mornings for a potter around the shops followed by lunch, a pint for him and a pot of tea for her in Busker Brownes. Mass at twelve in Salthill on Sunday, then home to read the papers and watch whatever match was on the telly.

Kitty had always been a home bird, happy keeping her house nice and rearing her children, and later, spending time with her beloved grandchild. They had often spoken to each other about how they never wanted to be a burden on their children as they grew old, but she had admitted that the thought of a nursing home filled her with dread. Her own mother had ended up in one, after she broke her hip and was left lying on the freezing floor in her kitchen for hours before she was found. That was one thing Kitty never had to worry about now.

He felt Cara could probably have done with a few more days off work after the awful few months she had put down, but that was the way it was these days. Everybody racing all the time. It was hard for the young people now, so many stuck living at home with their parents because they couldn't afford to rent, never mind get on the property ladder.

Cara and Kian were lucky they had bought when they did. They had a lovely house on the Clybaun Road, a semi-detached in a nice quiet estate not far from the retail park. If Billy and Kitty hadn't been in a position to help them with the deposit, they could have been at the mercy of the rental market now. Facing homelessness, like so many other families. Thank God for that at least. There had been a woman on the radio the other day crying after she'd had to hand the family dog to a rescue centre because their new landlord didn't take pets and no other accommodation was available. It would tear the heart out of you listening to it. The thought of having to give Ralph away, of how confused he would be, was just too sad. He was confused enough with Kitty gone.

Billy shifted in the armchair where he had been sitting for he wasn't sure how long now, just staring into space. The dog jumped off his lap, and stood looking up at him as if wondering what the plan was. He had teased Kitty for talking to the dog as if the animal could understand her, but had taken to doing the same thing when his wife had gone into hospital the last time and he had sensed she wouldn't be coming home. He had also started to keep the radio on for company all day.

'What time is it at all, Ralphie? I suppose I'd better ring Helena back. What did I do with my phone?'

The little dog cocked his head to one side, and lifted an ear as if listening intently to what Billy was saying. Nobody knew what had happened to his fourth leg: he had been brought into a vet in Barna with it badly damaged, possibly caught in a trap or hit by a car. Being short of a leg certainly didn't hold him back. As far as Ralph was concerned, he owned the Prom, and any other dog that had the neck to look sideways at him was yapped back into line, no matter their size or breed.

Billy wandered into the kitchen where his phone was sitting on the counter beside the radio.

The four o'clock news was on. Nothing but doom and gloom. Twenty-five people killed and more than fifty injured in a Russian rocket attack on a railway station in Ukraine. Another rise in the number of people now registered as homeless across Galway city and county, and 70 per cent of households nationwide facing energy poverty this winter in a worst-case scenario.

'Jaysus, it'd put years on you, wouldn't it, Ralphie?' The dog cocked his head again.

He turned the volume down. It seemed as though the whole world was falling apart around them. If Kitty was here, she would have pointed to the positive stories, the good things people were doing. But she wasn't, and never would be again.

'What am I supposed to be doing again? Oh, yes, calling Helena back.'

As he picked up the phone, it started to ring in his hand. 'Sorry, Helena, I literally just picked up the phone to—'

She cut across him, a panicked garble.

'Christ,' he said, to the dog, as he pulled out a kitchen chair and sat heavily into it.

11

He had to talk to his daughter. He couldn't even imagine the state she must be in.

Bloody Helena.

If she hadn't opened her mouth in the hospice, had kept her conversation with Kitty between the two of them, none of this would be happening.

And why the hell had she told Cara to talk to *him*? Couldn't she have said that, no, they'd been talking about something else entirely?

He sighed heavily. This wasn't Helena's fault. She had only been trying to forewarn him, worried about what on earth Kitty, in her morphine-addled state, might come out with.

And Cara had caught her on the hop.

No, this wasn't Helena's fault at all but, God Almighty, what a bloody mess. And what choice had he now but to tell Cara the truth?

Jesus Christ.

How was he going to explain it to her?

The dog whimpered, sensing Billy's distress. He reached down, patted the little head. 'It's OK, maneen, it's OK.'

It wasn't, though. Far from it. The day they had hoped would never come was finally here and, even worse, Kitty was gone and he had to face it on his own.

How the hell was he supposed to carry on without her for the rest of his own life? In a world dimmed for ever now that she was buried above in Rahoon. It wasn't one bit bleddy fair.

They had both been in agreement that not telling Cara the truth about her birth-mother was the right thing to do, although they had told her from a young age that she was adopted. She had loved the story Kitty made up about the mama bear who had given her precious baby bear to a family who wished and wished for her. And she had been such a happy, contented child.

As she got older, she had begun, naturally, to question more.
What happened to the other mama bear?
Did she miss her baby?
Was she not sad?

And Kitty and Billy had explained that sometimes when a mama is not able to take care of her own baby it makes her happy when she finds another special mama who can do it for her.

There had been a period around the age of nine or ten when Cara became anxious that Kitty would decide some day to give her away, like her first mama had. It had nearly broken Kitty's heart, trying to reassure the child that she was safe, that Kitty was her for-ever mama, they her for-ever family. Later, when she started to become more concerned with her appearance and fitting in, Cara had begun to ask if she looked like her birth-mother.
What colour eyes had she?
What colour hair?

Do I look like her?

They lied and told her they didn't know. That they had never met her mother.

When he heard that Kitty had told Cara about Lisa Fallon's disastrous experience with her birth-mother, he had been worried that their daughter would feel deceived by them if she ever decided to search for her mother but, as Kitty pointed out, that was the price they had to pay to protect her.

And they had got on with their lives and brushed the matter of Cara's birth-mother under the carpet where it was trodden down, like a flattened mouse. Unseen but always there. They had had to learn to live with the fear that their daughter would arrive home some day and tell them she wanted to find her.

As he sat at the kitchen table looking across at the empty chair where his wife would never sit again, Billy was pulled back in time to the same kitchen in the same house, but a different nightmare.

That evening Clodagh had gone to bed early complaining of a headache, completely out of the norm for a girl who was always on the go between hockey and swimming and friends. Kitty had a tart and a batch of queen cakes in the oven for a cake sale in school the next day, and the house was filled with the sweet waft of baked apples and rising dough.

When she went up to check on her teenage daughter, Clodagh had been clutching her head, and when Kitty touched her forehead, she realised she was running a fever. Then she had lifted her daughter's pyjama top, spotted the pinprick purple rash and shouted for Billy.

12

When Cara pulled up outside her parents' house, the home where she had grown up in blissful ignorance, Maura Carroll (or Hawk-eye as her mother used to call her) next door was out watering her rose bushes.

Shite.

That was all she needed.

Mrs Carroll was always fit to burst with the latest academic and sporting successes of her high-achieving grandchildren, and Cara really wasn't capable of indulging her right now.

She held her phone to her ear, and pretended to be in the middle of a deep conversation, pointing at the phone and mouthing, 'Sorry,' while Mrs Carroll waved frantically at her.

'Yes, of course I understand. It must be such a difficult situation for you all. I can come to the house and do the interview there if that would be easier for you.'

She kept the fake conversation going all the way up the path while the neighbour stood shamelessly eavesdropping from the far side of the low wall that separated the gardens. In the porch, she rooted around in a hanging basket filled with ancient pot-pourri and seashells until she found the spare key.

As she opened the door and stepped into the hall, like she had done so many times before, she was instantly struck by it. The absence, not just of her mother's physical presence, but something else. Some essential essence. The signature Kitty scent that had lingered even in the weeks when she had been in hospital and then the hospice: Comfort Original, Elizabeth Arden Eight Hour Cream and a heady hint of Shalimar. And something else that she couldn't put her finger on. Gone now. Her feet felt glued to the floor with the dead weight of her loss, the understanding that home would never be home again.

A yapping ball of frenzy came belting down the hallway towards her and the sickening wave of grief receded. The little dog was so delirious with excitement by the time he reached her that he almost completed a full back-flip in the air.

'Calm down, you lunatic.' She picked him up, let him lick her cheek. She could hear her mother's voice in her head: 'I wouldn't let that dirty tongue anywhere near my face when he spends most of his time licking his own willy.'

At least some things were still the same around here. She was glad her father had Ralph for company.

Paul came out of the sitting room. He was in his teaching gear, a short-sleeved shirt and chinos. He must have come straight from work. She wondered if Helena had called him. Or her father. His face looked strained.

'We're in here,' he said.

Her father was sitting in his armchair beside the window. God, he looked old today. The last weeks and months had taken so much out of him. He still had a fine head of steel-grey curls, badly in need of a wash now. And a trim. For a man who had always kept himself so well, he looked haggard.

He stood and walked towards her, reached out his arms. She took a step back and his face fell.

'I'm sorry, love,' he said. 'Not that we didn't tell you, because I still think that was the right thing to do, the best thing for you. I'm just sorry you had to find out the way you did.'

It was true! Jesus Christ!

If only she had made a different decision that day in the hospice. If she had gone in and sat by her mother's bedside instead of going in search of her father. If she could somehow backtrack those dozen or so footsteps and stop herself overhearing something that had pulled the world as she knew it upside down and inside out.

'So it's really true?'

Even though she had seen the unmistakable resemblance between Lucia Casey, herself and Maisie with her own eyes, she had still hoped there must be some other explanation. That she had got it all wrong. That she hadn't found and lost her birth-mother before she had even begun her search. That she wasn't long dead and buried, her body having been dumped in an isolated bog in the middle of nowhere.

She stood there, her gaze shifting from her father to her brother, the floor swaying beneath her.

Her father looked confused.

'But I thought ... Helena said you knew. That ...'

'I asked her if Lucia Casey was my mother and she told me I should talk to you.'

'Let's sit down so we can talk properly,' her brother said. 'Cara, you look like you're about to pass out. Please, sit down.'

'You knew.'

He nodded, his face grim.

Cara sank onto one end of the sofa and Paul sat at the other. Her father settled back into his armchair, and the dog jumped onto his lap. On the wall behind him hung photos of a younger Cara, a younger Paul. A large framed portrait of them all with Kian and Maisie, taken the day of her daughter's christening. Looking for all the world like a normal, happy family.

A pile of mass cards lay on the coffee-table – her father must have been going through them. The pretty new Carolyn Donnelly cushions her mother had bought in Dunnes needed a good plumping, she noticed absently, and the knick-knacks on the cabinet were coated in dust. The mantelpiece was now home to a variety of random objects: her father's wallet and car keys, a mug, a plate of sandwich crusts placed out of Ralph's reach. Her mother had hated clutter on the mantelpiece.

'Who else knows? Was I the only one who didn't? Jesus, you went to her funeral, you and Mum. I remember because I wanted to go with you, but you wouldn't let me, and you dropped me down to Aunty Helena's.'

Her memory of that day was so vivid, because she had been out playing with her cousin Gavin when he came off his bike and split his chin. She had never seen so much blood before. She could still see Gavin standing beside his fallen Grifter, eyes wide with shock, as blood poured from the gash in his chin that looked like a second mouth, soaking into the front of his Teenage Mutant Ninja Turtles T-shirt. He had collapsed, and Cara had run like the clappers across the field to his house to get Aunty Helena. She had to stay with Uncle Mike while Gavin was taken off to casualty to get stitched.

'Yes, we went to the funeral, we wanted to pay our respects to the family. You used to go everywhere with your mother,

her little sidekick as she called you, but obviously we couldn't bring you with us, and Paul was away somewhere with the lads so ...'

'I don't understand, though. How did you end up adopting me? Surely you couldn't just give your baby away to whoever you wanted, even back then.'

'Of course not, love. It was all legal and above board. We wouldn't do something like ... Oh, God, how do I explain?' He sighed, looked at Paul.

'Dad was worried about Mum, Cara,' her brother said. 'We all were, Maryanne and Helena too. She wasn't coping at all after Clodagh. Blamed herself. Clodagh was gone four years at that stage, and I was eighteen, living my own life. It wasn't that she replaced Clodagh with you, of course not, but having you to look after gave her a reason to get out of bed every morning.'

'But why didn't Lucia keep me? It's not as if she couldn't have afforded to. Sure her family are loaded.'

'They were different times, I suppose, love. Lucia was very young when she had you. There was still so much stigma back in the eighties around getting pregnant outside marriage, and the Caseys, especially her mother, were very religious.'

'Did she want to keep me?'

'I'm sure she probably did, but she was only sixteen when she got pregnant with you, seventeen when she gave birth. She was sent down the country. It was arranged through the church, an organisation that placed girls with families away from their own communities to have their babies. They'd come home months later with neither bump nor baby. Off helping a sick family member or doing a course, *mar dhea*.'

'What about my father? Do you know who he was?'

58

She had rarely thought of him, but she wanted to know what else they had hidden from her.

'No. She never said who he was, even though I know her parents tried to get it out of her. I've often wondered myself ...'

'Wondered what?'

'Well,' he looked at his hands, as if the answer lay in his palms, 'whether he might have been a married man who had maybe sworn her to secrecy.'

'So how did you and Mum end up adopting me? I assume Maryanne was involved.'

Her father nodded, shifting the dog on his lap. 'Maryanne told me Lucia was going to have a baby, and it was all being kept hush-hush. The baby was to be put up for adoption. Kitty was much closer to Maryanne back then. She had been very good to your mother after Clodagh and then when she had her hysterectomy. I was sick with worry about your mother. She was barely leaving the house, had no interest in anything. It was a desperate time.

'Then Maryanne came up with this idea that we could adopt Lucia's baby when he or she was born. I told her she was mad, but the more I thought about it, the more I felt it was something we should at least think about. Your mum was horrified when I said it to her. She roared at me, called me all sorts of horrible names. Accused me of not loving Clodagh as much as she did, of trying to replace her with a new baby. Of making her feel useless because she couldn't have any more babies herself. I knew it was the grief talking but ...'

'It was awful,' Paul said. 'Dad was in bits.'

'It was Helena who coaxed her into meeting you. It was a couple of months later, and you'd just been born so we knew you were a girl. I knew well that your mother only agreed to see you to get us off her back. She told me afterwards that she had no intention whatsoever of going ahead with any adoption.'

They had driven to Limerick, her father explained, where they met the family who had been hosting Lucia during her pregnancy. They must have sent her somewhere because there was no sign of her that day.

'You were only about ten days old, a tiny scrap of a thing. All dressed up in a little pink Babygro and a frilly hat. I'll never forget as long as I live the moment you and your mother locked eyes for the first time. You had been sleeping, but you woke when Mrs McNamara put you into Kitty's arms, and you gazed up at her so intensely, it was like you latched on to her with your eyes and you weren't letting go. And that was it. She sat there staring back at you, the rest of us afraid to move or say a word in case we broke the spell. She told me afterwards that it felt like she had known you for ever.'

13

Billy sat up for ages after they'd left, staring at the blank television screen, replaying the faded old footage in his head. There was no point in going up to bed: he wouldn't be able to sleep, and the flat duvet on Kitty's side would only depress him even more.

Paul had stayed for a while after Cara left. He had offered to spend the night in his old room, but Billy had told him to head on home. Let on he was going to get an early night. Paul was a good lad. Always had been. He'd been such a rock for Billy during Kitty's illness, particularly the last few really bad weeks when he'd gone straight from school to the hospice every day, sending Billy and Cara home to rest while he stayed overnight, sleeping in a recliner chair to ensure his mother was never left on her own.

Paul had known about Lucia, of course, he and a handful of others. Maryanne and her husband, Luke. Probably their children. Lucia's parents and her brothers. And Helena. That was it, though, as far as he knew anyway. Unless Lucia had told anyone.

They had been so naïve to think it was possible to protect Cara from the tragedy of her birth-mother's death.

'I'll talk to Cara, Dad,' Paul had promised, before he left. 'You and Mum only did what you thought was best for her and she'll see that when she has time to think about it. How could you even think of telling a child her mother was murdered and buried in a bog, for Christ's sake? She'd have been traumatised for life.'

'I know sure. I still think she was better off not knowing, but there's no going back now.'

The events of the day had brought up so much stuff. The drive home from Limerick after they had met baby Cara for the first time. There had been no motorway back then, of course. The rain had come down in slanting sheets, lashing off the windscreen, Cat Stevens singing about how the first cut was the deepest. Kitty had cried the whole way home, messy, snotty, noisy tears, four years' worth. Her stomach must have ached for hours afterwards.

Billy had wanted to pull off the road, but she had directed him to keep going with a flap of her hand, while she continued to sob and snort beside him. She had needed it, that feral unleashing of pain. She'd never get over losing her daughter – neither of them would: how could any parent ever get over something so cruel and unnatural? – but the physical outpouring of her torment seemed to have uncorked the anguish she had bottled up inside.

It had been about a week after what would have been Clodagh's seventeenth birthday when Cara came to join their family. There was surely never a child more ruined. Barely ever out of their arms. She was rocked, and kissed, and generally adored by Kitty, Billy and her besotted big brother. Overnight, Kitty had found her days were full again. Instead of revolving around her visits to her daughter's grave, she was kept on her toes caring for a newborn baby. At thirty-eight, the same age as Cara now, Kitty was regarded as an older mother. It was very different today: most women waited until their careers were up and running before they even thought about starting a family. And rightly so. Back in the day, women were expected to give up their jobs when they got married and say no more about it. They wouldn't have dreamed of questioning the decisions men made for and about them. It was just the way things were.

Only the year before Cara was born, the Lovett girl had died in a grotto in Longford, along with the baby boy she had just given birth to. That poor misfortunate. Only fifteen years old. And a few months after that, her younger sister took her own life, her heart broke, at the age of fourteen, not much older than Clodagh had been when she died. In the same month, the poor Hayes girl down in Kerry was put through a living hell when she was wrongfully charged with the murder of a newborn baby after a stillbirth. Accused by the guards of becoming pregnant with two babies by two different men at the same time. You couldn't make it up. Bastards, the lot of them. All those men, the guards and the priests and the judge, what they put that girl through. Even thinking about it made Billy feel ashamed to be a man. The shame and stigma that unmarried mothers had had to live with. No mention of the buckos who had got them into that condition and were allowed to waltz off into the sunset scot-free.

Kitty had never expected to love Cara so much, every bit as much as the children she had carried in her womb, she told Billy. He felt the same, but while Clodagh had been a typical daddy's girl, there was never any doubt about whose girl Cara was. She adored her mammy and never wanted to let her out of her sight. She had probably been a bit over-attached to Kitty when she was younger, but she had grown out of it. She had gone to college and got herself a good job in the local paper – Kitty had been thrilled because it kept her close. They knew plenty of people whose kids had emigrated to Australia and New Zealand, who had to communicate with their grandkids through screens. Kitty would have hated that.

Ironically, Cara wasn't dissimilar to Clodagh in looks, the same colouring, dark blonde hair and blue eyes. They were very different in personality, though. His older daughter had been so independent, feisty and stubborn as a mule too. She would have gone on to do great things if she had only been given the chance. Cara had been a quieter child, shy and happier in the company of her mother than out on the street playing with the other kids. She had become more outgoing as she got older, gained more confidence in herself when she got into journalism. It had been a source of great comfort to Kitty that she had lived to see her daughter married to a good man and become a mother.

She had worried about Paul, though. He had followed Billy into teaching, had a steady job and a grand group of friends, many from his own schooldays, but most of the lads were well settled by now, while Paul continued to play the role of groomsman and godfather. He had let a couple of lovely girls go over the years, but he didn't seem that bothered. There was still time for him yet – he was probably getting on a bit for kids, but he looked after himself and would make a fine husband for some lucky woman. Maybe someone who had her own children. He'd make a great dad. Had always been so good with Cara.

There had been crazy thunderstorms in Ireland the summer Cara joined their family, and that was long before there was any talk about climate change. Hundreds of farm animals were killed by lightning, giant hailstones damaged crops and there was severe flooding around the country. They had never seen the like of it before or since. An image pierced the surface of his memory: Kitty gazing out the kitchen window one evening at the dark purple sky, a worried look on her face, telling him she felt a horrible sense of foreboding.

It was two days later when she went to get Cara out of the pram in the front garden and found, to her horror, that it was empty.

14

Cara had been on her way to collect Maisie when Kian had finally seen her missed calls and messages, and rung her in a panic, wondering what was wrong.

'I'm coming straight home now, love,' he said.

She couldn't remember the drive to the crèche, had a vague impression of Chloe's smiling face, mouthing words at her, of the childcare assistant handing her Maisie's Bluey backpack. Maisie had been all chat about her day on the drive home. Cara had nodded and smiled, not taking in a single word.

She had plonked her daughter in front of the TV, a bowl of Rice Krispies on her lap, and sat beside her crackling with tension as she waited for Kian to get home. She wanted to go back in time, to unhear that conversation in the hospice. To unknow. But there was no unknowing the awful truth now.

Kian had come in and taken instant control of the situation. He wrapped his arms around her, held her tight. 'I'm so sorry, love.' He was the only one, apart from Alison, who knew how long she had been putting off the search for her birth-mother, how she had been waiting for the right time. A time that would now never come. 'We'll talk properly when Maisie's gone down but don't worry, love, it'll be alright.'

It'll be alright: her husband's mantra whenever she got herself worked up about something or other, a regular enough occurrence. It often turned out to be true. Not always, though. When her mother got sick that last time, it hadn't turned out alright. And now all hope of building a relationship with her birth-mother was gone. That wouldn't be alright either.

Kian turned on the oven to heat up the leftovers of last night's lasagne for their dinner, and handed her an ice-cold glass of rosé to drink while he bathed Maisie and got her ready for bed. She drank the wine faster than she usually would and poured herself a second glass. She didn't tend to drink much during the week, but she needed it tonight.

She went up to kiss her daughter goodnight, her blonde curls pouffed out around her perfect little face, like a dandelion clock. Maisie was half asleep, so fortunately it wouldn't be one of those nights when she clung to Cara, like a baby gibbon, insisting she lie beside her and cuddle her until she fell asleep. A terrible habit, everybody told her. Except her own mother whose motto had always been 'They don't stay small for long.'

'Night-night, Maisie Moo. Love you to the moon and back.'

'Night, Mama, lub you moon and back.'

They sat beside each other at the kitchen table with Cara's laptop in front of them, their dinner plates pushed to the side, her food barely touched. There was no point in eating when she knew it would go straight through her.

'I just can't believe they kept it from me all these years, that Mum didn't tell me before she died.'

'I suppose none of us ever know how we'll react until we're put into a particular situation,' Kian said, 'but if it was Maisie ... Well, I can kind of see where they were coming from, in trying to keep it from you. I mean, how could you even begin to tell a child something like that?'

'Yeah, I get that, but why didn't they tell me when I was older? Dad said they were always worried about me finding out. They should have been honest with me. It would have been a shocking thing to hear, but far less shocking than finding out like this.'

'I know, love. It's—'

'And the worst part is that I seem to be the only one who didn't know. Paul knew. And Helena and Maryanne. And the Caseys, of course. And God only knows who else. I feel like I'm the only one who was kept in the dark.'

'I still think, though, knowing your parents, Cara, that they did what they thought was in your best interests, whether or not you feel they were right. Jesus, it must have been an awful strain on them saying nothing for so many years, worried it could come out at any time.'

'Don't try to defend them, Kian. They took the easy option in not telling me. The more I think about it ... Mum actively discouraged me from searching for my birth-mother, and in such a sly way, telling me about somebody whose mother didn't want to know her. Christ, the whole thing is so fucked up.'

The anger that had been simmering on a low heat all afternoon was coming to the boil inside her skull.

'But even if they had told you, when you were in your twenties, say, or even your teens, it wouldn't have made any difference, would it? She died when you were a child so you still couldn't have met her.'

He was right, even if she didn't want to have to accept it. She had spent three years imagining a reunion with a mother who had been dead and buried for decades.

'I'm just so confused. Like, what relation is Maryanne to me now?' She tried to work it out in her head. 'My great-aunt through marriage instead of my aunt? And her kids are ... What? My first cousins once removed? It's insane. And I have grandparents and uncles and probably cousins out there who never in all these years tried to make contact. It just feels like such a ... I don't know ... such a kick in the teeth.'

'Look, love, it's going to take time for all this to sink in. You've had an awful shock today and the timing couldn't be worse, but it's going to be alright. You have me and Maisie, and we'll get through this together.'

She nodded numbly as he put his arm around her and pulled her into his chest. He didn't get it. How could he? He hadn't been given away at birth by a mother she had now lost twice. This could never be alright.

15

Kian couldn't get over the resemblance between Maisie and Lucia. Cara had gone into her search history and brought up the photo of her birth-mother she had found earlier.

'I can see a bit of you, but Maisie's the absolute spit of her, isn't she? It's mad.' He couldn't take his eyes off the photo.

Cara clicked onto the link to an *Irish Times* article published in 2012 on the twentieth anniversary of the discovery of Lucia's body and began to read aloud from the screen.

'There have been no developments in the case since two people were arrested in 1992 in the days after the discovery of her body. Two men, one in his twenties and one in his forties, were questioned for twenty-four hours each by gardaí before being released without charge.

'A garda spokesperson said they were appealing for anybody with information relating to the circumstances surrounding Lucia Casey's death to come forward now.

'"A lot of time has passed since this young woman's tragic death. We believe there are people out there who know what happened to her and have information that could help us get justice for Lucia," he said.'

The twentieth-anniversary report had run in a number of national and local newspapers, but apart from that, there wasn't a huge amount of detail about the case online. By 1992 none of the Irish papers had gone digital. It wasn't until 1994 that *The Irish Times* became the first newspaper in Ireland and Britain, and one of the first in the world, to establish an online presence.

'What about this one?' Kian pointed to a link towards the bottom of the search page: unsolvedmysteriesireland.com.

Cara clicked into it.

There were pages and pages of text with photos of the victims of unsolved murders, disappearances and crimes in Ireland. 'Where are they getting all this stuff from? It's not attributed to any source,' she pointed out. 'They're just putting all kinds of shite up and presenting it as fact.'

It pissed her off no end that she and her colleagues had worked their arses off studying journalism in college and being put through their paces in newsrooms, while any dope with a phone these days could put an un-researched, unsubstantiated and wildly unbalanced story online, claim it was fact and have it read and believed by thousands of gullible followers.

'There might be something in it, though. They've obviously lifted some of it from the news reports,' Kian said. 'They haven't even bothered trying to disguise it.'

'There should be a law against this sort of crap. No wonder the newspaper industry is on its knees with people just stealing our work and—'

'Well, that's not something you can sort out tonight, Cara. And some of these armchair sleuths do actually solve crimes.

Remember that Netflix thing about the cat-killer guy? It says here there were reports of a man seen hanging around outside Lucia's house in the days before she went missing, but despite numerous appeals, he never came forward.'

'We've no way of knowing whether that's true or not, though. I'll have a chat with Fitzie tomorrow, find out who covered the story for the *Champion* at the time. And I'll have a root through our own archives. At least I know the *facts* in those reports will be credible.'

16

Lucia
Kylemore
1984

It was a magical summer in so many ways, set against a soundtrack of Wham!, Madonna and Cyndi Lauper. It was the summer Bruce Springsteen released *Born in the U.S.A.*, Ronald Reagan visited Ireland, and an Irish missionary imprisoned somewhere out foreign was released. It was the summer of the big fiftieth-anniversary celebration of the opening of Kylemore House Hotel. And it was the summer Tommy discovered booze, and Lucia met her Mitchell Henry.

While her father was up to ninety getting the place ready for the big party, Lucia's mother was preoccupied with organising a special ceremony in the church in Letterfrack to give thanks for the safe release of the priest. At least she had stopped dragging Lucia with her to her endless prayer meetings and Stations of the Cross.

Her father had put his foot down when Lucia had woken the whole house three nights in a row screaming in terror after the last prayer meeting her mother had made her go to. It had taken place at the leader's house, in a dreary sitting room that reeked of damp and stale incense. Her mother and the other adults had started a weird kind of chanting, speaking really fast with their eyes closed and begging the Holy Spirit to pray through them. Praying for the gift of tongues.

And then one woman, with crazy hair that looked as if she had chopped it herself with a hedge clippers, had opened her mouth and in a deep mannish voice let forth a string of gobbledygook in a strange language. Lucia had been totally freaked out. As the other group members fell to their knees thanking the Lord, she wanted to flee from the room and its creepy atmosphere, but she was too petrified to move.

Then the same woman began an incoherent rant in her own voice about the Devil 'always prowling around, looking for ways to lead us into temptation'. The meeting leader had shushed her, told her she'd frighten away their younger members, but she had continued to sit and rave as everybody else got up and left. 'Trouble with her nerves,' Lucia's mother had said. 'Don't take a blind bit of notice.' That was easier said than done when Lucia was in bed at night, terrified to close her eyes in case the demon that crouched in the shadows at the foot of her bed came for her in her sleep.

Her mother might have given up bringing Lucia to any more prayer meetings, but rarely a day went by when she didn't tell her she should get down on her knees and thank God for all her blessings. She'd point to the poor Black babies on the Trócaire box who were starving to death every day, but Lucia tried not to look: the little babies with their beautiful brown eyes made her feel so sad. Lucia had more blessings than most, as her mother reminded her regularly. She'd never known a day of hunger, and very few girls of her age had their own pony.

Her father had bought Misty for her tenth birthday, glad perhaps to have one thing in common with his youngest child, his only daughter. He was master of the local hunt, his beautiful chestnut stallion Dynamo the pride of the stables. He had brought Lucia on a hunt with him when she was twelve and that had been the beginning and end of any kind of horsy camaraderie between them. She had been traumatised, had come off Misty shaking and crying, barely able to stand. She had vomited noisily into the hedgerow. The baying of the hounds, the roars of the hunters, the poor terrified fox running for his life, destined to be ripped to pieces, were all too much for her. Her father had been ashamed of her for making such a show of him but, to her relief, he never invited her to join the hunt again.

Tommy said Lucia's mother was 'a religious nutter' and she was inclined to agree with him. Her mother certainly seemed to spend more time in the church, or hanging out with Father Kenny, than she did at home these days. She took her duties as a minister of the Eucharist extremely seriously. Not just any Tom, Dick or Mary could fill the role, as she pointed out to her family. No, siree. She had been identified by Father Kenny as 'a worthy *acolyte*' for the honour, due to the 'exemplary Christian life' she led.

When she took those two steps up onto the altar, moving from the scratchy grey flooring to the plush red carpet of the sanctuary, above the ordinary people who filled the pews, her mother was raised to another level. She even stood taller there, chin out, shoulders back.

Lucia often thought her mother would have been much happier if she had joined the nuns herself, living as part of the Benedictine community in the Abbey, called to prayer five times a day. A quiet, peaceful life that would have suited her better than being married to a man who was married to a hotel, mother to three boisterous sons and a daughter who seemed to do nothing but disappoint her.

17

'Are you pulling the piss out of me again?' Fitzie stared at Cara, one eyebrow raised above his metal-framed glasses. In fairness to him, Cara had a well-deserved reputation for being a bit of a piss-taker among her newsroom colleagues, her innocent deadpan expression catching them every time.

She shook her head.

The gentle hubbub of conversation around them, and the tinkle of teaspoons against glazed ceramic was interrupted by the screech of a steam wand. She was sitting at the window overlooking Shop Street in 56 Central, their regular elevenses spot, opposite Sean Fitzgerald, editor of the *Connacht Champion*, and known to all as Fitzie.

Her mentor and boss was as far from the stereotypical hard-boiled editor as it was possible to be. Although he could be tough when he had to be, especially when standing up to management on behalf of his staff and their editorial independence, Cara and her colleagues in the newsroom knew how soft he was underneath. She had cried in his office on more than one occasion over the past few months during her mother's illness, and he had come out from behind his bombsite of a desk to give her a big hug. His door was always open, apart from Thursday mornings when the country edition of the paper was being put to bed. He was much more relaxed on Fridays when Kieran Murphy, the city editor, was in the hot seat.

The city edition was printing as they spoke, and would be on the streets by lunchtime. There had been talk for years of the press being sold off and, even worse, the lucrative city centre *Champion* property. She dreaded the change that was coming, still loved wandering down to watch the paper rolling off the presses and to inhale the pungent smell of the fresh ink and paper as the huge behemoth churned out the words she and her colleagues had written that week.

A young waitress put their coffees on the table in front of them, cappuccino for her, black Americano for Fitzie.

He was still speechless, a rare state for her usually loquacious editor. He was clearly having difficulty processing what she had just told him. He had always known she was adopted, but she hadn't mentioned anything to him about her plan to track down her birth-mother.

'Jesus, Cara. Are you OK?'

'Still trying to get my head around it, really. Not just that she was my mother but that I'm never going to meet her now. I've been awake half the night thinking about it. I know so little about her. I need to find out as much as I can now about who she was, and what happened to her.'

As she had lain in bed wide awake in the early hours, turning the whole thing over and over in her mind, her anger had begun to boil over. Her parents had been wrong in keeping this from her, and taking the risk that she wouldn't find out. It had been too high-stakes a gamble and she was the one paying the price.

She had finally drifted into a restless sleep at around four, and into a terrifying dream where she was falling from the sky, legs pedalling frantically, fingers scrabbling as she tried in vain to inflate her parachute, cursing herself for not listening to the air stewardess's safety talk.

'I covered the story myself. Sure it was huge at the time.' Fitzie grimaced. 'Sorry ...'

'Look, Fitzie, just forget she was my ... mother, OK? I need you to be completely open with me. There's been enough sneaking around behind my back. I want to know everything now.'

'I hear you. Well, it was pretty obvious from the start that there was something dodgy about the whole thing. She wasn't the type to take off on her own like that without telling anyone. Everybody who knew her said she was a quiet, shy girl. Johnny Browne covered the disappearance, from what I can remember, but he must have been off the day the body was found so I was sent back to Connemara. We got out there before the nationals, had a tip-off from one of the sergeants in Mill Street. Tony was sent out with me to get some shots. Christ ...' He shook his head. 'I still can't believe she was your mother.'

'That makes two of us.' She looked down onto the street below, the city's main shopping thoroughfare, where people were going about their daily business, sitting outside McCambridge's drinking coffee in recyclable cups, wandering into Boots and, even at this hour of the morning, going into McDonald's. A young busker had set up a guitar amp outside the bank at Lynch's Castle and a group of tourists had gathered to watch him perform.

'I don't think there was ever any mention at the time of Lucia having had a child, not even in the post-mortem report, but the bod— I mean *she* was in such a bad condition by the time they found her that it might not have shown up. Do you know who the ... who your father was?'

'No. She wouldn't say, apparently. She was sent away to have the baby, *to have me*, and it was all kept quiet. It's hard to understand with all their money why the Caseys couldn't have ...'

'Kept you? I know it seems crazy now, but back in— What year were you born?

''Eighty-five.'

'It was a different country back then sure. I know anything goes these days. Men marrying men, and fellas deciding to chop off their lads and be women instead, but even in the eighties, and that's not so long ago, the stigma around unmarried mothers was huge. So many girls forced to sneak off to England for abortions. Shocking, really.'

'As if they got themselves pregnant. Sickening to think that was going on when the priests got away with what they were doing for years,' Cara said.

'It is, but that's the way it was. Girls went off *to mind a sick relation* up the country and came home a few months later a lot trimmer around the middle. There'd be talk behind their backs for a while. Then people would forget and move on to the next thing.'

'I did a Google search, but there's not a huge amount of detail around the case. I'm going to spend some time in the archives this afternoon to see what I can find there, but I wanted to have a chat with you first.'

'Sure. Jesus. Let me think.' He lifted his cup to his lips and drank. 'Well, I remember she had a boyfriend who used to play trad music in the Crane. He was taken in for questioning after she was found, but released again. There was no evidence that he was involved.'

'Two people were arrested and let go. Do you know who the other person was?'

'It might have been a local lad but it's so long ago now that I can't recall exactly. There was also some suggestion at the time of a foreign-looking man seen hanging around Canal Road where Lucia was living with a flatmate, but I don't think the guards ever managed to track him down. Donie McGann was the sergeant in Clifden at the time. I know him well from when he was stationed in Salthill, used to play the odd round of golf with him. I can try to get a number for him if you want. He's well retired by now, but he might be willing to talk to you.'

'That would be great. I'd like to dig into this a bit more. I don't know ... I'm a bit all over the place at the moment but ... I mean she was only twenty-two. So young.'

'I know. It was desperate. I'll give Donie a shout when I get back to the office. Just let me know if there's anything else I can do.'

She thought for a moment. 'Would you know anything about getting access to a case file?'

He blew out a puff of air. 'I know it's bloody impossible with GDPR to get access to anything, these days. The cops are afraid of even looking up somebody on the Pulse system in case they get a slap on the wrist.'

'I meant for a family member to get access. If I applied as Lucia's daughter to get access to her file. Surely I should be entitled to that.'

'I don't think it's that straightforward. First, you'd probably have to show some kind of proof that Lucia was your mother. You'd have to go through the adoption services for that, and I can't imagine it being a fast process. Even then, you're not guaranteed they'll give you access. Look at that young fella whose body – well, part of it – was found on Inis Mór back in the nineties, and only identified last year. When his father tried to get hold of the case file, he was told they couldn't release it because his son was dead and not in a position to agree to the disclosure. Ridiculous altogether.'

'Yeah, I remember that. It was mad, alright.'

'All I'm saying is don't get your hopes too high. Try, by all means, but don't expect it to be easy. I think a good first step would be for me to reach out to McGann and see where that takes you.'

18

'Fucksake!' She stood in the stifling archive room, looking in despair at the chaos around her. Just the sight of all that dust made her nose twitch.

Binders of yellowing newspapers were thrown everywhere, on the counter, the shelves and the floor. The microfiche reader sat on an ancient desk, its screen caked with a thin layer of dust. A wonky chair stood in front of it, yellow foam protruding from a hole in the seat.

She couldn't remember the last time she had been in there, but it hadn't been anywhere near as bad as this. There had been some order, the binders arranged by date at least. It was going to take her ages to plough through this mess, but at least she wouldn't be interrupted in her task.

The newsroom across the corridor was deserted, phones, keyboards and clattering printers silent for once in the Friday-afternoon lull. Only Fitzie was still bashing away at his computer in his office at the end of the corridor, trying to get ahead of himself for next week. The man was a self-confessed workaholic.

She had missed calls on her phone from her father and Paul, text messages asking her to please call them back. She wasn't going to: she couldn't speak to or even look at either of them at the moment. Kian had called earlier to say they had been on to him too.

'I told your dad that myself and Maisie would meet him on the Prom for a walk in the morning, and that you need a bit of time to yourself right now. Paul will probably join us as well.'

'You did what?' Her temper flared. 'They don't deserve to see any of us after what they did.'

'I know you're angry with them, love, and I would be too in your position, but Maisie was asking about Granny Kitty again last night, wanting to know when she can see her again, can we go to visit her in Heaven. She doesn't understand that she's ... Well, I think it would be good for her to spend some time with your father this weekend.'

Cara had felt like arguing, but she didn't want to make things any worse for Maisie, who was missing her granny. She had never felt so conflicted, so angry. Hurt by the very people who had loved and cared for her all her life. She needed her mother, felt her loss as acutely as an amputated limb, but she was furious with her too.

She pulled a notebook from her bag and set to work to find the issues of the paper from December 1990 when Lucia had gone missing, and June 1992 when her body was found. Some of the binders were missing their covers, and pages had been ripped from some of the papers. It was a disgrace that this valuable archive was so neglected: there was history in these pages that you wouldn't find in any Google search. It should have been digitised years ago, but with all the cutbacks, there had probably been nobody available to do it.

The past two decades had seen the circulation for local paid-for weekly publications, like the *Champion*, fall by more than half, while the number of employees had also halved as papers 'transitioned to digital-based models'.

Some of her colleagues had taken the voluntary redundancy when it was offered, a few moving into the far more lucrative world of PR, and those who were left had been forced to take pay cuts. The high rise in the price of newsprint and spiralling energy costs meant the current environment was more challenging than it had ever been. Cara worried about the future of the paper, about her own future: she wasn't cut out for PR, for all the schmoozing. Even the thought of it was soul-destroying. It was all so stressful, especially given that she was the family's main source of income right now. Kian wouldn't be making a lot out of the school contract: he had priced it *competitively* to win the job, his goal being to use that contract to attract future lucrative jobs. She just hoped he hadn't priced it too competitively.

She had been searching for about ten minutes, already hot and sticky from hefting the unwieldy binders, when she found 'January to July 1992'. The newshound in her instantly sat to attention, adrenaline spiking. She dragged it onto the counter and flicked through to the issue of 26 June, the first paper printed after the discovery of Lucia's body two days earlier.

Unsurprisingly, it was the main story on the front page, an enlarged photo of Lucia smiling up at her. Cara pressed her hands over the brittle yellow paper trying to smooth down the line that ran through Lucia's right eye. Who had she been, this woman who had carried her for nine months, given birth to her and handed her away? She looked happy in the photo, her smile crinkling the edges of her eyes. What must she have gone through, though? How had she ended up in the godforsaken place where her body had been found?

She wondered if Lucia had thought about her much over the years. If she had pined for her, or if she had been able to get on with her life and put the experience behind her. She knew so little about the woman her birth-mother had been before she had met such a tragic death.

The story, under Fitzie's byline, explained that a local man out saving turf had found the body in the isolated bog nineteen miles from the family home in Kylemore: there had been a recent drop in water levels in the bog. Lucia could have lain there for decades if that man hadn't happened to be in that corner of the bog on that day.

She read on.

The state pathologist had been taken to the scene, where he was assisted by the Garda Technical Bureau. The body was fully dressed in the clothes the deceased was last seen in: a brown suede jacket over a pair of stonewashed jeans with a black leather belt, a baggy grey shirt with '1990 Vintage' printed on it, and black ankle boots with a low heel.

The body had been taken to the morgue at Galway Regional Hospital for post-mortem. Dr Hugh Guerin, the pathologist, had been unable to find any evidence of a fatal assault, as the body had lain in the bog for so long and had undergone significant decomposition. Gardaí were, however, treating the case as a murder investigation, given the circumstances in which the body was discovered.

The thought of Lucia lying there for so long, in that bleak bog, exposed to the elements, was horrendous. Connemara might be one of the most spectacular places in the world on a fine day, but there were few places drearier on a dark night in the depths of winter.

19

It was another scorcher of a day. Kian had taken Maisie down the Prom to meet Cara's father and give her time to read through all the archive material. No doubt she would be the topic of conversation, her father mounting his defence to Kian. She felt even less like talking to him today than she had yesterday. Even more furious at what her parents had done.

She was too exhausted when she got home the previous evening to go through the articles she had photocopied. Her lower back had been aching after hours of hefting the cumbersome files around, the physical pain a distraction from what was going on in her head. She had fallen into a deep sleep, waking in panic in the early hours from another falling dream, one in which she had been hanging onto a newborn Maisie by the fingertips of one hand as they plunged through the air.

She had no idea what time it was when she eventually drifted off, but skinny fingers of light were clawing their way around the edges of the blinds.

She took a mug of coffee into the garden where she settled herself at the rattan table in the shade of the parasol with her pile of pages. The sky was a glorious cloudless blue, a rare treat in this part of the world. Song birds twittered sweetly from the trees in next door's garden and a lawn mower droned lazily in the distance. Her mother would have loved this. Any sign of fine weather, she would have her shorts on and her sun-lounger out, soaking up the rays.

The loss thumped her, almost bringing tears to her eyes.

How could she ever accept that she would never see her again?

And how could her mother have kept the truth from her?

She had always felt she could talk to her mum about anything, which made it even harder to grasp that such a monstrous secret had been wedged between them all this time.

She pushed it away, and began to read the articles she had arranged by date from earliest to most recent. The next couple of hours flew by as she immersed herself in her research, writing notes in the margins and underlining important pieces of information as if she was working on a feature series with Lucia Casey the subject.

An unnamed source had told the *Champion* it was impossible to arrange a visual identification of the body given the damage caused by its submersion in the waterlogged ditch. A Seiko watch and a gold Claddagh ring recovered from the remains were identified as Lucia's, according to the same source. The family had appealed for anybody with any information to come forward and asked for privacy to grieve.

There was an interview with a neighbour of Lucia's, Maureen O'Flaherty, who had reported seeing a 'darkish' man hanging around the lower Canal Road area in the weeks leading up to her disappearance. She claimed to have seen the same man on at least three occasions when she brought her little Jack Russell out to 'do his business' before bed, but she hadn't managed to get a good look at him on those dark winter nights.

The neighbour described Lucia as 'a lovely girl. Very mannerly, always had a greeting for you, but kept herself to herself. She went to work and came home – you could nearly set your watch by her every day. We were all so shocked when she just vanished into thin air.'

It was bizarre. How could a young woman have disappeared without anybody seeing anything? And who was the man who had been hanging around in the dark?

The fine weather had brought the crowds out, and the narrow streets of the medieval city were heaving. Kian had suggested going into town for lunch, and even though she didn't really feel like it, she couldn't bear to be stuck at home with her head-wrecking thoughts. The city – a big town really – was like a non-stop party in the summer months with one festival following on the heels of another. They ate in the Front Door pub before taking a stroll down the pedestrianised cobbles of the city's Latin Quarter, absorbing the vibrant buzz of the area, with its pubs, restaurants and shops. Umbrellas and canopies had been set up outside to provide shade from the sun as opposed to shelter from the rain for a change.

Kian miraculously snagged a free seat outside Tigh Neachtain's where he sat with a pint, people-watching, while Cara and Maisie went into the Wooden Heart across the lane to browse the shelves of wooden toys and puzzles, puppets, spinning tops and paper-doll kits. The little toy shop, with its bright red door, antique window panes, and shelves of hand-made toys and games, had been there for as long as Cara could remember. She loved it most on winter evenings when the warm yellow light from inside spilled out onto the street, the shop almost seeming to glow. As a child, her own mother had often brought her in to admire the beautiful hand-stitched teddies.

It was one of the few family-run businesses that had survived from her childhood – the city centre was being taken over by mobile-phone and sports shops. Only a few hardy stalwarts like Anthony Ryan's department store, Fallers Jewellers, Hanley's Menswear, the Four Corners and O'Brien's newsagent's were still going strong.

'Look at this, Maisie! It's *The Princess and the Pea*.' She pointed to the little princess mouse lying on a tower of miniature mattresses inside a paper castle, a tiny pea hidden somewhere within. It was adorable.

'Me get, Mom?'

'No, Mays. Not today. Maybe for your birthday or from Santa.'

Another wave of sadness washed in. Her mother should have been with them today, Cara arguing with her over buying the toy for Maisie because she didn't want her getting too spoiled, but her mother inevitably winning the battle because 'That's what grandparents are for.' Her daughter would lose out on so much without Granny Kitty in her life.

'How about we get another animal for your collection?'

'Yay! Me need a widdle piggy.'

As well as the wooden piglet, Cara bought a little hand-cranked music box, its innards exposed, an exact replica of the one her mother had bought her as a child. She had loved watching the gears inside the box pricking out the tinkling tune as she wound the tiny handle. Watching Maisie's face light up as she turned the handle and the little box played 'Hey Jude' zipped her straight back to her own childhood and her father's beloved Beatles albums. The house was always filled with music, her mother and father singing along, knowing every word by heart. 'Hey Jude' had always been her favourite.

She had wanted for nothing growing up, surrounded by love in that house in Salthill. She had to keep hold of that in the midst of everything else that was going on.

20

Lucia
Kylemore
1984

'Where on earth is he, Zigs?'

Tommy's pony, a sturdy dun Connie, nickered at her from his stall.

'You're right, Ziggy. He's very bold leaving us waiting. And Misty's all ready to go, aren't you, my gorgeous girl?' she said, nuzzling her pony's swan-white neck.

Lucia had raced over from the Abbey after her morning's shift, glad to escape the stifling shop where two coachloads of American tourists had descended on them. She had made herself a quick sandwich in the kitchen, which she swallowed down while changing into her riding gear, then headed for the stables at the far side of the hotel.

Danny Conneely ran the stables for her father, organising treks for the guests and managing the stable hands. They did a bit of livery too for members of the local hunt. Lucia spent most of her time over the summer months helping to muck out the stables with Tommy, and groom the horses as well as looking after their own ponies.

Tommy sometimes grumbled that her father didn't give them a penny for all their hard work while their older brothers, who worked in the hotel when they came home from boarding-school in Dublin, were paid for their efforts. Lucia didn't care. There was nowhere else she would rather be than in the company of those beautiful animals.

Their usual routine was to hack the ponies as soon as she got back from the shop, but she had Misty groomed – all the mud from her rolling session brushed off, her tail untangled – and tacked up, and there was still no sign of Tommy. The grey mare nudged her head into Lucia's pocket now, searching for treats.

'Can you smell the mints off me, Miss?' She took a half packet of Polos from her pocket, placed one on her palm for the pony to take and popped another into her own mouth.

There was a loud bang from the next stall as Ziggy kicked his door.

'OK, OK, keep your tail on, Zigs. I wouldn't forget you, would I?' She threw a couple of mints into the food bucket hanging inside his stall. She had learned the hard way that Ziggy was a bit mouthy.

She was trying to decide whether to get Tommy's horse tacked up for him, or to head out on her own in case he wasn't coming, when she heard his voice. 'Most of the ponies belong to my uncle Marcus, who owns the hotel, but myself and my cousin, Lucia, have our own ponies here.'

Oh, flippit!

He must have been nabbed by a guest wanting to go out for a ride. They'd have to stick to the safe hacking paths now, wouldn't be able to take the horses out for a proper run.

'Here she is now.'

Tommy rounded the corner into the main covered stable area where Lucia was standing, a long row of stalls lined up on either side.

'Lucia, this is PJ. He's been sent out from Galway to spend some time in the schticks. Some third cousin seven times removed or something. PJ, Lucia.' Tommy jerked his thumb towards her.

She was gawping at the stranger. Intensely conscious of her red sweaty face, her filthy breeches and straggly hair, the stink of horse poo off her. He, on the other hand, looked like a model for Insignia deodorant who had never so much as broken a sweat. The most beautiful boy she had ever seen in real life. Thick blond hair, with a long fringe swept to one side. Sodapop Curtis blue eyes. Tanned face and arms. Ripped stonewashed jeans and a 'Dancing in the Dark' T-shirt. He didn't look like a PJ. He looked like a Rob or a Matt or an Emilio. Something far cooler than PJ.

Poor Tommy was like a scrawny child beside him, with his mucky breeches and his skinny farmer's tanned arms. She realised they were both staring at her. Waiting for her reply.

'Am ... hi.'

God, please make her think of something interesting to say. *Please, please, please.*

'Do you want to ride?' She flushed. 'I mean on a horse ... not ...'

Tommy snorted.

'He knows what you mean, you spa. You're hardly offering him the ride when you've just met the poor fucker.'

She flushed even more – she must be purple by now. She'd murder Tommy when she got him on his own.

PJ smiled, not appearing in the slightest embarrassed by all the talk about riding. 'Thanks for the offer,' he said, 'but I think I'll give it a miss if you don't mind. I've never been on a horse in my life. I'd probably kill myself.'

God, so polite too. He put the *liúdramáns* who had been in primary school with her to shame.

'I just brought him over to show him around the place,' Tommy said. 'I told him we'd give him a shout later if we're going to Lettergesh for a swim. He can take one of the lads' bikes.'

Mother of God. The thought of this hunk on the beach in a pair of togs made the blood rush to her privates. Then she realised he'd be looking at her in her swimming togs too and the blood rushed up to her face. Although she had been thrilled when she had finally started to develop breasts, albeit measly little ones, she was still far from happy with herself. She hated her naturally wavy hair and the freckles that popped up every summer, like sprinkles of pepper across her nose and cheeks.

Still, she didn't let any of that stop her going to the beach with the boys that evening.

And so the two musketeers became three.

On fine days, they cycled as far as Lettergesh or Glassilaun, where green fields edged by ancient stone walls faded into rock, then sand and finally clear green water.

They clambered up Dúchrach, PJ puffing on the steep rocky ascent to the summit while she and Tommy slagged the unfit townie. The Sacred Heart statue didn't look as eerie up close as it did from down below, his arms stretched to the sky, at the mercy of the harsh Atlantic wind and rain. On a clear day, the view over the Abbey and out over Connemara would take your breath away; on darker days, when it was shrouded in dark grey cloud, brooding and sulky, it looked like a volcano ready to blow.

21

Cara made a beeline for the one free table in the foyer of the hospital, ignoring the daggers thrown her way by a stocky man in a dressing-gown who was headed in the same direction. Usually, she'd have let the patient take the seat but after the hassle she had just gone through in trying to find parking outside, she was in every-woman-for-herself mode.

The heatwave had broken but it was still muggy, and her dress clung to her back by the time she found a space after driving around for nearly fifteen minutes. She swallowed half her Coke Zero in one long draught.

Her plan had been to get settled early in a quiet corner, and read through her notes again before her meeting with retired Sergeant Donal McGann – whose wife fortuitously happened to have a review appointment at the hospital after a recent surgery – but she wouldn't have time now and, anyway, there seemed to be no such thing as a quiet corner here.

A long queue snaked around the café, young medics with stethoscopes slung around their necks like fashion accessories, the odd patient in a dressing-gown and visitors taking a break from the bedsides of loved ones. There was a loud hum of conversation, the clanking and whistling of the coffee machine, the screeching of plates being scraped into bins, and the incessant ringing of the phones at the reception desk.

The irony of the setting didn't escape her. This was the hospital where Lucia had been working when she went missing.

'Cara?'

A red-faced man who looked about two steps from a heart attack stood beside her table.

'Yes. Donal, I take it?' She smiled up at him.

He nodded, then sat heavily onto the chair opposite her. He pulled a rumpled hanky from his pocket and mopped his face. 'God give me patience,' he panted.

'It's baking, isn't it? Look, thanks so much for agreeing to meet me like this. Can I get you a ...' she had been going to say coffee, but he looked like his blood pressure was already through the roof '... water or a cold drink or something?'

'Water, please. Plain, not that fizzy shite. Christ Almighty! It's fierce heavy, and it's a bloody satnav you'd need inside in this place. If I wasn't stressed before we got here, after getting an earful the whole way in the road from Clifden, as if it was my fault her wound got infected, I'd be bloody well stressed trying to find the friggin' outpatients department and then park within a mile of the place. I'm half tempted to go round the back and sign myself into the psychiatric for a break.'

Cara chuckled. The Irish really couldn't cope with heat like this in a country built for the cold. The poor man was practically frothing at the mouth. She went into the shop where the queue was shorter and bought two bottles of water for him and a KitKat. He looked like he could do with the sugar.

He guzzled most of one bottle, and made short work of the chocolate. Then, after blotting his face and forehead again with his hanky, he pulled some crumpled pages out of the back pocket of his jeans and smoothed them out. 'I jotted down some notes last night but, first, I just want to say that I'm sorry for your loss. When Fitzie rang me last week, it brought it all back. I was surprised to hear Lucia had a daughter, that was the first I heard of it.'

'I was surprised myself as you can imagine, but now that I know, I'm keen to find out as much as I can about her. I'm going to try to get access to the case files, maybe go through GDPR if I have to.'

'It's worth a try, I suppose, but what you'll get through GDPR will be so redacted, it probably won't be worth your while. I can remember nearly every detail of that case as clear as if it was yesterday, though. We don't get many murders in Connemara, as you'd know yourself, wouldn't be good for tourism. There was that poor girl back in Carraroe, of course, but the lad who did that is serving a life sentence, thank God. It's just a pity whoever was responsible for Lucia's death isn't alongside him where he belongs. I'll tell you everything I can.'

'Thanks Donal, I really appreciate this. Is it OK with you if I take notes?'

'Grand, yeah, as long as you keep my name out of it. Are you planning to write about it?'

'God, no. It'll take me a while to get my head around it, never mind anything else. I just want to find out what happened to her.'

As he talked, sharing details she hadn't come across in any of the press coverage, Cara scribbled in her notepad.

Lucia was last seen leaving the hospital after her shift, he explained. Her flatmate and best friend, Sandra Nolan, arrived home from Dublin airport at around eight p.m. to find the place in darkness and no sign of Lucia. She checked her bedroom where she found wrapping paper and a roll of Sellotape on the bed beside some presents waiting to be wrapped.

'It didn't look like she was planning to take off anywhere so.'

'No, not voluntarily anyway. Her jacket was gone, but she hadn't left a note, which the flatmate said was out of character. This was pre-mobile phones, remember, and Lucia rarely went anywhere alone, never mind venturing out on her own in the dark. It was a dirty aul' night too, wet and windy. The girls were planning to watch a video and it was Lucia's turn to make dinner.'

'What was the boyfriend's name?'

'She was doin' a line with a young lad she met at work, one of the porters. Colman Ryan. Known as Colie. They hadn't been going out together that long when she went missing. He was a trad musician, due to play in the Crane the night she disappeared.'

Cara knew the Crane well. One of the city's oldest traditional music venues, the pub had been around for as long as she could remember and was enjoying something of a revival in popularity.

Donal explained that when there was still no sign of Lucia by around nine that night, Sandra rang the Casey family home out in Kylemore and spoke to Lucia's mother, Annette, who said she hadn't seen or heard from her daughter for a few days, which wouldn't have been unusual. When there was still no sign of her an hour later, Sandra left the house and went to the

Crane to see if she was there, but the boyfriend said he hadn't heard from her.

'When Lucia still hadn't arrived home by midnight, Sandra started to get really worried. The following morning, the Monday, when Lucia failed to show up for work, Sandra again rang the family home where she spoke to Lucia's older brother, Phillip, who became very concerned when he heard she hadn't come home the night before. Her father, Marcus, rang Mill Street at that point to report her missing and to say the family were concerned for her mental state. She had suffered a bit of a nervous breakdown some years previously, had spent time in a psychiatric unit and they were afraid the same thing was happening again.'

Cara felt the heat rise in her chest. This was the first she had heard of her birth-mother having mental health problems. God only knew what kind of health issues she herself might have inherited.

It was now, Donal explained, hauling her attention back to him, that one of the neighbours reported seeing a strange man hanging around the place. However, nobody saw Lucia leave her house or being collected that Sunday evening, and it was highly unlikely she'd have left to meet a stranger on a dark winter's evening of her own accord. There was no sign of any foul play having occurred in the house so the main lines of thinking from the outset were that she had either left to meet somebody known to her, maybe straight from work, or may have gone into the river. The flatmate was adamant, though, that Lucia was in a good place mentally: there was no way she would have taken her own life. This was backed up by her boyfriend and work colleagues.

Pausing briefly to refer to his notes, the former sergeant told her that Colman Ryan had a solid alibi. He had been at the Crane all that Sunday evening and only left with Sandra Nolan shortly after ten o'clock to try to find Lucia.

Despite appeals for information in the local and national media over the following days, weeks and months, McGann said there wasn't a single verifiable sighting of Lucia. Nor despite an appeal for the tall, dark man who was seen in the lower Canal Road area in the days leading up to Lucia's disappearance, had anyone ever come forward. The gardaí had never succeeded in tracking him down.

Fast forward eighteen months, and the then Sergeant McGann had a call about the discovery of a body in Toombeola bog. 'It was in a bad way after submersion in bog water for so long, and the post-mortem was inconclusive in terms of a cause of death, as I'm sure you already know. However, although Lucia was fully dressed, it's highly unlikely that she dressed herself. Sorry to be so morbid especially when she was your mother but ... well, it's not easy to dress a corpse properly. You often find after a sexual assault or a murder where the victim has been dressed by the perpetrator that buttons aren't fastened properly, little things like that. In Lucia's case, not only was her shirt buttoned up arseways, but her underpants were on back to front. Our thinking was that she was killed somewhere else and transported to the bog after death.'

Cara thought of the smiling young face looking up at her from the newspaper, a quiet, innocent young woman by all accounts. She found herself praying that death had been swift, that she hadn't suffered long, hadn't known what was coming.

'I'm sorry, Cara, this can't be easy for you.'

'No, it's not, but I need to hear it. The man who was hanging around near the house, that sounds pretty suss, doesn't it, especially when he never came forward? Did you have any idea at all who he could have been?'

'None, I'm afraid, and there was no CCTV in the area at the time. He certainly was a person of interest to us but you learn to keep an open mind in these investigations. People have all sorts of reasons for not making themselves known to the gardaí, he could have been dealing to students in the college or up to no good of some other kind, and had nothing whatsoever to do with Lucia.'

'I read there was a man arrested soon after the body was found and let go again.'

'That's right. A local lad, Tadhg Ó Conghaile. A few cans short of a six-pack. His father owned the bog where the body was found, and Tadhg used to go out there saving turf with him. His mother gave him an alibi for the night Lucia went missing and the time around it. She said he was at home watching telly with her– that was all he did every night. Not the strongest alibi in the world, like, but that young fella wouldn't have had the brains for it. Or the stomach. He'd exposed himself at the public toilets in Clifden once, but was let off with a warning. The mother kept him on a tight leash after that. He was ruled out fairly quickly.'

'And the other man taken in for questioning, that was Colman Ryan?'

''Twas. He had a strong alibi for the evening she disappeared, but given their relationship, he had to be looked at. He was also ruled out early enough.'

'Do you know where he is now? Colman Ryan.'

'I couldn't tell you, love. I heard he went off the rails after the body was found, went heavy on the drink. Last I heard, he was out in Boston, but that's going back years.'

She circled Colman's name in pen. And Sandra Nolan's. She had to find them and discover as much as she could about who her birth-mother had been. About who she herself was.

22

She turned her phone to silent and tried to tune out the hubbub of the newsroom around her. She had eschewed going out for her usual mid-morning coffee with her colleagues, having a takeaway at her desk instead.

She had a backlog of work to get through, thanks to having spent so long with Donal McGann yesterday, and her brain felt stuffed with sodden cotton wool. Her sleep was still all over the place. She had been jolted awake from another falling dream at four a.m., her heart jack-hammering inside her chest. She had lain awake for a couple of hours, her racing mind refusing to power down.

She usually worked late on Thursday nights while Kian collected Maisie, but she'd be here even later than usual tonight.

Work had always been a sanctuary for her, her newsroom colleagues almost an extended family. Her career as a journalist was a huge part of her identity. She was good at her job, had won a number of awards, and gained a reputation for sensitivity and empathy in tackling difficult issues. She usually worked on autopilot, crafting sentences and paragraphs from her notes, presenting the key facts in the first few lines, then filling in the rest of the story. She was struggling to focus today, though. Her mind kept drifting away, her thoughts clamouring for her attention like toddlers tugging at her sleeve.

She dragged herself back to her screen where she was working on an interview she had done earlier that week with a couple who lived with their three children in one of the homes earmarked for demolition to make way for a new ring road around the city. The family were stuck in limbo, unable to sell up. The paper had been highlighting the need for a new ring road for decades, but it had been blocked every step along the way by those who would lay down their lives for a rare bog cotton, but seemed not to care that the city was being choked to death by traffic.

Her phone buzzed.

A WhatsApp message. Paul.

Her bowel clenched.

You free for lunch or a quick coffee? I'm just coming up Bridge Street.

'Shite,' she said, under her breath.

Her brother taught English and history at St Joseph's College, a boys' secondary school known locally as the Bish, located less than a ten-minute walk from the *Champion* office in Nuns' Island. He rarely came up town during his lunch break.

Her finger hovered over the message. She was torn. Her father and Paul were already devastated by the death of her mother and she knew that by shutting them out she was adding to their pain. She hadn't spoken to her brother in a week – it was actually a week today since she had found out about Lucia. It seemed longer and at the same time shorter. She had never gone so long without talking to Paul, or WhatsApping. But as much as she missed him, she also wanted to push him away. Her father too. It was still too raw.

She couldn't ignore his message, though – he'd probably get Caroline at Reception to buzz him up to the newsroom.

Sorry, up the walls. On a deadline.

He was typing: *Please, Cara, I really need to talk to you. Just 10 minutes.*

Feck him anyway. If she didn't go, she'd be too distracted with guilt to get any work done. She was finding it hard enough to wrangle the words on her screen into any kind of a coherent pattern and she could do with a break.

Quick cup so. See you outside McCambridge's in five.

Shop Street was buzzing as usual. Outside Lynch's Castle, a crowd was gathered around a group of buskers with guitars, violins and a banjo belting out a tourist-pleasing rendition of Ed Sheeran's 'Galway Girl'. The seating area in front of McCambridge's was wedged; she tried to remember the last time she had sat there with Paul before their mother's diagnosis, oblivious to what was coming. It was a shop she always associated with Christmas, of wandering around holding her mother's hand as they inhaled all the wonderful scents – coffee and spices and willow – and admired the fancy displays of hampers filled with gourmet chocolates and puddings and cheeses and wines. In her memory, her mother wore her red wool coat with the black velvet collar that always came out of the wardrobe at that time of year.

Her brother came out the shop door, a takeaway cup in each hand, and nodded to the corner seat his jacket was holding for them.

He handed her a cappuccino, a perfect chocolate powder leaf floating on top. 'So how are you doing? We've been so worried about you. Me and Dad, Helena too.'

He looked wrecked, like a man who hadn't had a good night's sleep in ages. He was still smartly dressed, her brother liked his style, but the stress of their mother's illness had aged him. She had always been able to talk to Paul about anything, but that was before. How could he possibly understand how she was feeling now? Not only had he not been handed over at birth by a mother who was murdered less than six years later, he had been part of the conspiracy of silence around her.

'I'm confused, upset, fuckin' angry. Pretty much how anybody would feel after finding out their whole life was a lie, I'd imagine.'

'I'm sorry, Cara. It was such a difficult situation. Mum and Dad didn't make the decision lightly. They really thought—'

'I don't care what they really thought, Paul. What they did, what you all did, was wrong. Wrong and bloody cruel. And I'm not in the right headspace to have this conversation with you right now.'

'OK, I get that. I just want you to know that I'm here for you. If you do want to talk or cry or just shout at me, whatever you need. We know you need time but please don't shut us out. Especially Dad. He's already struggling after Mum.'

'Do you think I don't know that? I'm sorry the timing isn't great for ye but it's not exactly great for me either – and I don't need you coming in to me at work and making things even worse by guilt-tripping me.'

'Ah, Cara, that's not what I meant at all. I'm sorry. I just wanted you to know that I'm here for you, not to make things worse. Jesus,' he said, covering his face with his hands, 'I just wish I could fix things for you but ... just please don't push us away.'

'There's no fixing this mess. You're going to have to give me time, you and Dad, to try and sort things out in my own head.'

'Yeah, of course.'

'Now, I really have to get back to work,' she said, getting to her feet.

He looked like he was about to say something else, but changed his mind again.

'Take it easy out there.'

Take it easy out there should be the epitaph on her brother's gravestone, his signature conversation sign-off. Like a lot of good advice, easier said than put into practice.

Despite being fit to drop after a long day at work, Cara had two more jobs to tick off her to-do list. The first was to stop at the Crane Bar on Sea Road.

Having failed to find any sign of her mother's old boyfriend online, she had decided to call into the pub to see if anybody there remembered him. The place was busy enough when she went in just after eight o'clock, a group tuning their instruments in preparation for a session. She had been hoping the bar staff might be able to help, but the hipster-bearded lad pulling pints, in a pair of jeans that must have been sprayed onto him, looked far too young.

She hovered around the top of the bar until he finished serving his customers and approached her with a smile. 'What can I get ya, love?'

'I was wondering if you could help me. I'm trying to trace a musician who used to drink here back in the nineties, a guitar player called Colman Ryan, known as Colie.'

'Never heard of him myself, but that's the man you want over there.' He pointed to a big white-bearded man sitting at the far end of the bar with a matching thatch of thick white curls, his huge paw curled around a half-drunk pint of Guinness.

'Mossie, you might be able to do something useful for once and help this lovely lady. She's looking for someone who used to play here back in the Stone Age.'

'Go 'way outta that, ya cheeky pup,' Mossie answered, before turning to Cara. 'Who're ya lookin' for, love, and what have they done?'

Cara headed down to his end of the bar and introduced herself, then ordered another pint for him and sparkling water for herself. She explained her situation and who she was looking for.

The older man stroked his beard thoughtfully, twisting the coarse hairs into a fine point. 'I remember Colie alright, played a few sessions with him meself. A nice lad, lovely guitar player.'

Bingo.

'Haven't seen him in years, though.'

Shite.

'He went to Boston after Lucia died apparently,' Cara said.

'I heard he went away alright, but I didn't know where. The guards pulled him in at the time. He was supposed to have been in a very bad way over it all. I'm afraid I wouldn't have a clue where he is now, though.'

Feck.

'But Paddy Moran might know. He'd have been close enough to him back then – they played together a good bit. He hasn't been here in a while, having chemo for prostate cancer last I heard, God help the poor fucker, but his brother-in-law Sean lives a couple of doors down from me. Sean was married to Paddy's sister Mary. She died of cancer a few years ago, started in the breast, I believe, but she was riddled by the end. Another sister died of the same thing. That bloody big C runs right through some families.'

Cara shook her head sympathetically. 'Awful bloody disease.' *Come on, for Christ's sake.*

'If you want to give me your number, loveen, I'll drop it into Sean on me way home, fill him in on the picture and ask him would he pass the message on to Paddy.'

'That would be great, thanks so much.'

'No bother at all, loveen, best of luck with it now.'

The last job on her list was to ring her father. She really didn't want to talk to him, had even considered asking Kian to do it for her, but she knew he would only say she was being childish.

He picked up on the second ring, as if he had been sitting by the phone willing it to ring.

'How ya love?'

'Hi.' She couldn't even muster up 'Dad'.

'Thanks for ringing. Are you OK? I was—'

She cut across him, getting straight to the point. No point giving him the false notion that she was wanting to play happy families. 'The reason I'm calling is that I need to apply for access to Lucia's case file, but to do that I have to be able to prove that she's my ... that I'm her ... I need to apply for my birth cert first.'

Cara had a certificate of adoption that had the legal status of a birth certificate, allowing her to apply for a passport and driver's and marriage licences, but had no details about either of her birth-parents. She had been vaguely aware of the Oireachtas debates about the Birth Information and Tracing Act 2022, which many adopted people had been waiting decades for as they had no statutory right to access their birth certs or adoption records.

She had read and heard some truly heartbreaking stories of mothers refusing contact when their children tried to track them down, but she had never really given much thought to the tormented lives these women must lead. They had had to endure the secret shame of giving birth out of wedlock, then to hide the existence of their child from their husbands and subsequent children, coping in silence with the pain and loss for the rest of their lives. She couldn't imagine having to live in the same world as Maisie without ever being able to see or touch her.

It had all seemed so removed from her before, as if she wasn't the same as other adopted people, didn't have that much in common with them because she was happy as she was and had never felt the urge to reach out to her birth-parents. Things were different now, though, and ironically, the timing couldn't have been better in terms of access to information.

When the legislation came into effect in October, she would be able to access any birth, early-life and care information that existed, including a copy of her original birth certificate. She had been in contact with a lovely woman at the Adoption Authority who had told her that the new Act also enabled people to access this information if their parent was dead. She advised her that if she could find out which agency had been involved in her adoption, it might speed things up.

Through her own research since, Cara had discovered that most applications where the mother was still alive were granted, but a substantial minority were refused, usually because the birth-mother did not consent. Almost a fifth of those who applied had been denied access to their own birth information last year.

Things had changed so much since Cara had been adopted in 1985. She was aware, of course, that there had been a steady decline in adoptions granted in Ireland since the 1980s but had learned that of the 863 applications for adoption made in 1980, about a quarter were family adoptions, many by grandparents or by parents who had remarried. This compared to 111 adoption applications made in 2021, most of which were for step-parents who wanted to adopt their partner's children and were granted over Zoom.

'Can you remember the name of the agency that was involved in my adoption?' she asked her father now. It was a long time ago, but surely her parents had kept some paperwork.

'We didn't go through an agency.'

'What do you mean? How could you not go through an agency?'

Was her adoption even legal? Nothing would surprise her at this stage.

'The law was different, you see. It's changed since but back then a birth-mother could choose to place her child with someone, usually a family member, if she felt they were suitable. That's what happened with you. It was all above board, I promise you that, Cara. We were assessed by a social worker and everything before we were recommended to the Adoption Board as suitable parents for you.'

'Oh, right.'

It all sounded very casual, as if kids could be swapped around willy-nilly within families, but then again, it was Ireland in the eighties. A lot worse than that was going on in front of blind eyes.

'Are you sure it's a good idea, love? Going down this road? I'd imagine that case file could be very upsetting and what good will it do at the end of the day?'

'I've been kept in the dark for long enough. I want to know everything there is to know now about my birth-mother and that includes all details of the investigation. I've no doubt it will be upsetting – the woman was murdered and dumped in a bog, for Christ's sake – but I need to know! Somebody out there knows what happened to her. Somebody got away with it.'

He sighed. 'Alright, love.' He sounded so defeated. Weary. Her heart went out to him. He must be so lost without her mother, pottering aimlessly around the house, the silence blaring in the absence of her endless chatter.

'Did you know her parents well, you and Mum?' She softened her tone. 'I never heard you talk about them.'

'No. We went to the poor girl's funeral that time, and we met them at Maryanne and Luke's wedding, of course, years earlier, but we didn't have any other dealings with them really. It would have been too awkward after ...'

'Of course. Anyway, I also wanted to let you know ... I've decided I'm going to reach out to the Caseys. To tell them I know now. And to see if they'd be willing to meet me.'

23

**Lucia
Kylemore
1984**

The fiftieth-anniversary celebrations were due to take place over the last weekend in July. It would also mark a month since their first kiss.

Lucia's first ever kiss.

She had been so nervous, afraid she'd get it wrong. *Just Seventeen* and *Smash Hits* were useless when it came to tips on how to kiss properly. If Victoria had been around, like she usually was during the summer, she could have asked her for advice. But Victoria was in Paris for three months learning to speak French.

She couldn't confide in Tommy about her massive crush on PJ. He'd just slag the arse off her and be bound to let it out. She still couldn't quite get over the fact that PJ had looked sideways at her in the first place. A boy who was so far out of her league he was in another galaxy, who could surely have the pick of any girl he wanted, yet he kept coming back to hang out with her and Tommy.

She had got over her initial awkwardness with him quickly enough, her shyness dispelled by his own easy-going nature, his interest in her and in what she had to say. She hugged herself at night in bed and dreamed of the two of them living in the beautiful home he had built for her, a happy, lively place filled with children, dogs and laughter. With a stable for Misty, of course.

'I don't get it. How can she be a grey pony when she's white?' he asked her now, tugging at Misty's tangled mane with a mane and tail brush.

He had started to join in the grooming rather than just stand there watching them. She had had to warn him about standing behind the horses. He had no idea how powerful these animals were, the damage one kick could do to fragile human bone. Misty looked angelic with her huge dark eyes, and she was usually pretty placid, but she could be saucy when the mood took her.

'I don't know to be honest. Grey horses can be born any colour, but their hairs gradually turn white as they get older. Her skin is actually black, look,' she said, parting the pony's hair to show him. 'Misty is fully white, but some greys turn dappled and the ones with speckles on their coat are called flea-bitten.'

She could talk all day about ponies, especially Connemaras, once she got started and he seemed keen enough to listen. She boasted about how they were the best performance ponies in the world.

'It's because they're native to here. They have to be hardy to survive in such a rocky, wild place. And they're known for their intelligence and calm temperament, although Misty is well able to let you know if she doesn't want to do something. She has a bould streak in her too. Don't you, my beautiful girl?'

One day they had managed to coax PJ onto Ziggy, his knees nearly coming up to meet his chin despite Tommy lengthening the stirrups as far as he could. He looked like a giant toddler on a donkey. He nearly lost his life when the horse started moving.

'Jesus Christ. Stop him. STOP!' he had roared.

Tommy and Lucia were bent over in hysterics. The pony was barely trotting.

'GET ME OFF! I'm going to fuckin' fall,' PJ roared louder.

Lucia grabbed the reins.

'How do I get off?'

She was laughing too hard to talk.

'Well, you've no fear of making the Grand National any time soon. Just pull your feet out of the stirrups, you feckin' eejit, lean forward and throw your left leg over the side,' Tommy instructed.

PJ flopped on the pony's back like a stricken whale, hanging onto his neck for dear life.

Lucia was down on her hunkers, her stomach muscles sore from laughing. PJ looked so ridiculous. If only she had a camera.

'You're so dead when I get off this yoke, Lucia Casey,' he had warned. 'You'd better start running now.'

When he'd finally managed to perform the most inelegant dismount she had ever seen, he had headed straight for her. She had taken off, haring around the back of the stables into the woods, he clumping after her in a pair of Phillip's old wellies that were a size too big for him. Her heart pounded in anticipation of being caught.

He had grabbed hold of the back of her top and she let out a shriek. Then he pushed her gently against the tree behind her.

Janey, he was gorgeous.

The long days spent outdoors had deepened his tan, making his eyes even bluer.

When he had leaned forward to kiss her, she had closed her eyes, grateful for the solid bulk of the tree holding her up.

24

Cara pressed the buzzer on the keypad at the imposing electric gates outside Maryanne's house on Taylor's Hill. She had been there once or twice with her mother when she was younger. A long driveway curved around a putting-green-perfect lawn to the modern architect-designed box in which Maryanne lived with her second husband.

The glass and stone house with its stunning views over the bay had been featured in the *Irish Times* property supplement. Maryanne had done well for herself, not only out of her divorce from her first husband, but in her second marriage.

The gate inched open as if reluctant to grant entry to Cara's lowly Hyundai. She parked to the side of the house, away from the top-of-the-range designer jeeps Maryanne and her investor husband Graham drove.

Maryanne ushered her in through continental-style double French doors to a large open-plan kitchen and living space that extended over the entire ground floor. Painted a stark white and floored with sleek black tiles, the space was vast, ultra-modern and, in Cara's opinion, utterly soulless. It took minimalism to a whole other level. Everything was hidden behind glossy white units, not as much as a cup or a plant or a family photo on show. The only bit of life in the place was the artwork on the walls, vibrant splashes of hot pink, petrol blue and lime green on huge white canvases. It was the kind of home you'd expect to find in Silicon Valley, where Graham spent much of his time, not so much in one of the most salubrious suburbs of Galway city.

She followed Maryanne to a seating area in front of the vast wall of glass that formed the back of the ground floor, and looked out onto a tranquil Japanese-inspired garden. A funky zebra-print rug lay prostate on the floor in front of the pristine white leather suite. Cara wondered if Maryanne's grandchildren visited often – the thought of Maisie running around this immaculate space made her blood run cold.

It was hard to believe Maryanne was from the same family as her mother and Aunty Helena – they couldn't have been more different. Her cut-glass accent was priceless, and she was an outright snob, but so unwittingly hilarious she got away with it. She genuinely didn't seem to give a crap what anybody thought of her. Cara wished she could be a bit more like that.

Graham emerged from somewhere at the other end of the house to welcome her, and asked if she would like to join himself and Maryanne in *a cheeky little mimosa* or if she would prefer some tea or coffee. Unlike his wife, Graham came from old family money in Kent and was genuinely posh. Cara would have loved a mimosa, especially if Graham was making it because it would be the good stuff, but she was driving and had promised to meet Kian on the Prom with Maisie afterwards. She opted for a coffee.

The last time Cara had seen Maryanne had been at her mother's funeral. Glamorous as ever, she had wafted into the funeral parlour on a trail of expensive perfume. At seventy-two, she could easily pass for fresh-faced, if ever so slightly shocked, early sixties, thanks to the various tweakments performed by her expensive cosmetic surgeon. Cara had never seen the woman without a full face of perfectly applied make-up and salon-fresh hair. Maryanne had every intention of 'ageing disgracefully', proudly showing off the neat scars behind her ears – from the face lift she had treated herself to for her sixty-fifth birthday – which meant she could no longer wear her hair tied back, a small price to pay, in her opinion. Today, her aunt's nipped and tucked body was head to toe in designer leisurewear, the logo too discreet for Cara to make out.

'So, Cara,' Maryanne said, dragging the elephant straight into the middle of the room, 'you must have got a dreadful shock finding out about Lucia the way you did. The timing wasn't great to say the least, for any of you, but I hope you can understand why ... Well, it would have been different if she hadn't died as she did. And it was such a worry for your mother, still playing on her poor mind at the end.'

'I'm still trying to get my head around it. If it was Maisie, I'd want to protect her, and I'd be worried about the damage finding out something like that could do to her but ... if they had sat down with me, when I was old enough, of course, and explained what had happened, yes, I'd have been shocked and upset but it would have been far less traumatic than finding out the way I did. Now Mum is gone and it's all just so ... shit.'

'I know, love.' Maryanne reached out and squeezed her hand. 'Just know that whatever they did, they genuinely thought it was the right thing.'

'Yeah, well ... I was wondering, do you know why Lucia gave me up for adoption, why she didn't keep me?'

Relinquish was the word the book she was reading used to describe giving up a child for adoption. A classic regarded by many adoptees as their Bible. She had looked up the word in the Collins dictionary. It meant 'to give up; abandon (a plan, policy etc); to renounce or surrender (something owned, a right etc); to let go (a grasp, hold etc)'. She couldn't imagine letting go of Maisie, abandoning her to get tangled in the branches of some other family's tree.

Graham delivered their drinks on a tray, Maryanne's cocktail in a delicate champagne flute, a strawberry doing the splits on the rim, Cara's coffee in a wide cup and saucer, vintage diner style. A discreet peep at the logo underneath showed Cara it was Ralph Lauren. Graham placed a matching milk jug and bowl of golden sugar lumps with tiny tongs in front of her, and a narrow rectangular china plate bearing a perfect row of pastel macarons. She'd take one to be polite but she wasn't a meringue fan, hated the phlegmy aftertaste.

'Thank you, my love,' Maryanne said, rubbing her husband's arm as he passed her. She turned back to Cara.

'Lucia was only seventeen when she had you, but you have to understand that we're not talking about a typical seventeen-year-old by today's standards or even when you were that age. She was a lovely girl, but very innocent for her age, probably mollycoddled by Marcus, Annette and her brothers, being the youngest and the only girl. Her pregnancy came as a huge shock to everybody. She'd never even had a boyfriend, not that anyone knew of anyway. We all assumed she'd never even been kissed. She spent most of her time with the horses out in Kylemore and Tommy, Simon's son. The two of them were thick as thieves.

'She refused to say who the father was even when they threatened to get rid of her horse ... They didn't mean it, of course, but they were afraid that maybe she'd been taken advantage of. Possibly by an older man. There were so many people coming and going between staff and guests. And she had always been such a good girl, so quiet and well behaved ... very different from my Victoria when she was a teenager, always giving me lip and pushing boundaries. Anyway, Lucia could barely look after herself, never mind a baby.'

'But surely the family could have helped her? Money wouldn't have been an issue.'

'It was never about money, probably more to do with shame and worry about what people would think. The Caseys were staunch Catholics, especially Annette. I'm talking real Holy Joes. Lucia was named after one of the children Our Lady was supposed to have appeared to in Fatima. Annette lost the plot altogether after she was found in that bog, went a bit loopy for a while, even had a grotto built in their garden at Kylemore. An awful gaudy thing. I haven't had any contact with any of them for years, not since Luke and I split.'

Cara was well aware that Maryanne's separation from her first husband had been far from amicable.

Maryanne continued: 'They're well into their eighties now, of course. Marcus is still going strong, from what Victoria tells me, still very involved in the business, although Phillip is more or less running the place these days. And Annette has Parkinson's – she's gone very frail apparently.

'But getting back to Lucia, you have to understand that they were different times. If a student nurse or a teacher got pregnant, she was out on her ear. A lot of women, not just teenagers, hid their pregnancies from their families. They'd just go away for a while and turn up again months later with nobody the wiser. Or take the boat to England. If Lucia had kept you, it would have been the talk of the place for years.'

'So you're telling me they were so afraid of what people would think they just gave me away? What was to stop them reaching out years later, when there wasn't so much ludicrous stigma attached to babies being born *out of wedlock*?'

'I don't know, Cara sweetheart, but I suppose the more time that passed, the harder it would have been ...'

'Do you know if ... Did she want to keep me?'

Maryanne looked longingly at her empty glass. 'I don't know if this will make things better or worse for you, but Lucia did want to keep you and I know she was very upset at having to give you up.'

Cara didn't know if it made it better or worse either. She wanted her mother to have wanted her. She didn't want to think it had been an easy decision to *relinquish* her. That she had been unwanted, disposable. She needed to hear that she had been very much wanted, even if she would never have swapped the happy upbringing she had had in Salthill.

'If it was me, if it was Maisie, I would have refused. I would have fought tooth and nail to keep her. No matter how young I was.'

'It wasn't as simple as that, love. Lucia didn't have a choice. Like I said, girls then didn't have the choices you girls have today. They had to toe the line and that was it. There were very few strong enough to fight back and Lucia certainly wasn't one of them. She hadn't been the strongest even before she got pregnant, mentally, I mean, and she had terrible baby blues afterwards. The family were so worried about her, but you have to understand, everything they did, they thought they were doing in Lucia's best interests.'

Jesus. She'd love to know how the people in this family gauged what was in their children's *best interests*. How could forcibly separating her from her baby ever have been in her birth-mother's best interests? And how could hiding the truth of Cara's beginning in life and her mother's horrifying death ever have been in Cara's best interests?

'I'm sure they must have tormented themselves over the years since Lucia's death. After all, if they hadn't made her give you up, she'd have been living a very different life and would probably still be alive. That has to haunt them.'

The thought hadn't occurred to Cara. She had been thinking only of how her adoption had shaped the course of her own life, but Maryanne was right. If Lucia had been allowed to keep her baby, her life would have taken a different direction. She would probably never have ended up working in the hospital and living in Canal Road. She might have got married and had more children, a family of her own. Had a life beyond the age of twenty-two.

'I'd like to meet them, Maryanne. The Caseys. My grand-parents at least. But I don't want to contact them out of the blue in case ... well, in case they're not keen. I don't think I could handle that right now. So I was wondering ... do you think, considering they're still close to the family, that Victoria might reach out to them for me? Or Andrew?'

25

She was in a special sitting of the District Court, shivering in the sub-zero air-conditioning, when she finally got the call. After three days of constantly checking her phone, she was beginning to wonder if anybody was going to bother getting back to her.

Maryanne had suggested Andrew would be the best person to reach out to his uncle Marcus. She had intimated that Victoria had a tricky relationship with her father, which wasn't surprising given the messy break-up of her parents' marriage, and wasn't that close to the Caseys any more. Maryanne's ex-husband Luke had always been a gobshite, according to Aunty Helena, who had never liked him. She referred to him as the Prick as if that was his given name. *I warned her he was a prick the first time I met him, but she still went ahead and married him.*

Cara realised she hadn't seen Luke at her mother's funeral, but why would he have been there? He and Maryanne had been separated longer than they had been married. Victoria, effortlessly elegant albeit painfully thin, and Andrew had come to the funeral parlour to offer their condolences. It was the first time she had seen either of them in years and, of course, she'd had no idea that they were her birth-mother's first cousins.

Maryanne had promised to call Andrew on Sunday after Cara left and ask him if he'd be willing to reach out to the Caseys for her. The lack of response since had strongly suggested that either he wouldn't, or worse. That he had contacted the Caseys to say she wanted to meet them, but they didn't want to meet her and he didn't know how to break it to her. Maryanne had given her Andrew's number so she could follow up herself, and she had added it to her phone contacts, but she had no intention of ringing him. She had already made the first move. The last thing she wanted was to look needy.

That morning Kian had told her to stop catastrophising or she'd drive herself to drink. She knew he was right, but she wasn't sure if she could cope with being rejected by her birth family. Again. Last night she had lain beside Maisie after she had fallen asleep just gazing at her. Drinking in every precious feature. Her soft unblemished skin, the delicate thready veins in her eyelids, the light seasoning of freckles that would go back into hibernation for the winter.

She couldn't imagine what it would be like to be separated from her, this little person who was more a part of her than anybody else in the world. Other than Cara's birth-father.

If he was alive.

Stop it!

Why was she torturing herself like this?

Nobody was going to separate her from her child. Kian was right: this way lay madness.

It was a week ago today that she had gone to the Crane and she had still heard nothing back from Mossie's contact,

Paddy. She would have to pop back into the bar and see if he was around. She had also tried to track Lucia's friend Sandra Nolan online and via social media. She had found dozens of women with that name and contacted a few through LinkedIn and Facebook, but without success.

She felt her bag vibrating under her seat. She rooted in its depths, pretending to scrabble for a pen while surreptitiously checking her phone. Her heart nearly stopped when she saw the caller name.

Andrew Casey.

A missed call and a WhatsApp voice note.

Bloody typical when she was stuck in court for at least another hour before the judge broke for lunch. Murphy's law said that if she left for five minutes to listen to the message, she'd miss the case she had been sent to cover. It was going to be a bloody long hour while her phone burned a hole in her bag beneath her.

The son of a former city mayor was up on a sexual-assault charge. Rumours of a spiked drink. He would be sent forward to a higher court for trial, the media prohibited from publishing his name to protect the identity of the complainant, but in a city the size of Galway most people would know who he was. She looked at him now. A nice-looking lad in a smart suit, sitting between his parents. They all appeared dead-eyed and exhausted. Had probably been dreading this day for months.

The word around town was that the boy, a second-year law student ironically, was vehemently denying the charges against him, his father telling anybody who would listen that the girl had been 'up for it', but changed her mind after the event when her boyfriend found out. It was possible, she supposed, but very few young women would willingly go through the nightmare of taking such a case to court because they were worried about their boyfriend being pissed off at them.

The minute hands on the clock that hung on the wall behind Judge Jarlath O'Donovan inched slowly past the noon mark. She had to endure a drink-driving and two drunk-in-public cases, the bread and butter of the District Court, before the one she was waiting for was finally called.

Her stomach had started to act up, the sounds cringingly loud in the court room. The former councillor's son stood, nervous and pale, while his solicitor spoke for him. Cara had to strain to hear him. Luckily, the judge was having the same problem.

'Speak up for goodness' sake, Mr Tiernan. How does your client plead to the charge?'

'Guilty, Your Honour.'

He'd obviously changed his tune. The councillor stared at his feet, while his wife, who looked like she was about to throw up, reached for her son's hand and gripped it tightly. The poor woman. Cara felt for her. She must be going through hell. Whether or not he was guilty, she would stand by her son. That was what mothers did.

'Very well. I'll remand him on continuing bail to appear before the next sitting of the Central Criminal Court in Galway, on condition that he continues to reside at his current address, surrenders his passport and does not apply for a new one or any other travel documents. He must also sign on weekly at his local garda station.'

The mother glanced in Cara's direction as she took down the judge's every word, aware no doubt that, even though his name wouldn't be printed, everybody would know her son had pleaded guilty to such a shameful offence. Cara didn't feel good that her report would add to the pain and stress that the woman was already going through, but she had to do her job.

She decided to wait until they were well gone from the building before she left – she didn't want the awkwardness of bumping into the councillor, with whom she had always got on well, in this setting. He might ask her to keep the report out of the paper, which wasn't in her power to do. It was one of the downsides of being a reporter in a small city. A former friend of her father had been so pissed off when she couldn't keep out his drink-driving case – incapable of understanding that she would have risked losing her job – that he hadn't spoken to her or her father since.

She stood on the steps outside the courthouse and pulled her phone from her bag. There was no sign of the ex-mayor and his family, just the usual tracksuit-and-runners brigade smoking and shooting the breeze. She pressed play on her voicenote.

'Hi, Cara, Andrew Casey here. My apologies for the delay in getting back to you. I was at a conference in Dublin and didn't get to talk to Uncle Marcus properly until Tuesday evening. Anyway ...' Cara held her breath, 'he's delighted you've reached out and the family are very keen to meet you. Aunt Annette is in bad health so isn't up to travelling into Galway, but they'd like to invite you out to Kylemore, if that would suit you. Give me a buzz back when you get a chance, and if it helps, I'd be very happy to meet for a coffee and a chat before that. Just let me know what suits.'

Adrenaline whooshed through her bloodstream as she walked back towards the *Champion*, making her heart beat faster and sweat pool in her armpits.

They wanted to see her.

26

Andrew had booked a table for two in the bar at Glenlo Abbey, a five-star hotel on the outskirts of the city, a short drive from the hospital for him, and quiet enough for them to have a private conversation. He had insisted he wanted to treat her to lunch when she had returned his call yesterday afternoon. Her coffee was being served when he arrived ten minutes late, effusive in his apologies.

A tall, striking man, he sported an impressive tan she suspected was imported from climes far sunnier and more exclusive than Salthill. His teeth were the kind of white and even you had to pay a lot of money for and his eyes a remarkable blue, which would have given Cillian Murphy a run for his money.

'I'm so sorry,' he said. 'Morning rounds ran late. I usually don't take a lunch break, just grab something on the go.'

A young waitress appeared at the table within moments of his arrival, depositing a double espresso in front of him. He was clearly a regular. He drained the tiny cup in one before fixing his full attention on Cara. 'So, Cara, I can't imagine how you must be feeling. You've had so much to deal with in such a short time. How are you doing?'

She had heard he was popular with his patients, was known for his good bedside manner, and she could see why. He gave great eye contact, made her feel like he genuinely cared.

She was well aware of Andrew Casey's reputation, of course. He had come back from Canada to take up the position of professor of obstetrics and gynaecology at University Hospital Galway, a position his father had held before him, and was a prominent voice in campaigning for better maternity services for Irish women in the wake of the Savita Halappanavar scandal in 2012: a young woman had died of sepsis in UHG after she was denied an emergency termination on legal grounds.

'It's been a lot to take in.' A thought struck her. 'Did you know Lucia was my mother? Before, I mean?'

He leaned forward, steepling his fingers with their neatly trimmed nails between them on the table.

'Yes, but only because Victoria overheard a conversation between our mother and yours around the time Lucia went missing. When we asked Mum about it, she told us Lucia had given a baby up for adoption when she was a teenager and that baby was you. She warned us not to say a word about it to anybody.'

The young waitress appeared beside them again. 'Would you like to order now or do you need more time?'

'I'll go for the salmon, much as I'd love the burger, and a sparkling water, please,' Andrew said, patting his non-existent belly. 'Would you like some more time, Cara?'

'I'll have the caramelised pear salad, please.' She would have loved the burger too, and a side of the mouth-watering Parmesan and truffle aioli fries, but she didn't want to look a complete hog in front of him.

'So, as I said on the phone, Marcus and Annette were thrilled to hear from you. They had thought about reaching out themselves over the years but ... Look, I'll let them talk to you when they see you. Phillip and Hugh are going to be there too. Denis lives in Chicago so he won't make it this time but, hopefully, you'll meet in the not too distant future. It's obviously going to be very emotional for you all, meeting for the first time. Especially after what happened to Lucia.'

'The not knowing what actually did happen must be a nightmare for them. Do they have any idea at all themselves about who might have been involved?'

He shook his head. 'Not really, no. They're convinced that the man who was seen hanging around by the canal was somehow involved, especially when he never came forward to rule himself out of the garda enquiries. But they've had to accept that they'll never know. It's the only way they could try to move on with their lives. Not that they'll ever get over it, especially Aunt Annette. The year and a half that Lucia was gone was just hell. She went down to nothing, and Uncle Marcus was trying to keep the business going in the middle of it. They had the press camped out at the gate and then when she was found, in that dreadful place ... None of us will ever forget it. It was horrific. The kind of thing you read about in the papers but never expect to happen to anyone you know, never mind your own family.'

The irony didn't escape Cara: that Lucia's parents had made her give up her daughter and ended up losing their own. She wondered why they hadn't felt compelled to reach out to her in the years after Lucia's death, a flesh-and-blood connection to their lost child.

There was a lull in the conversation as their food was served. Andrew forked some pink flakes of fish away from the fillet and dipped them into the green foam they had been served with. He looked directly at her. 'Cara, this is a bit awkward and ... The last thing I would want to do is offend you or cause you any more upset than you're already going through but ...'

Had they changed their minds about seeing her? She felt her temperature begin to rise despite the climate-controlled coolness of the bar.

'It's just that Annette, as I think I mentioned, isn't in great health, and Marcus is concerned that, given your job, the whole thing isn't dragged up again in the papers.'

'God, no! I have no intention of writing about this. I mean, it's so personal. To me, this isn't a story, it's my life. To have found out about Lucia the way I did ... It's just so huge. I'm still trying to process things. Please assure them that I would never do that.'

'I will. I know that will give them great comfort. I really hope I haven't offended you. I did say I thought it was very unlikely that you would want to go public with it but they were a bit anxious about it after what they've been through.'

'I totally understand. All I want is to find out as much as I can about who my birth-mother was. What she was like. I'll never have the chance to meet her so I'll have to rely on people who knew her to help me do that.'

How could she explain to him the deep need inside her to vacuum up every speck of detail about her mother, to fill the empty spaces inside her with it like a kind of emotional Polyfilla? It was only by finding out who her mother was that she would discover who she herself was now. Not the old Cara who had drifted through life pretending that the separation from her natural mother only days after her birth hadn't been that big a deal: to the new Cara it had been a huge deal, especially now that she was motherless and rudderless in the world.

27

Lucia
Kylemore
1984

The day of the fiftieth-anniversary celebrations of the hotel opening had finally arrived and the whole place was on high-doh. A former taoiseach was coming and a couple of former government ministers, Uncle Joseph's cronies. All the local politicians would be there with their wives. A controversial high-court judge had been invited, and a few famous actors and actresses. Bagatelle were playing and there was even talk of Gay Byrne showing his face, which her mother wasn't a bit happy about. The heady scent of the massive floral arrangements in the entrance hall and ballroom overpowered the fumes of fresh paint. All kinds of fancy food had been ordered in. There was even a red carpet.

When Lucia had tentatively suggested that all of the guests be given a posy of violets to wear for the dancing, like the old days in Kylemore Castle, her father had looked at her as if she was an imbecile. She and Tommy had been ordered to stay well out of the way until the party that night and to be on their very best behaviour. Her mother was nowhere to be seen, probably at the church with Father Kenny praying for all their souls. A lifelong Pioneer, Annette Casey wasn't impressed by the amount of alcohol that had been ordered in for the big night.

Lucia and Tommy's brothers were strutting around the place like cocky penguins in their tuxes. Tommy and PJ had gone back to Tommy's house to change into their rented suits, and Lucia was on her way to Aunt Maryanne's room to see the dress she had brought out from Galway for her. Her aunt, who was staying in the hotel for the weekend, had come to the stables earlier to tell Lucia she had somebody coming to her room to do her hair and make-up that evening, and wanted to treat Lucia to have hers done as well. Lucia had jumped at her offer. Her mother didn't approve of her wearing make-up, and Lucia had never had much interest in her appearance before, but she wanted to look her best tonight.

Her hair had been teased into her first ever up-style and the beautician had worked a miracle. Lucia couldn't quite believe it was her in the mirror. Her hair was pulled back off her face emphasising her petite features, and showing off cheekbones she hadn't known she had. Her eyes looked bluer than normal and her freckles weren't quite so freckly. She turned to the side now in front of the full-length mirror in her aunt's bedroom. The dress was a deep blue taffeta that came to just above her knee with a gorgeous ruffled hemline. Aunt Maryanne had brought her a pair of low-heeled shoes, covered with the same fabric as the dress – Lucia hadn't thought about shoes and owned nothing even vaguely suitable.

Her aunt had great taste, always looked so stylish. She was very bold, always taking the Lord's name in vain, even in front of the kids, but great fun. Lucia envied Victoria having a mother like that. A mother you could talk to about anything. When Lucia had started her periods, it had come as an awful shock to her. She hadn't a clue what was happening, had no idea that it happened to all girls, not just her. She didn't have friends to talk to about that kind of stuff and wouldn't have dreamed of telling her mother that blood was coming from her private parts. When the bleeding stopped and came back a month later, soaking through the wads of toilet roll she had stuffed into her underpants, she confided in Sister Breda that she thought she was dying and asked her to tell her parents.

Instead Sister Breda gave her a packet of sanitary towels and told her how to use them. She explained that it happened to every girl when she became a woman, even the nuns, and that it meant she could now have a baby. She gave Lucia a note to give to her mother when she went home, and the next day, her mother brought her to the hot press and pointed to where a cardboard box of Lil-lets was tucked away down the side of the immersion out of sight of the men of the house.

Aunt Maryanne came out of the bathroom, the height of glamour in a long purple dress with a strapless sequined top, her hair tumbling in curls onto her shoulders. Like something out of a film. Lucia wanted to tell her how beautiful she was, but she always felt so shy around adults, even nice ones like Maryanne.

'Oh, Lucia, show me you.' She turned to face her aunt.

Maryanne opened her mouth dramatically wide. 'Wowee, you look absolutely fab. I knew that blue would suit you.

Wait until everyone sees you. You'll be the belle of the ball tonight.'

Lucia turned back to the mirror. She cared about only one person's reaction and, for once, she felt good enough to warrant his attention. 'Thank you. I love it, the hair and make-up too. I don't even look like me.'

'Well, now you know how you can look when you put a bit of effort in. I'm always saying to Victoria that you'd be gorgeous if you did yourself up. It takes work to look that good.' She laughed.

Lucia would have loved to tell her aunt about PJ, about the weird fluttery feeling she got in her belly when she thought about him. Which was most of the time. She'd love to ask Aunt Maryanne if she thought it was possible that he liked her too. The kind of things she could never in a million years talk to her mother about.

If it was possible to burst with nervous anticipation, there'd be bits of her splattered all over the bedroom. Aunt Maryanne was insisting they wait until all the other guests had arrived at the hotel before they made their grand entrance. Like Cinderella at the ball. But Lucia just wanted to get there. To see him. To take in his reaction when he spotted her. The ugly duckling all dolled up. She took a sip from the glass of champagne Maryanne had given her. She grimaced. It was too bitter, needed a splash of Ribena or something to sweeten it.

It wasn't quite the fairytale entrance Lucia had envisaged, with all eyes turning to stare in awe as they descended the staircase. When they stepped into the foyer, a butler in a top hat led them inside to the Connacht Room for the drinks reception. People stood around high tables and sat in little groups by the fireplace, which was filled with chubby cream candles dripping wax. The women fluttered around in dresses of every colour and style imaginable. The men were all in identical penguin suits, some waistcoats having to work harder than others to restrain the bellies inside them. A few heads turned to smile in Maryanne and Lucia's direction, but most people continued their conversations. Lucia didn't recognise many of the important people her father had invited.

She scanned the room. No sign of PJ and Tommy. She spotted her brothers outside on the terrace with a group of snooty-looking boys and girls their own age. Must be their friends from boarding-school. A lot of back-slapping and guffawing going on.

'Maryanne, you look wonderful.' Her father came to greet them. 'And Lucia. My, my. Don't you scrub up well? Thanks, Maryanne, I appreciate you helping. I hardly recognise her out of her filthy jodhpurs.' He looked Lucia up and down admiringly. As if she was a mare at the horse sales. *Any vices? Does she stand well for grooming? How is she with boxing? Does she take the bit easily? Is she easily spooked or fairly bombproof?*

'Maryanne, you know the Honourable Mr Justice Horan, of course,' her father said, as he drew her aunt into a nearby group, leaving Lucia standing awkwardly alone at the door. What was she supposed to do? She couldn't see anybody her own age and she certainly wouldn't be welcome in her brothers' company. The thought of trying to make conversation with strange adults filled her with dread. She backed out the door, and wandered through the Grand Hall where a pianist was tinkling at the keys and a few stragglers were still arriving.

The double doors to the ballroom stood wide open. The room had been transformed. Huge arrangements of fat purple and blue hydrangeas burst from vases on every table. The chairs were spruced up for the occasion in ivory jackets to match the newly painted walls, and the freshly varnished floorboards were gleaming. The chandeliers sparkled from above and the flames from the tall slim candles in the polished candelabras danced slowly in the draught from the open French doors leading to the gardens. Her father and his staff had done an amazing job. Their hard work had really paid off.

She decided to check outside for the lads. Heading back through the hall, she spotted her mother standing in a huddle with Father Kenny and some of the members of her prayer group. She was wearing a beige dress, a long shapeless thing. In their dull drab clothes, they looked out of place in the midst of the tropical birds around them. As if they thought they had been invited to a funeral, not a party.

Lucia backed down the corridor again past the ballroom, not wanting her mother to catch sight of her in case she ordered her home to scrub 'that muck' off her face. She slipped in through the breakfast room and out the French doors onto the terrace that wrapped around the hotel. It was still bright out. She surveyed the garden, which had also been dollied up for the occasion and was studded with lanterns awaiting darkness. Still no sign of the boys.

She flopped onto the wrought-iron bench on the terrace, rightly fed up now. She had been looking forward to this night for weeks, had dreamed of PJ sweeping her off her feet, dazzled by her. What a fool she was. As if a fancy dress or hairdo could change who she really was. Yes, they had kissed and, yes, his eyes did seem to follow her a lot, but that was probably because she was the only girl around the place. Why would he pick somebody like her when he probably had his choice of the girls at home?

'Boo!'

'Arrgh!' she shrieked.

Her cousin was standing beside her, beaming from ear to ear. Swaying slightly.

'Jesus Tommy, you big eejit. You nearly gave me a heart attack.'

'Ooh, look at you, all dickey doo!' He whistled, then dragged a chair across the patio, and collapsed into it. He was definitely well on it.

'Where were ye? Where's PJ?'

'We were looking for you. He's gone back inside to see can he find you. And to get us some more drink.'

Her spirits lifted, and her stomach skittered. *He was looking for her.*

She was about to suggest they go after him when the man himself rounded the side of the house, balancing three champagne flutes in his hands.

'I found her, Peej. She's hiding out here away from everyone.'

'I'm not hiding ...' She tailed off. *Holy crap.* He was so handsome in his tux. And the way he was looking at her. As if ...

'Lucia, wow, you look ... beautiful.' He couldn't take his eyes off her, stood there just staring at her.

'Will you gissa drink, ya clown, and stop staring at her like the eyes are about to fall out of your head?' Tommy said.

PJ handed them a glass each, and settled himself on the bench beside Lucia, close enough that his arm was touching hers. The energy crackled between them.

Tommy knocked back his drink in two swift gulps.

'Take it easy, Tommy, will you? That stuff's strong. He's already had about four,' PJ said.

'Go away out of that. That's only like Lilt compared to the poitín. Speaking of which ...' Tommy pulled a naggin of Powers out of the inside pocket of his jacket. 'Who wan's a drop of the good stuff?' He lifted the bottle to his lips and took a deep slug, shuddering as it went down. 'Fuck me. Tastes like shit, but you get some buzz off it.'

'What are you at drinking whiskey on top of the champagne? You'll be sick as a dog.'

Tommy laughed and took another slug.

'It's not whiskey. It's poitín the clown is drinking,' PJ said

'Ah, God, Tommy. You haven't an ounce of sense,' Lucia chided. 'If your father catches you in this state, you'll be grounded for the rest of the summer.'

'Fuck 'im. I don' give a fuck,' Tommy slurred. He took another slug from the naggin, screwed the cap back on and fumbled around for his pocket.

'Here, I'll mind it for you, Tom. Just chill out there for a while,' PJ said, winking at Lucia. He put the glass bottle under the bench behind his feet.

'A'right, Peej, thanks.' Tommy slumped sideways in his chair and closed his eyes.

PJ took a sip of champagne, wrinkling his nose.

'It's rotten, isn't it?' Lucia said. 'You can have mine if you like. I'm not drinking it.'

'Nah, you're grand, thanks.'

There was silence for a minute or two. He turned his head towards her. 'You look lovely. Your hair suits you like that.'

'Thanks.' She looked at him, and glanced away, embarrassed.

His hand was so close to hers, she wished she could reach out and touch it, but she could never be so forward. Even though they had kissed four times when they had managed to lose Tommy, their spare wheel. None of the heroines in her books ever made the first move. Finally, after seconds that seemed like aeons, he moved his hand and reached for hers. She raised her eyes to him again, forced herself to hold the stare this time.

Then Tommy, who had thankfully fallen asleep, let out a loud snort that broke the tension. Lucia giggled.

'Do you want to go for a walk?' PJ asked, nodding towards the woods beyond the stables.

'Yes,' she answered, squeezing his hand tighter.

28

The sky above her was a glorious Marian blue as Cara dipped down into the Inagh Valley, the mountain-flanked landscape bathed in the breathtaking Connemara light that had inspired so many artists and writers. For once the peaks of the Bens weren't shrouded in wispy white cloud.

It was a very different scene from the last time she had travelled this road on her way to a spring wedding with Kian at Rosleague Manor near Letterfrack, a much more typical Connemara day. It had been like driving through a painting entitled *Four Seasons in One Day*, the bog carpeted in purple heather, gorse and bog cotton. When they had passed the entrance to the Kylemore Manor hotel that day, she had reminded Kian that her aunt Maryanne had been married to one of the owner's sons, oblivious to her real connection to the Casey family.

She drove slowly and carefully, conscious that in this part of the world, the blackface mountain sheep ruled the road. The bright splotches on the long bedraggled fleeces that draped over their jet black bodies – denoting their owners – made it look for all the world as if they'd just been paint-balling. Easy to believe there were more sheep than people in Ireland when you drove through here. The Connemara sheep, with their curved horns, were exceptionally hardy – they had to be to survive in the rugged, rocky terrain and to withstand the cold, the wind and heavy rain of the harsh, mountainous climate, particularly over the long dark winters.

Today, though, only the merest hint of a breeze tickled the surface of the lake as Cara drove past. Sheep pottered along the roadside, a few raising their heads to peer in at her as she passed, as if they were wondering what her business was in these parts, but most taking no notice of her. There were few houses along this stretch of valley, and only one hotel. At intervals along the way, there were pull-off areas for tourists to stop and take photos; many were busy today with rental cars and tour buses.

Emerging at the other end of the valley, Cara turned left in the direction of Kylemore. The lake came into view on her left, the mountains looming over both sides of the road, picture-postcard perfect. No matter how many times she drove along this road, the scenery never got any less spectacular. She pulled into the verge across from Kylemore House, a lovely old property that had been converted into self-catering apartments, and got out of the car.

She stared across the still lake and took a few deep breaths, hoping to absorb some of its serene energy. She caught the coconutty waft of the yellow furze that always reminded her of suntan lotion and holidays abroad. Song birds chattered and chirped gaily as they flitted from bush to tree, and from somewhere on the slope behind her came a plaintive bleat.

She was nervous, there was no denying it. She needed to get her thoughts together. Today was a big deal for her, meeting her biological family for the first time.

She was grateful to Andrew for setting up today's gathering, and for the time he had taken out of his own hectic schedule to paint for her a vivid portrait of a young Lucia and what sounded like a half-feral childhood as she and her cousin, Tommy, were let run wild through the bogs, mountains and lakes of Connemara. A different era when kids weren't wrapped in cotton wool and banned from climbing trees.

He had told her of Lucia's great love of horses and of how she and Tommy had spent much of their free time hanging out in the stables with their ponies. Andrew said he had bumped into Lucia a few times in the hospital when he was a medical student and she was working as a nurse's aide, and he remembered thinking she seemed to have developed a bit more confidence in herself and was happy.

Cara had soaked it all up.

Kian had warned her to *manage your expectations* before he'd left for work that morning. She knew he was just worried about her, didn't want her to be hurt any more than she already had been, but she wished he could have been a bit less glass-half-empty.

'I'm not expecting to meet the Waltons, Kian,' she had said. 'They haven't exactly been bombarding me with birthday and Christmas cards over the years.'

She hadn't mentioned to him that she had been a bit disappointed that today's meeting was taking place not in the family home but in the more impersonal setting of the hotel.

'Just be careful, OK? This isn't like chasing a story. You're heavily emotionally invested here.'

He was right, of course. She knew fairytale reunion stories were the exception to the rule, and she was trying hard not to get her hopes too high but that was easier said than done. The falling dreams were almost a nightly occurrence now.

She got back into the car and followed the road towards Kylemore. It was clogged with tourists inching along as they took in the scenery, the road too winding to chance overtaking. Then, to her right, rising from the wilderness, there was the Abbey, which, on a fine day, was perfectly reflected in Lough Pollacapall directly in front of it. The vast estate of more than a thousand acres was made up of mountains, lake and bog, like the rest of Connemara, but the Benedictine nuns who had set up home here at least a century ago had done an incredible job in restoring the original period rooms and Victorian walled garden, carving out woodland, lakeshore and riverside walks from the wild beauty of the landscape.

The boarding-school had provided the daughters of wealthy families with the finest of educations before it closed in 2010 due to the decline in vocations. There had been a big feature in the *Champion* earlier in the year on the nuns' plans for a new monastery on the site with a monastic chapel, a guesthouse for visitors from around the world, and a spiritual education centre.

Driving past now, in the knowledge that her own mother had attended the Abbey as a day pupil, it felt different. Cara vowed to return some time later in the year, when the place wasn't thronged with tourists, to do the full tour. She'd bring Maisie to see the Connemara ponies and the adorable little Kunekune pigs. She kept going, past the extensive Abbey estate, then indicated right to turn into an elegant gateway and past a large sign for Kylemore Manor Five-star Resort.

Set in the heart of what was now known as Connemara National Park, the manor had been built by Neilus Casey in the mid-1930s as a small luxury hotel in a Gothic style similar to the neighbouring Abbey to cater for the parents who came to visit their daughters at the school. It also became a popular haunt for well-heeled Americans in search of their Irish roots, and an expansion in the 1950s saw it more than double in size, to include a large stable block and tennis courts. The hotel had closed for nearly a year in the 1970s when Marcus had overseen another significant expansion and an entire renovation of the property. Since then, he had opened an award-winning spa, achieved five-star status, and Kylemore Manor had been named in numerous top-hotels-in-the-world lists. Cara had known all this before she'd found out about her connection to the place.

The long driveway wound up through scenic woodland, the trees leaning across from each side to embrace in the middle, creating a dark leafy tunnel, before it opened on her left to field and bogland where two grey ponies raised their heads from grazing to watch her pass. On a large set of formidable gates to her right, a sign bearing the head of a German shepherd, mouth twisted in a vicious snarl, warned that the property behind them was private and protected by guard dogs. She couldn't see far beyond the gates where another driveway curved through the woodland to the Casey residence where Marcus and Annette lived and where her birth-mother had been reared. She could only imagine how luxurious it must be if the hotel was anything to go by. Maybe if today's meeting went well, she might be invited there some day.

29

She rounded a soft bend and the hotel stood before her in all its glory, the imposing stone edifice mellowed by rows of hanging baskets, late-summer perennials in blues, purples and yellows spilling over the sides. A mini-me of the neighbouring Abbey, with its romantic tower and turrets, mullioned windows and oriels, the brooding presence of Dúchrach in the background.

The car park was about a third full, many of the hotel's wealthy patrons probably touring around Connemara for the day, and Cara found a spot close to the flight of stone steps that led to the front entrance. Tables and chairs had been set up outside under a navy and cream striped awning and a handful of guests sat reading papers and basking in the sunshine. They had probably been warned to bring raincoats and wellies, certainly wouldn't have been expecting sunscreen weather in this part of the world.

A hulking wooden door stood wide open leading into a vast dark-panelled foyer tiled in black and white chequerboard. Pleasantly cool. The subtle earthy scent of hydrangeas came out to meet her; giant vases of the plump blue blooms stood on the marble fireplace and at either end of the heavily polished reception desk. The wide sweeping steps of the grand staircase, carpeted in a rich claret, split off into two smaller flights going in opposite directions to a first-floor gallery, around which were grouped some of the bedrooms.

She stole a peep at that evening's tasting menu, displayed on a stand outside the Michelin-starred Henry's Restaurant. Heavy on fish. Scallops, trout, lobster, roe, eel and sea urchin teamed with a random list of foods as ordinary as bread and butter and potato and as exotic as lovage, rose and sea buckthorn. Her own lunch had consisted of the remnants of a banana sandwich abandoned by Maisie.

Cara approached the elegant desk. The receptionist, in a crisp white blouse and tailored black trousers, greeted her with a smile.

Her nerves began to kick in as she was led through the foyer, down a corridor and into what appeared to be a small sitting room with a sign on the door saying 'Reserved for private function'. Her gut tightened and her heart picked up speed. The receptionist walked straight in without knocking and gestured for her to follow.

Cara found herself in a high-ceilinged room with intricate cornicing. Perfectly pleated curtains framed double-height windows that looked out onto the gardens at the side of the hotel and the field beyond where more horses grazed. Another huge fireplace, a magnificent Gothic-style mirror propped on the mantelpiece, formed the centrepiece of the room, an elegant deep blue sofa and mustard yellow armchairs arranged around it.

The room managed to be cosy yet stylish. It was also empty. She had assumed the Caseys would be sitting there chatting among themselves before she got there, and she had made sure to arrive exactly on time. She could feel troops of butterflies amassing in the pit of her stomach, their fluttering setting off a wave of nausea. She perched on the edge of one of the armchairs beside the fireplace, facing the door.

After an interminable five minutes or so, a tall man entered, with thinning salt-and-pepper hair and greyish-blue eyes. Phillip. Lucia's eldest brother. Cara's uncle. She recognised him from the photos she had seen online. He bore no resemblance at all to his younger sister.

She stood to greet him.

'Welcome to Kylemore, Cara. I'm Phillip. It's wonderful to meet you. Please ...' he gestured to the armchair where she had been sitting '... make yourself comfortable.'

She sat back down and he took the seat opposite her.

'I've asked our receptionist, Roisín, to arrange for some refreshments to be sent in. Hugh is on his way over from the house with my parents.'

She knew that Hugh, the youngest of Lucia's brothers, ran a successful portfolio of bars and restaurants in Ireland, just as Denis, the middle brother, did in the States.

'As Andrew may have told you, my mother isn't very well. She's eighty-four now, and she's failed a lot in the last year or so, I'm afraid. She is, of course, looking forward to meeting you but, well ... this is a very emotional occasion for us all, nobody more so than you, of course, and, em ... stress exacerbates her condition so we don't talk about what happened in front of her. She gets too upset. I hope you don't mind me ... I know you must have so many questions and I really don't want you to feel that I'm putting restrictions on our conversation today but if you wouldn't mind ... just in front of Mother ...'

'Don't worry, Phillip. Andrew has already spoken to me about it. I won't mention anything in front of her. I can't even begin to imagine what she must have gone through, what you all went through, and I certainly don't want to cause any further pain to anybody. All I wanted was the opportunity to meet you all, and to learn as much as I can about Lucia.'

Relief softened his features and he sat back, crossing his legs. 'Thank you for being so understanding. We're probably a bit over-protective of Mother but she's been through so much already. She could have done without being hit with bloody Parkinson's on top of everything else.'

'It can't have been easy for any of you. And I don't know if Andrew already told you, but I just want to reassure you that it was never my intention to write about this. I wouldn't dream of it.'

That was true although she couldn't deny it would make a great piece. The nationals would be all over it. Readers would lap it up. Lucia Casey's long-lost daughter reunited with her murdered mother's family. It was the kind of article Cara would read with interest if she wasn't the long-lost daughter involved. Her job was to report on the news, though, not to be it.

'Yes, he did say that and, I must admit, it came as a relief. The thought of it all being dragged up again, especially now with my parents so much older ...' He shook his head. 'Anyway, tell me, do you like the job? We read your series on the Tuam babies scandal, a great piece of journalism.'

Cara felt a rush of pride at the thought of her grandparents and uncles reading the articles that had won her a national media award, that they had been following her career when she was unaware of their connection to her. 'Thank you,' she said. 'That was a really tough series to work on, but I do enjoy it, most of the time anyway. It's like any job, I guess, you have good and bad days, but I can't imagine doing anything else.'

She wondered if the others were ever going to arrive, was keen to switch the focus off herself.

'The hotel is looking great. Have things picked up since Covid?'

'Don't mention the C word but, yes, business is booming again – we're busier than ever, in fact. Of course, we've had to increase our rates with the price of gas and electricity gone through the roof thanks to that madman in Russia, but fortunately our clientele can afford to pay.'

He launched into a long anecdote about an Oscar-winning movie director and his husband who came over from LA to stay at the hotel every Christmas with their two Chihuahuas, flying into Knock airport on their private jet. How the director had mentioned in an interview that the worst part of the pandemic for him had been missing their annual trip to Connemara and how the publicity from that one interview had led to a flurry of bookings for the next year.

Cara nodded as her gaze swept the gallery of framed photos on the back wall, recognising most of the faces pictured with various members of the Casey family. Politicians, actors, authors, a celebrated Irish poet, an artist renowned for his paintings of the Connemara landscape, even a rock star or two.

Phillip's monologue was finally broken when an ageing waiter, tucked neatly into a black waistcoat, arrived with tea and coffee on a silver tray. She wondered if he had worked there all his life. After ascertaining that Madam would like coffee, he poured it from an antique silver pot into a fine bone china cup with a matching saucer. He left and returned minutes later with a cake stand bearing the prettiest petit fours she had ever seen, each one a miniature masterpiece. Bite-sized cakes, chocolates, biscuits and, of course, the ubiquitous macarons.

With a sweeping flourish of his hand, Phillip invited her to help herself and, despite her jittery stomach, Cara couldn't resist.

She was about to ask Phillip to pass on her compliments to his pastry chef when the door opened again and a frail elderly woman in a wheelchair was pushed in by a man Cara assumed to be Hugh. Phillip stood and Cara followed suit. She had come across very few photos of Annette in the press – she had little to do with the business, according to Maryanne, and was dressed now in a pale pink cardigan buttoned to the neck and heavy wool trousers, a cashmere sack of kindling.

They were followed into the room by a remarkably well-preserved Marcus Casey, who had to be well into his eighties also, but looked years younger than his wife. There was an awkward few moments while Hugh struggled to manoeuvre his mother's wheelchair between a high-backed chair and the sofa and nobody spoke.

Cara took the opportunity to size up Marcus Casey, her *grandfather*. The man cut an impressive figure, despite his advanced years. He had to be over six foot, as tall as his sons even at his age. His blue eyes were still sharp and bright ... eyes the same colour as her own, as Maisie's. A dapper and leaner version of his eldest son, hair more silver than grey but still thick. Still holding on to traces of his handsome looks. He wore a well-cut navy sports jacket over a lightly striped shirt and a contrasting spotted tie.

Hugh finally wedged his mother's chair into position and Annette, Mrs Casey, her grandmother – whatever she was supposed to call her – reached a trembling hand towards her.

'Come here to me, *a stór.*' Her voice was as shaky as her fingers.

Cara moved towards the old woman, and crouched awkwardly in front of her chair. Annette laid a hand on either side of her face and gazed into her eyes as if meeting a newborn grandchild for the first time, which in a strange way she was, albeit in the body of a grown woman.

Tears coursed a track through the crepey gutters of the old woman's face as she ran her fingers over Cara's temples and her forehead, her cheeks and her chin. As if she was blind. Cara held her breath, not sure what to do or say.

'I'm sorry. We thought it was the right thing ...' A strange sound erupted from her throat, somewhere between a guttural sob and a wail.

'Now, now, Mother. Don't be getting yourself all upset.' Marcus lifted his wife's hands away from Cara's face, and placed them gently on her lap. Cara unfolded herself, moved back slightly. 'We'll all sit down and have a nice cup of tea and a chat.'

'Wait, I have something I want to give her.' Annette reached out for Cara's hand again, pressed something hard and warm into it.

'I had it blessed for you. Wear it on a chain around your neck, close to your heart. It will bring you special graces.'

Cara looked at the silver disc in her hand: Our Lady on one side, a cross and bar entwined with a large M on the other. A miraculous medal.

'Thank you,' she said, touched.

The waiter reappeared, and poured for the new arrivals, while Hugh introduced himself, a slimmer, warmer version of his older brother.

'We've been really looking forward to meeting you,' Marcus said, as he settled himself into the armchair across from her where Phillip had been sitting. His sons sat either end of the sofa between them. 'We were so surprised when Andrew called, pleasantly so, of course. It was a call we had been afraid to hope for but, much as we wanted to, we always felt it wasn't our place to go against your parents' wishes. We were aware they hadn't told you about Lucia, and we had to respect that. We knew they had only your best interests at heart.'

'I've been looking forward to meeting you too. It's ...' She was completely lost for words.

She couldn't believe this was actually happening. It was like a dream, more than she had even allowed herself to dream. That the Caseys hadn't just regifted her, like an unwanted present, and got on with their lives as if she didn't exist, but had kept her alive in their thoughts and, more than that, had hoped she would reach out to them some day.

'We've heard you have a little girl,' Hugh said. 'I recently became a grandfather for the first time, and I'm completely besotted. A little boy, named Marcus after his great-grandfather. It's taken me by surprise, to be honest. I was always working while my children were growing up, missed out on so much, but I'm hoping to try to make up for it now. This is him.' He pulled out his iPhone and proudly displayed a photo of a beaming baby.

'God, Hugh, you'll bore the poor girl to tears,' Phillip said. 'The way he goes on about that child, you'd think there'd never before been a baby born.'

'Not at all,' Cara replied, grateful to Hugh for subtly cracking the ice and dialling down the emotional thermostat in the room.

'Do you have any photos of your little one?' Hugh asked.

'Of course.' She pulled out her phone, scrolled through until she found one where Maisie was looking at the camera and smiling. 'This is Maisie. She's three now.'

He took her phone from her. 'Oh my God.' He was staring at it, his eyes watering.

Cara hoped he wasn't going to cry.

'It's unbelievable. It's like looking at Lucia at that age. Look.' He turned the phone around to show the photo to his parents and brother. 'She has her eyes and her smile. Isn't it uncanny?'

There was an excruciating silence and the room seemed to hold its collective breath as Cara watched the colour drain from Marcus's face, his mouth twitch. It wasn't possible for his wife to get any paler than she already was, but she opened her mouth and let out another strangled wail.

30

Lucia
Kylemore
1984

Even after she'd missed her period three months in a row, it hadn't occurred to her that there could be a baby growing inside her. Even after all the talk about that poor girl who had died in the grotto. Her mother had banned Gay Byrne from the house in disgust after he had begun to read out the letters on the radio from all the other unmarried girls who had got themselves into trouble, and no Gaybo meant no more *Late Late Show* on Saturday nights. It had never happened to anyone she knew, though, and it wasn't something she had given much thought to when she did it with PJ.

The only sex education her mother had ever given her was to remind her regularly that her body was 'a temple of the Holy Spirit' and that she had to keep it pure. She knew her mother would be horrified if she knew what she had done with PJ, not just once but three times, and she had no intention of ever telling her. That was supposed to be a secret between her and him, one that made her heart feel like it might burst with joy whenever she thought about it.

The one thing she did know about pregnant women was that they had big bumps. Her tummy was flatter than it had ever been – she had actually lost weight, if anything. She had gone off breakfast, unable to face the thought or smell of food in the mornings. She had no idea that that was a sign. Just like she had no idea that her bras getting too tight was another. She had just assumed her body was developing and had even asked her mother if she could have some new bras a couple of sizes bigger.

She wasn't sure how her mother had copped it, whether it was the bras, the not eating breakfast, or that she had stopped using the sanitary towels from the hot press. Maybe a combination of everything.

However she had found out, Lucia would never forget the day her mother had confronted her about it. It was the end of November, a dark, drizzly evening. She had got soaked cycling home from school and had just changed out of her sodden uniform into her cosy flannelette pyjamas in her bedroom. She had planned to take out the last letter she had had from PJ, like she did nearly every day after school, and reread it for the hundredth time. She missed him so much, treasured the memories of their time together. He had written only twice since he'd gone home at the end of the summer, but he was a boy and she knew boys weren't the best at soppy stuff like that.

'Lucia, I'm going to ask you a question and I need you to tell me the truth,' her mother had said, in a tight, strained voice. 'Did you ... did you lie down with a boy?'

Lucia froze. She knew what her mother meant but how had she found out? Nobody knew, apart from herself and PJ. She couldn't tell her the truth. Her heart thumped and she felt her face grow hot, her shame betraying her. 'What do you mean?'

Her mother caught her chin and twisted her head to face her. 'You tell me the truth right this minute, Lucia Casey. Did you fornicate with a boy?'

She had never heard that word before but she had a fair idea of what it meant. Her mother's right eyelid was jumping like mad and there was a crazy look in her eyes. Lucia was in big trouble.

'Why are you asking—'

'DO NOT LIE TO ME, you little tart. Don't lay another sin on top of the ones you've already committed. Did you do it?'

Lucia couldn't answer. Her cheeks were blazing now. She couldn't look her mother in the eye, so she stared at the floor instead.

That was all the answer her mother needed. She sank onto Lucia's single bed, her head in her hands, her fingers entangled in her hair. 'Stupid girl,' she muttered over and over. 'Stupid, stupid dirty girl.'

Lucia wanted to say she was sorry, but she was afraid to open her mouth.

Her mother left the room then, flew down the stairs, still muttering under her breath.

Lucia heard the front door slam, a car start, and tyres crunching over the gravel on the driveway before the house fell silent.

She wasn't allowed back to school after Christmas. Never went back. The story was that she had gone to a private clinic, 'trouble with her nerves'. The stigma of that was far less shameful than the truth. Uncle Luke had come out to the house to examine her the weekend after her mother had confronted her and confirmed her suspicions. Lucia was pregnant, over four months gone. She was due around mid-March of the following year. The week after she turned seventeen.

Lucia was warned not to tell a soul about the trouble she had got herself into. She wasn't even brought to the family GP in case word got out locally, but driven to Uncle Luke's private clinic in Galway for her check-ups.

She was subjected to endless interrogations by her mother, her father and Father Kenny as to the identity of her baby's father, but she wouldn't give his name. Nobody knew, not even PJ. Tommy would probably have suspected if he had known what was going on, but he was back in boarding-school by then and oblivious to all the drama going on at home.

There was no way she could tell. They'd never let PJ come back to Kylemore.

It was Father Kenny who made the arrangements for her to go down to the McNamara family in Limerick and stay there until the baby was born. During those endless months as her belly swelled in a strange bed in a strange place and she pined for her pony who, she knew, would be pining for her, she dreamed often of a girl giving birth under the stars. Crying out in pain. Cold and frightened and all alone. And her poor little baby, no blanket to wrap around his naked newborness. No loving arms to welcome him to the big scary world, no mother's heartbeat to comfort him.

The thought of the birth terrified Lucia, even though she knew she would be in a hospital with nurses and doctors to look after her. She tried to put it out of her mind as she helped Marie McNamara mind her children and clean her house. She had no idea how they were going to get the baby out of her and was too afraid to ask.

As she changed the nappy of Mrs McNamara's adorable baby, patting Johnson's powder onto his soft skin, his chubby legs kicking in the air, and felt her own baby kick inside her, something began to change. And as the weeks went by and her baby's kicks got stronger, so too did the feeling, until she was sure. She wanted to keep her baby.

31

Cara read back over her interview with the mother of a suicidal ten-year-old one last time to check for typos before she sent it for subbing. It had been one of the toughest interviews she had ever done. She had spent most of the previous afternoon with a woman whose child told her every day of his life that he wanted to be dead, and who was quite literally – she had broken down in the interview – crying out for help for him. She wasn't the only parent in Ireland on suicide watch for her own child, sleeping next to him every night for fear of what he might do. Children and teenagers in desperate need of help were being left on long waiting lists with some admitted to adult psychiatric units inappropriate for their needs.

She would do her best to highlight the plight of this mother and her child, to raise awareness of the abject state of child mental-health services in the country, but she felt as if she was banging her head off a brick wall. She had been writing about the dire gaps in mental-health services for years, but what difference had it made? At every election, the politicians promised change, but the change never came. Not the real change that was needed anyway. And what did come was so slow and pitiful as to make no difference to the large number of families suffering so much. Too late for many.

She stuck her head into Fitzie's office to update him on her visit to Kylemore, but he was on the phone. Spotting her there, he waved her in, holding up five fingers. She wandered over to the window, and pulled back the dusty beige blinds that she suspected had once been cream. It was still warmer than usual for the time of year, but the sun had absconded, and a layer of cloud moved in, making for a heavy day.

She yawned deeply. She was so tired today, had stayed up until after midnight last night talking to Kian. It had taken her ages to fall asleep, so many thoughts tumbling around inside her head. Her birth-family – not just any family but one of the most successful and respected hoteliers in the country – had not only welcomed her with open arms but had been hoping for years that she would reach out to them.

While their welcome was more than she could have hoped for, it had flung more fuel on the flames of the anger she felt towards her parents for keeping the truth of her birth-family from her. By not telling her, they had robbed her of a relationship with her grandparents, her uncles and their children.

Once they had got over the initial shock of Maisie's resemblance to Lucia, Marcus had deftly changed the subject back to Cara and her job with the *Champion*. Annette had dozed while he and the boys shared some of their fondest memories of Lucia as a child, staying well away from her teenage pregnancy and the tragic end to her life.

Before she left, Marcus had asked if she would like to visit them again, at the house next time, where she could look through Lucia's childhood photo albums. She told them she'd love to and he had asked her if she would bring Maisie with her. The invitation had extended to Kian, but she knew it was Maisie they really wanted to see.

'So how did it go?' Fitzie asked.

'Really well. Much better than I'd hoped. It's very early days, all of us just getting to know each other but they've invited me back, with Maisie and Kian.'

'I'm delighted for you, Cara,' he said. 'I was worried after everything you've been through. You never know how these things will go. Sure you know yourself. Anyway, I hope things continue to work out. Have you heard anything back from the guards yet about the file?'

'No. My request is *being processed* apparently and there's a long backlog, but I've been thinking about it and I'm not sure I'll bother going down that road now. I want to know who Lucia was, and now that the family are open to talking to me about her, I'm not sure there's much point in getting her case file. I mean, I'm hardly going to solve it if the guards couldn't figure it out over all these years.'

'It's hard to see how it would benefit you, even if you did manage to get hold of it. I can't imagine it would be pleasant reading. How about the boyfriend? Did you ever hear anything back from your man in the Crane?'

'No, but again, I don't know how much point there is in pursuing him. They weren't even going out together that long. For now, I have enough going on with the family and trying to get to know who Lucia was.'

And she meant it.

But that was before she opened the text message on her phone the following morning to find out that Mossie from the Crane had come through for her after all.

32

She'd thought nothing could shock her after finding out that Lucia Casey was her mother, but she was wrong. What Colman Ryan told her shocked her all over again. It was two days later before she and her mother's old boyfriend managed to speak to each other on the phone due to the five-hour time difference between Boston and Ireland. It was morning for him, lunchtime for Cara.

He had been living in the 'next parish over' for years, he told her, had moved there a few months after Lucia's body had been found. He had been working as an orderly at Mass General Hospital for the best part of thirty years, and still played music in a popular trad band called Cabbage.

Colman hadn't lost his accent despite all his years in the States, his strong Galway 'howya' travelling the distance between them as if he had never left. It amazed her that some people who lived abroad for years never lost their accent, while others, like her, had been known to pick up a sing-song twang after a weekend in Cork.

Cara had hoped her mother's ex-boyfriend might help to shed some light on the type of person Lucia had grown into after leaving home, and he did, but he also dropped a bombshell she wasn't expecting.

'Pregnant. But I don't … How did this not come out? It wasn't mentioned in any of the press reports or the missing-person appeal.' Why had Donal McGann not said anything? If it was true, surely the father of Lucia's baby would have had to be a strong suspect. 'I met with one of the guards who investigated the case and he didn't mention anything about her being pregnant.' The pulse throbbed in her neck as her heart rate accelerated.

'I dunno, to tell ya the truth. I didn't have a clue meself until Sandra told me a week or so after she went missing. I nearly died when she said it.'

'Why would she tell Sandra, though, and not you?'

None of this made any sense. Donal had said Colie had gone heavy on the drink after Lucia's death. Had it pickled his brain?

He took a deep breath before answering. 'That's somethin' I'll never know the answer to, love. Maybe she wasn't sure how I'd react, like. We were only together about six months when she went missin'. I'd have supported her if she was pregnant, but I've had to come to terms with never knowin' whether she was or she wasn't, or what happened to her.'

'Did nobody else know? Did you not tell the guards?'

Such an important detail in the case of a missing young woman would have been all over the media if the guards had released it. And surely a foetus would have shown up in the post-mortem, no matter how decomposed the remains.

'I said it to no one. The way I saw it, if the girl was pregnant it was her business and no one else's. She was old-fashioned that way. She wouldn't have wanted it all over the papers. When she wasn't married, like.'

Jesus! It was the 1990s they were talking about, not the 1890s. Surely having *a child outside wedlock* wasn't such a big deal then, even if homosexuality was still treated as a crime until 1993, as ludicrous as that was to believe.

'Sandra said it to the guards, though, I do know that,' he said. 'She was ragin' after because it was never printed in any of the papers, and when she got on to them about it, she was told the family were sayin' it was all lies. Sandra said Lucia done a test and all. She'd seen the result. She had no way of proving it, though. She told me one of the brothers came up to her outside work one day and threatened to sue her if she didn't stop spreading lies about Lucia. She was fierce upset about it at the time.'

'Bloody hell.'

Cara had grabbed a pen and her spiral pad and started to take notes. 'Did you ever meet the family?'

'No. Apart from the cousin, Victoria. I found her a bit snooty, but Lucia got on well with her. I doubt very much I'd have been good enough for Lucia in the Caseys' eyes. Shur me own mother said as much to me. She wasn't a bit happy when I told her who I was going out with, and that wouldn't have been like Mammy at all, getting involved in my business. She warned me it would all end in tears, and shur wasn't she right too, just not in the way she thought.'

Cara wondered if he had been right. Would her mother's family have been justifiably concerned as to whether a porter could keep their daughter in the style she was accustomed to? Or would they have been glad she had found somebody who made her happy, no matter the size of his wage packet? She didn't mention her visit to the Caseys: it was clear he didn't have much time for them.

'I did love her, you know, even though we weren't together all that long. I never met anybody like her after that.'

Colie talked almost nonstop for the next hour. It was as if his memories of Lucia, kept on ice all these years, had been defrosted by Cara's call and were gushing out of him now. Cara wondered if, like unrequited love, Lucia's tragic death had kept her alive in his mind all these years. He too described her as having been 'young for her age'; it certainly seemed to be the general consensus.

'There was something very naïve about her ... I think that was why the kids on the ward loved her so much. She was brilliant with them. And the parents. They couldn't speak highly enough of her. She used to go back after her shift some days and sit with the kids, playing that hippo game and colouring in. She was always thinking about them, even when she wasn't working. Picking up little bits and pieces, like crayons and stickers. She loved that job, even though it was hard, dirty aul' work at times.'

There was silence at the other end of the line for a few seconds. She wondered if he was all talked out.

'She did tell me about ya,' he said. 'She found it really hard to talk about, but she never stopped thinking about ya. I don't know if you know this, but she wanted to keep you so badly. They wouldn't let her. It broke her heart.'

His voice had gone hoarse, but he cleared his throat and kept going.

'I left Galway fairly sharpish after I was cleared by the cops. I was so fucked up, I'd probably have got meself into trouble if I stayed. What really maddened me, though, was that if they'd been doin' their job properly, they'd have tracked down that lad that was seen hangin' around the Canal. That was no fuckin' coincidence, like. But sure, lookit, no point going on about it now.'

'Did you ever meet anybody else, Colman?'

'*Ara*, I met a few quare wans over the years, but none that ever stuck so I reckon you could say I'm a confirmed bachelor.' She could hear the smile in his voice. 'I'm well settled out here. I've some great friends – we're like family for each other really. It's hard not bein' able to get home. I couldn't risk it, though. I send home money for the mother to come out to me every year so at least I get to see her. We're hopin' Biden might do something for us. No sign of it yet, though.'

Colie was one of thousands of undocumented Irish living and working under the radar in the US, afraid to come home in case they were refused re-entry, missing out on so many important family occasions over the years. Births, deaths and weddings. So many Christmases.

'Before I let you go, would you have any idea where I could find Sandra Nolan?' Cara asked. 'She doesn't work in the hospital any more and I've searched online but haven't been able to find her.'

She had decided not to bother pursuing Lucia's friend, but after her conversation with Colie, she had to talk to her.

33

Lucia
Galway city
1990

'What time are you on break, Luce?' Sandra stood at the door to the ward where Lucia was in the middle of tucking in the corners of a starched white sheet.

'In a couple of minutes. Whenever Susan gets back from hers.'

'Perfect. I'll see you in the canteen.'

Lucia gave her friend a thumbs-up. Then she turned to the child in the faded Superman pyjamas sitting in the chair beside the bed she had just made. He looked as sick as he was. Like a shrunken little man, grey and gaunt, his head so shiny it looked as if it had been polished, the skin stretched taut over his skull. Dara's father had shown her a photo of him before he got sick, his cute little face beaming out from under a mop of blond curls. Every last follicle of that lovely hair had been targeted and killed by the chemo drugs as they destroyed every rapidly dividing cell they could find, good and bad.

'Well, Your Highness, how's that for you?'

'Hmm, it'll have to do, I suppose.'

'Go 'way out of that, you cheeky pup.' She swatted him gently on the head.

Dara was one of her pets. This was his third time back in the unit since she had started working there nearly a year ago now. He broke her heart. Those huge blue eyes that continued to sparkle despite the toxic drugs being pumped into his little body. His undefeated sense of mischief. Always the ring-leader for whatever antics the kids on the ward got up to, until inevitably his tank ran dry and he collapsed onto his bed and slept for hours. She couldn't even begin to imagine how his mother coped, seeing him being poked and prodded and poisoned. No hope of a cure. Little hope of him ever graduating childhood.

He had been so ashamed of himself this morning. He'd called her over, whispered to her to pull the curtains around them. 'I had another accident.' He couldn't even look at her. After weeks of relying on a catheter, it took a while for his brain to remember to wake him before his bladder released. She had blinked back the tears: they were useless to the poor child.

She had run him a bath, pouring in plenty of the Matey bubble bath his mother had left in his bedside locker, the blond-haired, blue-eyed sailor on the bottle a ringer for Dara himself. Before. She had sat beside the bath, as the child lay back in the bubbles, and made up another of the stories he loved about Misty, the super pony. She had promised him that some day, when he was well enough, he could come to Connemara to visit the pony. His mother had agreed, tears in her eyes. She rarely cried in front of Dara.

After Lucia had dried him and sprinkled baby powder onto his scrawny body, pretending he was a piece of steak she was seasoning as he wriggled and giggled, she let him pick a fresh pair of super-hero pyjamas from his cupboard.

'Now hop back in here and read your comics while I go for my break,' she said, handing him a couple of *Beano*s and plumping the pillows behind his back as she inhaled his clean, fresh scent. 'I'll be back in a while to check on you.'

She dropped off the soiled bedding in the sluice room and stopped at the nurses' station halfway down the corridor to let Sister Maureen know she was going on her break. The woman barely acknowledged her – she was like a bag of cats today, but she was like that most days. Lucia often wondered why she stayed in the job if it made her so miserable. She herself had been on since six and was parched.

Sandra waved at her from the back of the canteen where she was sitting in a small group. Salt-N-Pepa's 'Push It' was pumping from the radio. Lucia's mother would have curled up and died if she'd heard Lucia's work pals singing along to the racy lyrics. She queued at the counter, taking a cold can of Club Orange from the fridge and a Twix. Her work was very physical, long hours on her feet. Lifting and bathing and changing beds, scouring bedpans and, while it wasn't part of her job, trying to coax morsels of food into her little patients. She loved it, though, and looked forward to going into work every day even though, no matter how hard she wished for it, she couldn't cure her little charges.

It was Sister Breda who had suggested Lucia would be good with children. Sister Breda, who had never given up on her, who had written to her every week while she was in the hospital in

Dublin. The only one who had. Victoria had sent the odd letter and Tommy had sent a postcard out of the blue about a month after she was admitted, but she and Tommy had drifted apart after that summer, as the booze, the love of his life, tightened its grip on him.

Lucia would never have believed, during that dark time, that one day she would be living in Galway, happy and independent away from her family. She wouldn't have believed she could ever be happy.

She still thought about Maeve every day. The pain would always be part of her, she imagined, but it wasn't so raw and sharp now. It was more like the dull ache of a tight muscle, one that clenched tighter whenever she saw a mother pushing a pram, tiny fists emerging from the blankets. She had come back from Limerick a shell of herself. Hollow body and soul. A mother but not.

Before that she had never spent much time around small children. Never realised she was such 'a natural', as Marie McNamara kept telling her. And, indeed, the McNamara children had really taken to her, following her from room to room, screaming with laughter when she pretended to fend off their teddies as they attacked her. *Again, again.* Mad for snuggles on the sofa or in her little single bed. Especially the baby, with the rolls of fat on his arms and legs she loved to nuzzle, his pudgy arms reaching out for her every time he saw her.

The closer it had come to her due date, the more she had known that there had to be a way for her to keep her baby. How she knew she was having a girl she couldn't say. She just did, and she was going to call her Maeve. The biggest shock, when the baby finally arrived after a traumatic labour, was not the strength of the love she felt for the tiny creature, it was her perfection. They had taken her away and cleaned her up, dressed her in a soft yellow Babygro and a matching cap, then let Lucia see her.

She could have stared at her for ever. She simply could not fathom how someone like her could have produced something so perfect, so beautiful. Tiny doll's hands with ten perfectly formed fingernails. Huge dark eyes wide open in shock at finding herself in this too-bright scary world. As Lucia held her baby close, cradling her fragile head, she looked into those beautiful eyes and promised to keep her safe. To make sure she always felt loved and protected.

They stole her while Lucia was asleep. She never even got to say goodbye. They said it would be easier on her that way. All she had left was the soft white blanket that Mrs McNamara had knitted for her. She had howled from a place deep within her soul. Harsh, guttural sobs that physically hurt. She cried the whole way back to Kylemore in the car as she clutched the blanket that had swaddled her baby in her first days and hours on earth, her father silent in the driver's seat beside her.

'It's for the best. You'll see that some day,' were the only words he spoke for the entire journey.

Even Misty, poor Misty, so happy to see her home, so sensitive to her pain, couldn't console her. When the tears were still flowing two weeks later, her stomach muscles in spasm from crying and hunger, her parents started to lose patience. Threatened to take Misty away if she didn't pull herself together. By then, something inside her had snapped and she no longer cared what they did. Even if they took her beloved pony. She didn't care whether she lived or died. The idea of eternal sleep was quite comforting. Her appetite had died, her tears dried up. She didn't have the energy for hunger or even feeling.

She was packed off to a private clinic in Dublin where she spent the next four months or so in a blurry tranquillised no man's land. Neither dead nor alive. Being weaned off the medication was a fresh hell, like a lump of meat being thawed after months in a deep freeze.

Sister Breda's letters formed a tenuous link to her former life. The nuns were all praying like mad for her. She sensed that Sister Breda had guessed the real reason for her leaving school so abruptly. She would have loved to confide in the kind-hearted nun, but she had been warned by her parents not to tell a soul. In every letter she wrote, the nun reminded Lucia that she was a good person, stronger than she knew. That she had it inside her to get through this tough time and could call on the Lord any time she needed help. While she realised that Sister Breda's faith was far more Christian than her mother's, Lucia had no interest in calling on the Lord. If he could allow her baby to be taken from her, he certainly wasn't somebody she was willing to rely on now. No harm in letting the nuns pray for her, though: they probably had a more direct line to him than she did.

She had made a couple of friends in hospital. Noelle was from Roscommon, an inpatient like herself. Manic depression. She had been as high as a kite when she was admitted, hadn't slept for six days, she said. They pulled her back to earth with injections of sedatives that knocked her out for most of the next couple of weeks. When they finally managed to get her medication sorted, and she emerged groggily from under her covers, she started hanging out in the TV room where Lucia spent a lot of her time. Noelle was her first real girl-friend, the kind of friend she had always dreamed of, if not coming down off a manic high in a psychiatric unit. They talked for hours about everything and anything. Noelle came from a very ordinary family. Her father worked in the bank, while her mother stayed at home. There was an older sister and a younger brother. Nobody knew where Noelle's illness had come from. There was no history of it in the family. Just bad luck. She told Lucia how much she hated the side effects of her medication, the weight gain, the thirst and the constant weeing, which was why she had come off it, unknown to anybody until it became clear to everybody.

Lucia confided in Noelle too, told her what it had been like growing up in her family, of how the constant putdowns had crushed her self-esteem to smithereens. She told her how they had stolen her beautiful baby from her and given her away. How she could never forgive them and how the thought of going back to them, back to that life, made her feel utterly hopeless.

A girl who liked to call a spade a spade, Noelle told Lucia she needed to get as far away from her family as she could. And then she should go to the guards and demand they get her baby back. 'They can't just steal your baby, for fuck's sake.'

It wasn't as simple as that, as Lucia had pointed out. How could she possibly look after a baby on her own? Where would they live? What would she do for money? Painful as it was, Maeve was better off staying where she was for now. Not a day went by when she didn't think of her. The Maeve in her head had big blue eyes and blonde pigtails. Every birthday, five of them now, and every Christmas, Lucia went to the Augustinian Church and lit a candle for her daughter. She didn't bother with the church apart from that, didn't even go to mass any more.

Her other friend at the hospital had been Dolores, a Filipina nurse's aide, not much older than Lucia. She lived in a two-bedroom flat in Dolphin's Barn with her parents, grandparents and siblings. Dolores worked long, hard hours and her family's living conditions left much to be desired, judging by the little she gave away, yet she always had a smile on her face. She might not have had a lot, but she was content.

The more time she spent with Noelle and Dolores, the more Lucia began to imagine another life for herself. What if Sister Breda was right and she was stronger than she knew? As she watched Dolores carry out her menial duties and saw the satisfaction she derived from her work, she began to wonder where she could find such contentment in her own life.

It hadn't happened overnight. She did a certificate in childcare at the Tech on Father Griffin Road in Galway, staying with Uncle Luke and Aunt Maryanne three nights a week, and getting the bus in and out from Threadneedle Road. She became closer again to Victoria, who was studying medicine in University College Galway. She got work experience at a playschool in Letterfrack and, while she enjoyed being with the children, she hated living at home after her taste of freedom. When Dolores rang to tell her they were looking for a nurse's aide at the paediatric unit in the Regional in Galway, she applied straight away. She still couldn't quite believe that she had got the job. That she was free. Living with Sandra in their cosy home a stone's throw from work. *Happy as two little piggies in shite*, as Sandra put it. She had never felt as safe and secure as she did in that two-bedroom house beside the Canal. Had never really felt *home* before. She couldn't remember the last time she had gone back to Kylemore. She had been there just once since Misty had died the previous December. She missed her pony, missed the special Connemara light and the air, the mountains keeping watch, but not enough to go back.

She rarely thought about PJ. He had never returned to Kylemore after that magical summer, had stopped replying to her letters. She had been so hurt. Her first love, tainted now.

As she carried her drink down to where her friends sat, somebody called her name. 'Lucia. Hold up there.' She turned. Her heart skipped. Colman Ryan. With his cheeky smile.

'Are you coming to the session in the Crane tonight?' he asked. 'Sandra said she'll try to talk you into it.'

She hesitated. She wasn't that keen on crowded pubs, but she didn't want to turn him down. And she was dying to show off the new brown suede bomber jacket Sandra had talked her into treating herself to for her birthday.

'Am ... I'm not sure yet.'

'*Ara*, come on, you're only young once. It'll be a bit of craic,' he coaxed. 'If you decide you want to leave early, I can walk you home.'

'Maybe. We'll see sure,' she said, turning towards her friends, a shy smile playing at the edge of her lips.

34

Maisie had been unusually clingy that morning at drop-off. Cara had to force herself not to go to the back of the Little Tots building and peek through the window to see if she had settled.

In the front porch, a group of Lululemoned mums were making arrangements to meet for coffee before walking the Prom. Cara felt the familiar FOMO pang – for herself and for Maisie because the mummy playdates inevitably led to kiddie playdates. They had stopped inviting her after the first few weeks of being told that, much as she'd love to, she was afraid she had to go to work.

It wasn't as if she wanted to be a stay-at-home mum, even if it had been an option financially, which it definitely wasn't, but a more flexible structure, like maybe working three days every second week, would be ideal. More time to spend with Maisie and less time feeling guilty. Time to go for coffee every now and then with the Lulus and to arrange playdates for Maisie and her little pals.

She and Kian weren't big spenders, but they needed two full-time salaries to cover their mortgage payments, the car, his van and all of their outgoings, especially when prices were only going one way. Kian was trying to get his business off the ground, and like all small businesses, facing cost challenges due to high inflation and rising energy prices. She knew he was stressed about the budget on the school contract, but any time she brought it up, he changed the subject, which didn't fill her with confidence. And God only knew what lay ahead for the newspaper business. They hadn't been on a sun holiday since Maisie was born and wouldn't be going away any time soon.

She could have done with a couple of days off this week. She doubted she had even had five hours' sleep last night. Her head had been filled with Lucia, the idyllic upbringing in Connemara described by her family such a stark contrast to the way in which her life had ended. And then the questions raised by her conversation with Colman. Could she have been pregnant? Surely not, but why would the friend make it up? She had left a message for Donal McGann to call her yesterday but had heard nothing back from him yet.

Things were building up on her at home and at work. The house was like a pigsty. Laundry was piling up, clothes and toys thrown everywhere, and the place was in desperate need of a good hoovering, but she couldn't muster the energy in the evenings to do anything beyond make dinner.

It wasn't helping that Kian was pressuring her to stop *punishing* her father and Paul by rarely returning their calls, and not joining him and Maisie when they visited her father or met him on the Prom for a walk. It tugged at her conscience, like a permanent stitch, but Kian couldn't possibly understand how conflicted she felt.

He had started on about it last night when she was already too tired to think. 'You can't go on like this for ever, love. It's not fair on anybody. There has to come a point where things go back to—'

'Normal? Well, that's not going to happen, is it, Kian? Because there's nothing normal about this situation, and unless you can dig up a time machine from somewhere, things can't ever go back to the way they used to be.'

'I know that, and I know how shit this is for you, but I'm just saying you can't cut them out for ever. You've always been so close to your father and Paul. You need each other now more than ever and Maisie needs them too. She's started to ask why you're not coming when we call down to see your dad. She might be only three but kids pick up on this stuff.'

She had got up off the sofa. 'I really don't need you loading more guilt onto my shoulders, Kian. I'm just about keeping it together as it is. I'm going to bed.'

He had come up after her, apologised and put his arms around her, but long after he had fallen asleep, she was awake mulling over his words.

She was so horribly torn. Of course she missed seeing and talking to her dad and brother but she was too angry and upset to be around them right now, especially when she was trying to assimilate her birth-family into her life, the family they had connived to keep from her. She knew the situation couldn't go on for ever, just as she knew deep inside that, in pushing away her father and brother, she was pushing away the grief at her mother's death that hovered over her.

She had been nearly twenty minutes trying to write the intro to a straightforward news story on the opening of a new public menopause clinic in Galway. Her brain was refusing to cooperate, her thoughts reverting to the same default position.

Had Lucia been pregnant and, if so, why had it not been mentioned in any of the press reports?

She decided to call Donal McGann if she didn't hear back from him in the next hour or so.

She had rung the hospital earlier and left a message for a guy called Marty Mannion, who, Colie had told her, had worked in the Regional with him back in the nineties and was a brother of Sandra's husband. Sandra was a Mannion now, not a Nolan, which explained why she had been so hard to track down.

It was later that evening before she heard back from Donal and told him what Colie had suggested. 'I mean, it can't be true surely, although I don't know why he'd make it up ... It wasn't mentioned in the papers or at the inquest. And I'm sure you'd have said something about it if it was true.'

'No, Cara, there was no truth in it. Any foetal remains would have shown up in the post-mortem. There was nothing like that.'

'Jesus. Why the hell would he make up something like that?'

'I don't blame him. It was the flatmate who spread that rumour after Lucia went missing. She was the one who told the Ryan lad. And he was gullible enough to believe her. As if his girlfriend wouldn't have told him herself if she was pregnant with his baby. Lucia's family were very upset about it at the time, as if they weren't going through enough of a nightmare.'

'But why would she do that? It just doesn't make any sense unless ... Is there any way she was involved in what happened to Lucia? Could she have been trying to cover up something with this story of a pregnancy? To make it look like Lucia had gone off to get rid of the baby or something?'

'Look, sometimes with these cases, you'll have people who get their kicks from the drama of the situation,' he said. 'The Nolan girl was mad keen to go to the papers with her story, even though there was no proof, apart from her say-so, that Lucia was pregnant.'

'Colie said one of Lucia's brothers approached her at work and threatened to sue her if she didn't stop.'

'Well, I can't say I'd blame him if he did. I'd probably have done the same thing myself in his position. You can't just go round making up stuff like that about people. The papers probably wouldn't have printed it anyway although the tabloids might have run with it. They don't seem too bothered about being sued or about verifying the facts of what they're told.'

When she got off the phone from the retired garda, she had an email in her inbox from a pathologist whom she knew from covering inquests, and whom she had contacted the day before. She confirmed what Donal had said. If Lucia had been pregnant when she died, it would have shown up during the post-mortem. If, however, she had been pregnant and lost the baby, it wouldn't have shown up after such a prolonged period of submersion in the bog, even though the uterus was the last muscle to decompose.

There was something off here, something not right. Maybe Donal was right and Lucia's friend had, for some strange fucked-up reason, made up a story about her missing flatmate being pregnant. Or maybe something else was going on. Either way, Cara felt a strong compulsion now to talk to Sandra Mannion and dig deeper into her birth-mother's case.

35

They drove down into the Inagh Valley, Cara barely taking in the wild beauty of the scenery around her. She was filled with nervous excitement at the prospect of meeting her birth-family again, in their home this time, and introducing her husband and child to them. Kian was driving, Maisie conked out in her car seat, head back, mouth wide open. The mountains were sullen today, a layer of cloud pegged low over the landscape.

They came out of the valley and curved around the road towards Kylemore, slowing at the Abbey as usual to take in the stunning view. She checked her watch. Two minutes to three. Perfect timing.

Kian indicated to turn right off the main road onto the Casey property, and she reached a hand back to squeeze Maisie's knee gently. 'Wakey wakey, Maisie pet.'

Kian pulled in beside the intercom at the stately black gates guarding entry to Fatima, the name of the house, according to an elegant sign set into the high stone wall that surrounded the property. He lowered his window and had just reached out to press the buzzer when the gates began to part before them, sleek and soundless.

'Come on, Maisie, we're here now.'

Her daughter gave a long stretch and rubbed her eyes.

There was no sign of the vicious guard dog threatened by the notices on the gate. Two cars were parked at the side of the house: a black Range Rover that looked fresh from the showroom, alongside a stunning dark green Jaguar. Kian pulled in beside them, and Cara was on her way to release Maisie from her car seat when she stopped in her tracks.

Holy fuck.

When Maryanne mentioned that Annette had had a grotto built in the garden, Cara had expected a little shrine, but this yoke was full-sized, like something you'd see in the grounds of a church. Carved into the side of the mountain that formed the boundary wall of the garden, it was quite an extraordinary sight. The centrepiece was a large statue of Our Lady, looking benevolently down upon a smaller statue of a girl in a white veil on her knees, her painted plaster hands joined together in prayer.

Cara was standing beside the car staring at it when she heard the front door open behind her and she returned to extricating her child.

'Hello, hello.' Marcus stepped out onto the paved turning oval at the front of the house to greet them, a wide smile on his face. 'You must be Kian,' he said, shaking his hand robustly. 'Welcome to Kylemore. Wonderful to meet you.'

He turned to Cara and Maisie, who had tucked herself in shyly behind her mother's legs. 'It's lovely to see you again, Cara.' He moved towards her and, for a moment, it looked like he was going to hug her, but he gave her arm an awkward little squeeze instead. 'And this must be the little lady I've heard so much about.' He bent towards Maisie. 'What's this your name is again? Hmm, let me think. Oh, yes, Daisy, isn't it?'

Maisie shook her head and clung tighter to Cara.

'Oh, dearie me. Well, I know it sounds like Daisy. Let me think. Oh, I know, Crazy. Your name is Crazy, isn't it? That's a lovely name for a pretty little girl like you.'

Maisie started to giggle, her need to correct him overtaking her natural shyness. 'Me not Cazy. Me Maisie.'

'Oh, Maisie. Yes, that's it. I'm an awful silly old goose, amn't I?'

'Dilly ol' doose,' Maisie agreed, with a beaming smile.

He bent down to her level again, indicated with a wiggle of his index finger that he had a secret to tell her. She leaned forward conspiratorially, and he whispered loudly in her ear, 'A little birdie told me you don't like cake, Maisie, *especially chocolate cake.*'

Maisie looked at him in horror. 'No. Me do like cake. Chockette my best kind.'

'Well, that's very good to hear because we made a big chocolate cake as today is such a special occasion for us all. The day we meet you for the first time.'

The ice well and truly crushed, he ushered them in through the wide doorway in front of him into a spacious entrance hall.

'Phillip is inside with Mother but unfortunately Hugh can't make it today,' he explained. 'He's out of the country on business, but he hopes to come next time. We don't see much of Denis, these days, I'm afraid, but he'll try to get back before the end of the year to meet you all.'

As Marcus talked, Cara took in as much about her surroundings as she could, conscious that this had been Lucia's home for most of her short life. Similar to the hotel in design, the Casey home was just as tastefully decorated apart from gaudy splashes of religious iconography that jarred in such a setting. A metal holy-water font lined with slimy green algae and inscribed with the words *God Bless Our Home* was attached to the wall just inside the door. A stunning watercolour hung above the fireplace, blood red poppies and yellow-yolked daisies so real she felt as though she could reach in and pluck them. A Kenneth Webb original, if Cara wasn't mistaken, the British impressionist landscape painter who had made Connemara his home, the landscape his muse.

On the opposite wall hung a huge gold crucifix, a suitably tortured-looking Jesus pinned to it with silver nails. And beside that a picture of the Sacred Heart – once a quintessential part of so many Irish households along with a photograph of Pope John Paul II – this version of Jesus gazing beseechingly heavenward in the garish red glow. Maryanne clearly hadn't been exaggerating when she said Lucia's family took their religion seriously.

Marcus led them into a large, sunny living room with a wide bay window, showcasing another oversized fireplace, and more beautiful pieces of art. Annette was almost lost in a double winged chair, a heavy tweed blanket over her legs, a fire blazing in the hearth beside her.

Phillip came forward to greet Kian and shake his hand, then bent to say hello to Maisie, who was scanning the room for cake, and giving her an awkward pat on the head.

Annette reached for Cara's hand, her tremor worse today, pulling her closer. 'Thank you for coming out to see us again, dear, and for bringing the little one.' Her voice was feeble and wispy.

'Thank you for inviting us. Maisie, come here and say hello to ... your, em ...' She had no idea how to introduce her daughter to the grandmother she had met only once herself.

'Nanette,' Marcus said, dissolving the awkwardness of the moment. 'That's what all the other grandchildren and great-grandchildren call her. 'And they call me Gandy. Phillip's eldest lad, James, couldn't pronounce "Granddad" so he called me Gandy and it stuck. I'm happy to share a name with another great man.' He chuckled.

All of the other great-grandchildren.

Cara felt a warm wave wash over her. Her daughter was being treated like the other Casey children, those who had always been part of the family. It also solved the problem for Cara of how she should address her birth-grandparents.

'Come and say hello to Nanette, pet.' She beckoned to her daughter.

Maisie, however, wasn't quite so enthusiastic at the prospect of getting any closer to the very old lady in the big chair. She shook her head at Cara and hid behind Kian.

Normally Cara wouldn't push it, knowing her daughter would come out of herself when she'd had time to get used to the strange adults, but Annette's twiggy, quivering hand was reaching out towards her. Cara widened her eyes at Kian, signalling for him to coax the child into getting with the programme, but as he tried to peel her fingers off his leg, the little monkey tightened her grip. Annette's arm was still hovering in mid-air, shaking harder now. Cara could feel sweat gather beneath her arms and above her lip. It was far too warm and she was too close to the fire.

She was about to suggest they give Maisie a few minutes to settle when Marcus bent down beside the little girl and whispered something in her ear. Then he held out his hand to her. There was no way she would take it, Cara knew. She was far too shy. But, to her amazement, Maisie reached out a pudgy little hand to Marcus and allowed him to lead her to his wife. Cara couldn't believe it. Was Marcus some kind of child whisperer or had Maisie somehow sensed her blood connection to these people?

A painful lump of emotions lodged in her throat as Maisie stood before her great-grandmother and the old woman held the little face between her hands, her eyes wet. She leaned forward to brush a kiss on Maisie's temple, muttering what sounded like a prayer. Cara couldn't make out what she was saying apart from 'The Lord taketh away and the Lord giveth.' Wasn't it supposed to be the other way around?

Then Maisie opened her mouth: 'Nanette got chockette cake for Maisie?'

The room erupted into laughter, even Annette joining in as Maisie looked round in bemusement. So that was how the wily old divil had done it: old-fashioned bribery.

After the chocolate fudge cake had been brought in and served, Marcus took Maisie and Kian out to see the treehouse in the garden while Cara began to look at the photo albums that had been brought to her. Marcus had told her she could take the photos away and get them copied if she wanted. There were christenings, birthdays, communions and confirmations. Lucia in jodhpurs on her pony, in swimming togs on the sand, in school uniform on her first day at Kylemore Abbey. Lots of photos of her with her cousin Tommy, his brown eyes brimming with mischief. There were photos of her as a teenager in a uniform of T-shirts with either riding breeches or shorts, always with the same shy smile.

As she leafed through the pages, crinkled now with age, some having long lost their stickiness, Annette and Phillip provided commentary until the old woman nodded off, sitting upright in her chair. Phillip explained that this happened all the time, her body worn to exhaustion by the constant tremors. As she continued to flick through the albums, the only sounds a soft whistling through Annette's nostrils and the squeals of her daughter from outside, Cara felt an immense rush of gratitude towards these people for welcoming her and her little family into their home and for offering her the opportunity to feel closer to her birth-mother. It couldn't have been easy for them, her appearance in their lives stirring up so many painful emotions, but they had opened their arms to her.

She slipped a photo out of its sleeve. In it, Lucia looked about three, the same age as Maisie now. In gingham shorts and red wellies. They could have been twins. This was definitely one she would be getting copied and framed. Then she came across a picture of a teenage Lucia at a ball in a blue dress with matching shoes, her hair and make-up done. She looked so different.

'Wow, she's beautiful there,' she said, holding it out to Phillip.

'That was the night of the fiftieth-anniversary party. Before she ... em ... before she had you.'

She hadn't had any intention of bringing it up, hadn't heard anything back from Sandra Nolan's brother-in-law and didn't even know if he'd heard her message. She checked to make sure Annette was still asleep, lowered her voice just in case. 'Was that the only time she was pregnant? When she had me?'

Phillip looked confused.

'Sorry, I hadn't planned to bring it up. It's just that I've been talking to Colie, her boyfriend, and he said ...'

'Oh right yes, I see where this is coming from,' he said, his jaw tensing. 'Please don't ever mention this in front of Mother. You have no idea how upsetting it was at the time. It was that girl, Lucia's flatmate, who spread the rumour. We have no idea why. We were already going through absolute hell, and for her to start spreading such a blatant lie ...' He shook his head. 'It was dreadful. I actually had to call to the hospital to beg her to please stop, to think of my parents but she just kept lying directly to my face. I don't know if she was some kind of fantasist or if she got some kind of sick pleasure out of all the drama. The guards told us it wasn't unusual for people to do that kind of thing. We'll never know why she did it. My father hired a private investigator, a retired detective with a great track record, to look discreetly into the case when more than a year had passed and the guards still had no answers for us. He got nowhere either so we've had to learn to accept that we'll never know what happened to Lucia.'

'I didn't realise a private investigator was involved and I'm sorry for bringing it up. I just wondered, you know.'

She had wondered how the family had been able to accept not knowing how Lucia had met her death, and who had been responsible, but it was beginning to make more sense now. They had tried to find answers themselves, hadn't simply sat back and done nothing, and for that she was glad.

Maybe she, too, would learn to be more accepting of her mother's fate in time.

36

She invited her father and Paul for a barbecue on Sunday evening. It was a spur of the moment decision. She had enjoyed her first night of unbroken sleep in months after the visit to Kylemore the day before and woke feeling energised and refreshed. She knew her father was struggling, and she couldn't keep pushing them away for ever.

Kian had been delighted when she suggested it and even offered to take Maisie into town that morning to pick up some tasty salads while she tackled the house. 'It's the right thing to do, love. Time for us all to try to move forward now. Together. Especially when things are going so well for you with the Caseys. Maisie is all excited about Grandad and Paul coming over.'

They had sat up together the night before after they'd got Maisie off to sleep, flicking through the photo albums again, Cara providing the commentary for Kian and picking out the many she wanted copied.

'It looks like an idyllic childhood, doesn't it,' Kian had said, 'growing up in such a beautiful place, the best of everything?'

'Yeah. These photos have really helped ... It's just lovely to know she had a happy childhood, a good life despite the awful way it ended.'

She hung one wash out to dry, and put another on. She gathered every stray item of clothing, every toy and random misplaced object from around the house, and put them back in their places, then scrubbed the bathrooms, hoovered, mopped and polished until the place was as close to gleaming as she could get it. She was ready to collapse afterwards, but it was worth it for the satisfaction of her clean, tidy surfaces and almost empty laundry basket. Plus the bottle of her favourite rosé Prosecco that was chilling in the fridge, the organic anti-hangover one.

It turned out to be a lovely evening: the sun had bullied its way back through the clouds late in the afternoon and they set the table in the garden. Their neighbours were doing the same – she could hear the twins two doors up squealing from their trampoline, their tow-coloured heads bobbing over the fence as they bounced. The air was rich with the scent of charcoal and sizzling meat, a hedge trimmer whirred in the distance and Coldplay were playing through Kian's beloved Bose portable speaker. Ralph was sticking close to the barbecue, on the cadge as always.

Paul was pushing Maisie on her swing as she screamed, 'Higher, higher!' and her father was sitting back with a bottle of beer in his hand, smiling as he watched them, his eyes soft. Cara had been taken aback when he'd arrived with Paul. He had aged so much over the past couple of weeks since she had seen him. It struck her again how lonely he must be, rattling around that big house on his own, nothing but silence to fill the spaces her mother had left in every room. She hadn't been back there herself since the day she'd found out about Lucia.

A spasm of guilt ripped through her. This was the man who had reared her, pushed her on so many swings, held her hand, picked her up when she fell, wiped her tears. Celebrated every success with such immense pride.

At the same time that he and her mother had been keeping a dark secret from her. He turned to her now, clearly conscious of her eyes on him.

'Mum would have loved this,' he said.

'She would, Dad.'

She took a sip from her glass. There was a strain between them that had never existed before.

'I'm glad things seem to be going well ... with the ... with Lucia's family. Kian was filling us in. All we ever wanted was for you to be OK, to be happy.' He sighed. 'Maybe we did the wrong thing in not—'

'I'm not ready to talk about it, Dad. Maybe down the line when I've had more time ...'

'Whatever you need.'

She had finished reading the Bible-for-adoptees book, and while it explained a lot, it hadn't made her feel any better. If anything, maybe a bit worse. The author described the separation between mother and infant at birth as a *primal wound*. That the baby may only have been a few days or weeks old when the separation occurred made no difference: they had shared forty weeks with a person with whom they probably bonded in utero, a person to whom they were biologically, genetically and, even more importantly, emotionally and spiritually connected.

The author pointed out that it took human infants a year to attain the degree of maturity that the young of most other mammals had at birth. During this time, she maintained that though the physical body was born, the self, or core being, of the infant was not yet separate from the mother but was psychologically contained within her. The mother provided a container for the child's developing ego, just as she had previously provided the container for their developing body. This concept made sense to Cara, who had struggled to separate psychologically from Maisie during the first year after her birth, feeling at times as if they were the one person.

They managed to have a nice evening, despite the absence of her mother. She felt less untethered, more relaxed, although that was probably due in part to the Prosecco currently fizzing through her veins. Not all, though. Cutting off contact with her father and brother had been like cutting out her heart to spite her brain. It wasn't fair on anybody.

Maisie had insisted on Uncle Paul putting her to bed, and judging by the shrieks of delight coming from upstairs, he was being attacked by her giant panda again. It would take ages to settle her now, but mellowed by alcohol, Cara didn't care.

Her father shook his head, smiling. 'Will that eejit ever get sense? He's like a big child.'

'He is. She's in her element, though. He's such a natural with kids. It's a pity he never had his own. He'd have made a great dad.'

'Your mother used to say that, too, but I don't know. He seems happy enough as he is and that's the most important thing.'

'Yeah, I suppose.'

She had left her phone charging upstairs all evening and it wasn't until after her father and Paul had left and a hyper, overtired Maisie was finally asleep that she checked it and saw she had a missed call from an unknown number and a voice message. She called 171.

'Hello, Cara. It's Sandra Mannion here. I got your number from Marty, my brother-in-law. He was off on holidays and just got your message. I can't believe it, Lucia's girl ... I'm so thrilled to hear from you. Give me a call back when you can and we can chat and maybe arrange to meet up in person.'

37

Cara had just raised her hand to ring the doorbell of the end-of-terrace house, its window boxes painted a pretty pansy purple, when the door was pulled open by a woman with a mop of frizzy copper curls, a wide smile and warm brown eyes.

Sandra, she assumed, clamped a hand to her mouth and her eyes filled with tears.

'Oh my God.' The tears plopped over her lower eyelids and Sandra wiped them away with the back of a hand, reaching out the other to Cara.

'Come in, love. What am I like leaving you standing there? It's just ... I wasn't expecting you to be so like her.'

She ushered Cara inside, still wiping tears away. 'Is it OK if I give you a hug?'

Cara allowed herself to be squished into Sandra's bosom. She felt positively petite in the other woman's arms. Sandra had the most enormous boobs Cara had ever seen or been squashed so tightly against. When she had spoken to Sandra on the phone on Monday morning, her mother's old friend had explained that she was living in Dublin with her husband and four boys, but would be more than happy to come to Galway to see her. Cara had protested that she didn't want to put her to that kind of trouble.

'It's no trouble, believe me. Eric and the boys can manage fine without me. They're all big and bold enough to mind themselves. I could do with a break from them, to be honest. Four lads under one roof plus Eric, who's the worst of the lot, they've me driven demented. I haven't been home in far too long and my mother's not getting any younger.'

'Bring her in here till I get a look at her, will ya, Sandra?' A croaky voice came from the other end of the narrow hallway, the walls of which were almost completely papered with family photos. She recognised a young Sandra smiling out from under a white veil, the same lovely brown eyes.

'Mammy's dying to meet you,' Sandra said, as she released her. She guided Cara ahead of her into a cluttered, cosy kitchen where an old-fashioned cream range was pumping out heat.

'C'mere ta me till I see ya, loveen.'

Sandra's mother was an older, scrawnier version of her daughter. She sported a set of the generous breasts that obviously ran in the family, although hers were sitting on her lap. She was sunk into a high-backed armchair beside the stove. She patted the chair beside her. 'I'm Bridie, love. I've been dyin' to meet ya. Sit in here beside me. Ah, Gaw help us, you're the head off her. Isn't she, Sandra? The pretty little faysheen.' She tutted sadly.

'She is, Mammy. I can't get over it.'

Cara couldn't get a word in edgeways as the two women talked over each other and Sandra poured tea into cups. The table had been properly laid with the good china and a pristine embroidered white tablecloth that Cara suspected came out only for special occasions. There was enough food for ten people: homemade fruit scones with a slab of butter in a dish and a jar of Chivers strawberry jam, an apple tart and a huge plate of Jacob's Kimberley and Coconut Cream biscuits. On the other end of the table there were two photo albums, and some framed pictures of a younger, slimmer Sandra with Lucia.

'Will ya get the nice napkins out of the press, Sandra, for God's sake? The matching ones. Where did ya find those aul' yokes?'

'They're grand, Mam, will ya stop? A napkin's a napkin, for feck's sake.'

'Ah, fer ... I'll get them meself.'

As Bridie made a half-hearted attempt to stand, muttering under her breath, Sandra told her to stay where she was, rolling her eyes as she went to fetch the napkins. It was a well-rehearsed dance, Cara could tell.

The house reminded her strongly of Granny Joyce's house in Grattan Road, long since sold, modernised beyond recognition and vastly appreciated in value. The same fuss that was made for visitors. The genuine warmth of the welcome. Not like the estate where she and Kian lived, neighbours waving to each other as they passed on their way to and from work, and from dropping kids here, there and everywhere. There was very little popping into each other's houses for tea and biscuits, and if there were scones, they were usually shop bought.

They wanted to know all about her.

Was she happy?

Did she like her job? Lucia would have been so proud, her daughter writing for the paper. Imagine that.

How was she enjoying being a mammy? What did she call her? Maisie, what a beautiful name. Had she any photos of her? Oh, wasn't she gorgeous and the image of Cara and Lucia.

Would she have another scone?

Would she like her tart heated? A small biteen of ice-cream with it? Ah, go on.

'Listen to us jabbering on,' Sandra finally said. 'Sorry, Cara love, you came here to talk about Lucia, not to get the third degree from a pair of nosy aul' bats. I pulled out all the photos I could find of her. It's hard to believe she's over thirty years gone. Where did that time go?'

Sandra handed her a framed photo of a much younger version of herself with Lucia, wearing happy smiles and paper Santa hats, and surrounded by the detritus of Christmas dinner – pulled crackers with their entrails spread across the table, half-empty wine glasses, dessert plates bearing the remains of custard and jelly – in the kitchen where they were sitting now.

'This is one of my favourite pictures of her – I had it framed for Mammy cos she loved it too. That was a lovely day. It was the Christmas before she went missing. The first Christmas she didn't spend in Kylemore. She was rostered on that day so she came here after her shift instead of going home. She was in great form, wasn't she, Mammy?'

'She was, love.' Bridie smiled, sadly.

Sandra was flicking through one of the albums. 'Look at this one of her and Colie. It was taken in Canal Road. She was so happy-looking there.' Sandra handed her the photo. 'The quality's not great – no such thing as camera phones back then.'

Cara held the slightly blurred photo. Colie and Lucia were in a kitchen, in front of an old-fashioned teak kitchen unit, he standing behind her with his arms around her waist. Lucia must have been twenty-one or -two, but she could have passed for a teenager. She was smiling shyly and Sandra was right, she did look happy.

'God, she was so young-looking.'

'Sure she was constantly asked for ID – it used to drive her mad. She didn't just look young, she was ... not immature, but she had a real innocence about her. Oh, she was just the loveliest person you could meet, wasn't she, Mammy?'

Bridie nodded. 'She was one in a million.'

Sandra continued: 'I only got to know her when she moved to Galway. We just clicked straight away. We were working on the same ward and I had started just a few weeks before her, was finding my feet as well.'

Cara buttered another half-scone for herself while Sandra reminisced.

'She hadn't an ounce of confidence in herself when she started at the Regional, God help her. She was convinced she was thick stupid, but she had so much going for her. She was warm and kind and funny and she was really starting to come out of herself too.' Sandra explained that they had been living together for a while before Lucia told her about the baby she had been forced to give up for adoption. 'She found it very hard to talk about. The more we got to know each other, the more she opened up, though. And to Mammy too. Ye used to have great chats, didn't ye, Mammy?'

'We did. She started coming over the odd time with Sandra for dinner, and the two of us hit it off like a house on fire. She used to say she felt really at home here. Our house certainly wasn't anywhere near as fancy as what Lucia was used to, but she didn't care. She'd been so lonely for so long. We used to spend hours sitting here at this table talkin' about everythin' and anythin'. She always wondered if you were happy, love. She worried about whether you were being looked after right, whether you were loved as much as you deserved to be. She didn't even have a photo of you to look at, Gaw love her.'

Cara felt a sharp pang of pity for the young woman looking up from the photos. She picked up another from the table, took in the image of Lucia in a blue tunic with teddies on it, her hair tied off her face, waving from the bedside of a bald child in a pair of Fireman Sam pyjamas, with an oxygen tube in his nose. There was a half-finished Spiderman jigsaw puzzle on the over-bed table in front of them.

'That poor little ladeen died a few weeks after that photo was taken. Lucia was in a bad way after it. She got far too close to some of them. She would have learned with time not to get so involved, but sure she never got the chance,' Sandra said wistfully. 'You can take all these photos away with you and get copies made, if you like, Cara.'

'That would be great, thanks, Sandra. It's lovely to have them. The Caseys gave me some albums too. I met them for the first time a couple of weeks ago on my own, and again with my husband and Maisie last Saturday.'

Sandra and Bridie's mouths pursed in unison and she felt the temperature in the room drop. There was clearly still bad feeling between them and the Caseys.

She turned to Sandra. In for a penny, in for a pound. 'There's something I wanted to ask you about. Colie said you told him

Lucia was pregnant when she went missing. He said he had no idea himself.'

Sandra looked at her mother, who nodded at her. 'Well, that makes the decision a lot easier. I was humming and hawing about whether I should mention it or not. I didn't know if Colie'd say anything to you. Lucia hadn't even had the chance to tell him before she went missing. She *was* pregnant, Cara. I know that for a fact. I got her a test and I was with her when she found out it was positive. She was terrified of her family finding out, but I think Colie would probably have stood by her. She knew me and Mammy would be there for her either way. Nobody knew, only us. And her cousin Victoria. I thought it was a mistake telling her, but Lucia said she had kind of guessed it.'

'But I checked with Donal McGann, the sergeant who was investigating the murder, and he said she wasn't pregnant. That it would have shown up in the post-mortem if she was.'

'I don't know why nothing showed up. Maybe the poor girl was too badly damaged after being buried in that place so long. I even wondered at the time if there had been some kind of cover-up. The Caseys knew people in high places. I thought they might have got to the pathologist or the coroner because it just didn't add up.'

What the hell? A cover-up? Was Sandra another bloody conspiracy theorist?

Sandra took in the sceptical look on her face.

'All I can tell you is that I am one hundred per cent certain she was pregnant when she went missing. I didn't tell the guards initially in case she came back and was annoyed at me for letting it out. And then when I did tell them, the family point blank denied it. Poor Colie didn't know what to believe,

I'd say. I threatened to go to the papers myself because I felt the guards weren't taking me seriously, but Phillip came into me at work and said Mr Casey would sue me if I did. Accused me of making it up to get attention. I was in bits over it all, wasn't I, Mammy?'

'You were, love. Bad enough that poor Lucia was after vanishing into thin air without you being called a liar on top of it. Sure what benefit was there for Sandra in saying the girl was pregnant if she wasn't?'

'We kept hoping she'd turn up, that there'd be some explanation but we knew she was in trouble from that first night she didn't come home. We just knew it.'

Bridie took over again. 'There was one evening she called here a week or so before she went missing. She was talking about trying to get you back after she'd had the baby, saying the adoption had been forced on her, and she was going to a solicitor to see what her rights were. We were a bit shocked. You'd have been five or six by then and it sounded kind of mad, but she got so angry and upset when we tried to say it to her.'

'Yeah,' Sandra continued. 'We'd never seen her like that before ... She said we couldn't understand because we'd never had a baby stolen from us. We put it down to pregnancy hormones at the time because it was so unlike her. The following week, she disappeared and we never saw her again.'

'So you never went to the papers?'

'No. My heart was broke over the whole thing. And then when she was found, it was such a terrible time. I never thought we'd be sitting here all these years later, though, still not knowing what happened to her.'

Despite her initial suspicions of Sandra, Cara couldn't help but be drawn to her and her mother. It was clear how much they had loved and cared for Lucia. And they were adamant that she had been pregnant. Unless they were incredibly accomplished liars, they genuinely believed it.

Yet it hadn't been true, according to the gardaí and the post-mortem report. Had Lucia lied to them about the pregnancy and, if so, why? Could that lie have had something to do with her death?

Cara needed to get hold of the case file. She might find something in there, a loose thread to follow to try to find out what the hell had happened to her birth-mother.

38

Lucia
Galway city
1990

The night it happened, Colie had been plastered. They had been at the afters of the wedding of one of the porters at the hospital and the drink was flowing. She reminded him to pull out, but it was too late. She hadn't been that shocked when her period, due two weeks later, hadn't come. The thought of telling them at home made her feel like puking, but there was a kind of feverish excitement inside her too.

She told Sandra very early on, knew she could trust her not to say anything. She had never had a friend like her before. Sandra was like the sister she had never had and, indeed, Lucia had been welcomed into the Nolan family with open arms when her friend had brought her home to Mervue to meet her mother. Bridie hadn't let being widowed young get in her way: she had reared three children, who were each a credit to her, and who all adored her.

Sandra got a pregnancy test from a nurse she knew at the hospital, and they had waited until they got home that evening for Lucia to do it. As they sat on the edge of the green bath in their tiny bathroom, waiting for the result, Lucia felt herself hoping the line would turn blue.

She wasn't ready to tell Colie yet, wasn't sure how he'd take the news. They hadn't been going out together that long, and although he was kind and seemed fond of her, he might run a mile if he heard he was going to be a daddy. She was fond of him too. At times, something about him reminded her of Tommy, although her feelings for him were nothing close to what she had felt for PJ. She didn't think she could ever feel that aching love for any man. The kind of love that people dismissed as teenage hormones, but that she thought came along maybe once in a lifetime if you were lucky.

None of that mattered now, though. All that mattered was the tiny creature growing inside her belly. While the ideal situation would be for Colie to support her in rearing their baby, she would manage either way. She had Sandra now and Bridie, who was insisting that she would mind the baby for Lucia while she was at work. Lucia would be the kind of mother that Bridie was: steady and loving, there for her child no matter what.

She hadn't planned on telling Victoria, certainly not when she hadn't even told Colie. They had arranged to meet in Lydon's on Shop Street for tea and buns on one of Victoria's rare afternoons off. Victoria had been waiting when Lucia arrived from her own shift. She looked dog-tired. She was on rotation in Casualty and working mental hours.

'I've ordered the usual for us,' Victoria said, before doing a comical double-take. 'Wow, Lucia, you look ... fab. Your skin is glowing.'

Lucia had reddened, flustered by the unexpected compliment. Her cousin rarely noticed her appearance, certainly never commented on it. Unconsciously, she pressed her hand to her still flat belly. Victoria's eyes bored into her, moving from her treacherous cheeks, to the hand, then up to her chest to take in the breasts that were straining against her blouse.

The room grew louder around them as if somebody had turned up the volume.

Lucia couldn't make eye contact with her cousin, afraid her eyes would betray her too. Two women at a table across from them were huddled together, not talking. One looked as if she had been crying. Lucia wondered if she had just received bad news or …

'Oh, my God, tell me you're not.'

'Not what?' Her eyes met Victoria's briefly. She was such a useless liar.

'Are you pregnant?' Victoria asked, in a low, dramatic voice.

Lucia was wondering if medical students were taught how to tell somebody was pregnant just by looking at them when the buns her cousin had ordered granted her a short reprieve. She stared intently at the tiered cake stand as if deliberating over which of the selection to go for: the chocolate eclair oozing cream, the meringue the size of a snowball, the pink iced one or, her favourite, the dome-shaped coffee bun.

'Look at me, Lucia. You are, aren't you?'

'What? No, no, of course I'm not,' she said, willing her eyes to stop darting about.

Victoria completely ignored the cakes. *Oh Janey. This was bad.* She usually dived straight in and grabbed the choux slice, devouring it in two bites, before selecting her next victim. You picked what you wanted from the stand, only paying for the ones you'd eaten. She and Victoria had been known to put away three each. Today, Lucia would struggle to get one down. She didn't need a mirror to tell her she was puce red.

'Lucia, look me in the eye and tell me the truth.'

Flippit!

Victoria knew she was going out with Colie, but she had promised not to say anything to Lucia's parents or Andrew. Lucia didn't want word of her new boyfriend getting back to Kylemore. She lifted her eyes to her cousin's, opened her mouth to deny the truth, but she couldn't lie straight to Victoria's face.

So she had admitted that yes, she was pregnant, and she had confided in her cousin her plan for after the baby was born.

Victoria had sworn not to tell anybody, least of all their families, until Lucia was ready. After the birth. It might turn out to be a good thing that Victoria knew because Lucia's family would have to find out at some point and better that the news came from somebody within the family. It might soften the blow.

This time, though, there was no way they were going to take her baby from her.

39

'I just don't know what to believe. The family are convinced she wasn't pregnant and Sandra is convinced she was. She and her mother seem like really decent people and her mother believes it too. What could they have to gain by making up something like that?'

Cara was in 56 Central sitting opposite Fitzie on Monday morning, their coffees cooling on the table between them as she told him about her visit to the Nolans on Saturday.

'What about the cousin she was supposed to have told? Have you managed to get hold of her yet?'

'No, actually, I haven't.' He had just reminded her that Victoria hadn't returned her call from a few days ago. 'I left a message for her but she hasn't got back to me yet, which is surprising, given how responsive the rest of them have been. I'll have to try her again.'

'I suppose there's always a chance that Lucia was in the very early stages of a pregnancy and it didn't show up in the post-mortem,' Fitzie said. 'Maybe the body was just too badly decomposed.'

'I just ... There's something not right here, Fitzie. I can feel it in my gut.'

Whether her newshound antenna had picked up some subtle vibration from the ether or the spirit of her dead mother was trying to help her solve the mystery of her own death – a scenario that had seemed quite plausible in the early hours of the morning, but utterly farcical in the cold light of day – something had been niggling at her since she'd met Sandra and her mother. They had just seemed so credible. So genuinely upset at being accused of lying about the pregnancy.

It had been hours later on Saturday evening when Cara realised that she had forgotten to ask Sandra about the man who had been seen hanging around near the house on Canal Road.

'Still nothing from the guards?' Fitzie asked.

'Zilch.'

Despite numerous emails and phone calls, all she'd had back were the same stiff responses telling her that her *request is still being processed*, and advising her there was *a long backlog of requests at the moment*. She had to wait until next month to apply to the Adoption Authority for access to her birth cert and other personal information when the new law came into effect. God only knew how long she'd have to wait to receive it.

'I'm thinking of calling on the gardaí to open a cold-case review of Lucia's death.'

It was the first time she had spoken this thought aloud. She hadn't even mentioned it to Kian, but Fitzie had always been a great sounding board for her. He had a way of stepping back from a complicated situation, of looking at it with an objective eye and finding a simple clarity.

He nudged his glasses up his nose, thinking. 'Well, you've nothing to lose by asking, but, again, don't get your hopes up. That cold-case unit is totally under-resourced. They only do a handful of cases every year.'

'I know. I was reading about it.'

She had been shocked at what she read. The justice minister had confirmed earlier in the year that fourteen cold cases were under investigation by the unit. Only fourteen out of hundreds of serious unsolved cases, all involving devastated families, who were crying out for answers about what had happened to their loved ones. Some didn't even have a grave to visit. In one article she had read about an incredible woman who had spent years trying to get justice for her sister, a mother of three who had been stabbed to death in a brutal attack up the country. She eventually ambushed a senior investigating officer at the cold-crimes unit in Dublin, with a bag of scones, butter and jam, and insisted that he listen to her. Incredibly it had worked! As a result of her persistence and devotion to her sister, two men were serving life sentences for the contract killing.

As she had lain awake last night, Cara realised that Lucia deserved somebody to battle like that for her.

'Would you consider going public with it?' Fitzie asked, pulling her out of her head into the busy café where people chatted around them, crockery clattered and serving staff bustled past.

'Public? God, no. I don't think so, anyway.'

'Well, maybe it's something you should think about. It might improve your chances of having her case looked at again or speed it up if you launched a public appeal for her case to be reviewed. The national press would wet themselves over it, and it would certainly blow steam up some garda arses.'

She really didn't want to have to go public with her personal story, didn't feel comfortable at the idea of being the interviewee instead of the interviewer, but she realised that, despite her promise to the Caseys, she couldn't rule it out if she was serious about getting justice for Lucia.

40

It was gone nine on Thursday evening and she was rushing to get the last of her court reports finished for the following day's city edition. The son of well-known local property developer Johnny Burke was charged with possession of cocaine for sale or supply. He was pleading not guilty even though he had been caught red-handed with the gear in the boot of his flashy jeep and was clearly under the influence of his own product when stopped by gardaí. Cara had taken an instant dislike to the young Burke as he sat in court beside his father, a couldn't-give-a-shit smirk on his cocky face.

She would normally have her court copy finished and sent through for subbing by early afternoon, but she was running behind and still had a news story on the rental crisis across the city to write up. The pressure, combined with fatigue, was causing her to hit the wrong keys and make stupid mistakes. God only knew what time she'd get out of here tonight. There was only the sub-editor, Orla Roche, and the city editor left to put the paper to bed. The newsroom was quiet, apart from her frantic typing and the rattling of the old windows in their frames as hail hurled itself against the glass. There had been a storm warning, and the forecasters had managed to get it right on this occasion. She ignored the message light flashing on her landline. It would have to wait until she had finished her court reports; if it was important, they'd have called her mobile.

Her brain was wired and tired at the same time and she was finding it increasingly difficult to focus on anything properly. Things had started to pile up again at work and at home, her stress levels increasing concurrently.

She was aware that she was in danger of becoming consumed by the idea of getting justice for her birth-mother but, as she had pointed out to Kian last night, 'Somebody out there knows.' All she needed was for one person to remember something they had seen or heard, one dangling thread that could unravel the whole thing.

'I don't know, Car,' Kian had said. 'The family won't be happy about it and I wonder if you should be doing anything to jeopardise that relationship when it's all so new and you're just getting to know each other. I'm worried about you. I think you're trying to distract yourself from ... your mum being gone. You have to admit you're getting a bit obsessed with this cold-case stuff. Even when you're here, you're off somewhere else in your head.'

'Maybe you'd be *obsessed* too, Kian, if your mother had been murdered and the person who did it had got away scot-free,' she had spat. 'I'd like to think I might be a bit more supportive of you in the same situation.'

'I didn't mean it that way, love. I'm just afraid you're going to run yourself into the ground the way you're going. You're not sleeping, you're fading away ... Maybe you should make an appointment to see Dr Byrne.'

It annoyed her that he was right. Again. Nothing she ate, no matter how bland, seemed to agree with her, her gut spasming in protest. Her clothes were starting to hang off her. But she knew there was nothing her GP could do, only prescribe more medication for IBS that didn't work. It baffled her that nobody had managed to come up with an effective treatment for such a common and debilitating condition.

Even when she was with Kian and Maisie she wasn't really with them, not mentally anyway, her mind fixated on Lucia and the cold-case review. And while there was an element of trying to distract herself from the grief that lurked in wait for her, it was more than that.

She had considered forgetting about the whole thing, as Kian had suggested, and just getting on with her life, grieving her mother and continuing to bond with her birth-family. It would certainly be a lot less hassle, but it wouldn't leave her alone. She found herself returning again and again to the official page of the Garda Serious Crime Review Team – the proper title of the cold-case unit – on the website, peering at the thumbnail images of the missing and murdered whose cases were currently under review. A tiny photo of each tragic person and a one-line description. Murdered on a date unknown between ... Last seen leaving a certain place at a certain time on a certain date. Most going back to the eighties or nineties. Each with loved ones out there somewhere who had no answers.

It wouldn't be easy to get a review of Lucia's case, but she felt compelled to try because there was a chance that the publicity around a fresh investigation might spur somebody to come forward with new information.

She had decided she was going to do it, had already typed up a formal request for the SCRT. She hadn't submitted it yet: she had to tell the Caseys first and, hopefully, get them to understand why she needed to do this. It wouldn't be an easy conversation and she wasn't looking forward to it, but all she could do was assure them that she wasn't trying to drag anything back up, or to traumatise anybody again. This was about trying to get justice for their daughter and sister. For her mother. Surely they should want that too.

Bleary-eyed by the time she sent her last court report to the sub-editor, she started to gather up her bits and pieces. She hadn't been going to bother listening to the message on her landline – its blinking orange light had been annoying her all night – but something made her pick up the receiver and access her voicemail.

41

Lucia
Galway city
1990

When she admitted to Sandra that Victoria had guessed she was pregnant, her friend had grimaced. 'Oh, God. You'll have to tell Colie now. It'd be terrible if he heard it from someone else.'

'She's promised she won't say a word to anybody until I tell her she can. I don't want them finding out at home until it's too late for them to try to make me change my mind.'

It was clear that Sandra thought she had made a mistake in telling Victoria, but Lucia trusted her cousin. Her friend made it no secret that she had very little time for Victoria, that she thought she was 'up her own arse'. And there was no denying that Victoria could be a bit uppity at times, especially when she was with her boyfriend, Barry, a former boarding-school buddy of Andrew's and a fellow med student in Galway. It was also true that Victoria could be a bit thoughtless, but the bond with her cousin went back a long way and she was the only member of her family Lucia had any kind of a close relationship with since she and Tommy had drifted apart.

'She said I really need to make an appointment to see my doctor, to make sure everything's OK with the baby and get into a maternity clinic. I'm just worried about Uncle Luke finding out if my records are in the system.'

'I'd say that's highly unlikely. Look, Lucia, I wouldn't see eye to eye with Victoria on much, but I agree with her on this. You have to make sure you get all your scans and stuff.'

'I know, I know. I don't want to go to Dr Ryan at home, though. I know it's supposed to be confidential, but ...'

'I'll get you an appointment with my doctor. Remind me to ring him tomorrow.'

As it happened, the following day was so busy at work she forgot to remind Sandra. She had planned to ask Colie to call to Canal Road that evening to tell him about the baby, but that conversation never happened either because he had to work late covering somebody else's shift and she was on lates for the next few nights.

And then she talked to Victoria, deciding to wait until after her scan so she could tell him when the baby was due, and fill him in on her plan to get Maeve back.

42

Pulling into the car park at Glenlo Abbey some eight weeks after she had first met Andrew Casey, Cara thought it felt more like eight years. So much had happened since then. And at the end of it all, she'd been left with far more questions than answers.

Which was why she had to try to speed up access to that case file. It would contain details of every interview that had been carried out around the time of Lucia's disappearance and death. Somewhere within it could be that loose thread.

She had missed a call from Sandra and rang her back but it went through to her voicemail. She had also put in another call to Victoria and left a message. She would have to ask Andrew to ask his sister to give her a buzz. And she needed to ask him if he had a number for his cousin, Tommy.

Her mother's cousin had sounded half pissed in the garbled message he left on her work phone, either that or he had some sort of health condition that made him slur his words. From what she could make out, he had just found out about her, and had had no idea that Lucia had been pregnant or had a baby back in 1985.

'Not one of them had the decency to tell me about you, I had to hear it from someone down in Veldon's last week. Anyway thass neither here nor there now. I heard you were in the hotel recently and I just wanted to say I'd love to meet you the next time you're out this way. Even just for a cup of coffee or sumthin'. Myself and Lucia were great pals until ... Well, anyhow, if you're coming out again, give me a shout. OK. I'll go now. Bye, bye, bye, bye.'

It was unlikely Tommy would be able to shed any light on what had happened to Lucia as they had drifted apart by the time she'd moved into Galway, but Cara was still keen to meet her birth-mother's closest childhood friend.

This time Andrew was in the bar before her, an empty espresso cup in front of him. He was still sporting a healthy tan in October. For a few minutes they chatted about the dire weather and the even worse traffic. Andrew ordered another espresso for himself and the same for Cara. She needed the caffeine, having had so little sleep again last night.

'I really appreciate you coming to meet me,' she said, nervous now about his reaction to what she was about to spring on him. 'I wanted to run something by you before I speak to Marcus and Phillip. It's just that ... well, I want to dig a bit more into Lucia's case.'

He looked at her blankly.

'I've been on to the gardaí trying to get access to her case file but that might never happen and, well, I've decided to call for a cold-case review.'

Andrew visibly paled beneath his tan. 'But why? I mean, Phillip told you about the private detective, didn't he? He spent months on Lucia's case, Uncle Marcus paid him a small fortune, and he got nowhere.'

'A lot of years have passed since then and maybe somebody who couldn't come forward before might be willing to now. You read about these cases all the time. Somebody who's been afraid to speak turns up with a piece of vital information. Somebody out there knows what happened to her, Andrew. Maybe more than one person.'

'But, Cara, can't you see how ...' he stared at her, palms raised, searching for the right word '... how horrendous it would be for Marcus and Annette, for the whole family, if you did this? The press would be all over it again. These people have spent years trying to get over what happened. The last thing they want is for it all to be—'

'And the last thing I want is to cause anybody any more pain. What I want more than anything is to build a relationship with you all. But I also feel strongly that as Lucia's daughter I must do this for her. It's not right, Andrew, that the person who took her life when she was only twenty-two has been able to carry on living their life with no consequences.'

He sighed. 'No, it's not right, Cara, of course it's not. And I understand why you feel the way you do. I'd probably be the same if I was in your position. But the reality is that the likelihood of a cold-case team *solving* the case at this point is slim. The number of cold cases that are actually solved is minuscule. There's usually a bit of hype in the media, then it dies down and nothing comes of it. You have to ask yourself if it's worth putting the family through that hell again. If the guards and the PI couldn't solve the case, it's highly unlikely that, no offence, a reporter on a local paper can. This is real life, not some bloody Netflix series.'

She was taken aback at his reaction. She had known he wasn't going to be hugely enthusiastic but she had hoped that, being a bit more removed from the situation, he might have understood, and even been willing to help her to bring the family around to the idea. She saw now that this had been wishful thinking. It would be extremely difficult, if not impossible, to build a relationship with her birth-mother's family if she continued down this road. And she hadn't even broached the matter of going public if she had to.

43

The phone call from Marcus came that evening. She had been horizontal on the sofa pretending to watch *Ozark*, but finding it impossible to focus on what was happening. Kian paused the TV while she went into the kitchen to take the call.

She had been expecting it. She and Andrew had left things fairly amicably, with her promising that she would take some time to think things over (although her mind was pretty much made up) and not do anything without informing the family first.

Marcus sounded shaken on the phone, older and far less assured than usual. He said he was ringing to tell her that Annette had been admitted to hospital with breathing difficulties, had gone downhill very quickly over the past twenty-four hours. Things were not looking good.

'Please promise me, Cara, that you won't do anything rash ... not until ... I don't know how much time she has left. We're waiting to hear from her consultant but we might be talking weeks, maybe even less ...' he said. 'Just please wait until we can sit down and discuss it between us, the boys too ... later. There's stuff you don't know about Lucia ... what she did to you ... when she wasn't in her right mind ... and I just ...' He sounded exhausted.

'Of course I won't, Marcus. I promise you that. I'm so sorry to hear this. Please tell her I was asking for her and let me know if there's anything I can do to help.'

'Thank you, I will. Phillip and I will keep you updated. Oh, and before I go, Andrew mentioned you were looking for a number for Tommy. I don't have one but I can ask Simon, his father, for it if you want. He lives with him. But if you want my advice, I really wouldn't draw him on you. I'm ashamed to say it about my own nephew, but the man is a pity, the village drunk. You can't believe a word that comes out of his mouth and he'll probably only play the poor mouth. That's what he does. He's put Simon – and his mother, when she was alive – through hell over the years. They tried their best, God knows, but some people, I'm afraid, can't be helped.'

After the call ended, she sat looking at the phone in her hand as a maelstrom of emotion swirled around her. More death. Her birth-mother's mother now. Before she'd had a chance to get to know her.

And what had Lucia tried to do to her? What else had they kept from her?

She went back in to Kian. 'I need to talk to Dad.'

44

Paul had been at home with her father when Cara rang to say she was calling down. That there was something she needed to ask their dad about. She wondered how many evenings her brother spent keeping their father company, felt a sharp sting of guilt at her own neglect of him.

When she put the key in the door that night and walked into the hall, as she had done so many times before, she was struck again by the absence of her mother. She inhaled deeply trying to catch even a faint hint of her, but there was nothing. Not a trace. Only the greasy smell of fried food overlaid with the reek of wet dog. The sense of loss was so intense she felt like turning on her heel and running from it.

'Cara?' Paul stood at the kitchen door, Ralph wriggling furiously in his arms, trying to get free. 'Are you OK?'

'Yes, just coming.' The weight of her grief pressed down on her as Cara moved down the hallway towards the kitchen where her mother would never again turn from the sink to greet her with a smile, her face lighting up.

Her father was sitting at the table with a mug of tea in front of him. He looked happy to see her, but dishevelled and still badly in need of a haircut. It was unlike him to let it get so out of control; he had been going to Healy's barbers on High Street the first Saturday of every month for as long as she could remember. He had obviously missed a couple of Saturdays. The house looked dishevelled, too, clutter piling up on countertops and across the table. Newspapers, junk mail, mugs, plates and cutlery, a knife covered with butter. There mustn't be a spoon left in the drawer. Her mother would have had a fit if she'd seen the state of the place. Cara felt bad that she wasn't doing more to help, but she was barely staying on top of things at home as it was. She must talk to her father about getting a cleaner in for a couple of hours a week, and going for a trim. She wondered if he was eating properly, or sleeping, but pushed the thought away. She couldn't deal with any of that now. She needed to find out what Marcus had been talking about.

As Paul made her a cup of tea and searched the presses for biscuits, she explained that Marcus had called her earlier that evening to say Annette was very sick in hospital. 'He said something strange then, that there was stuff I didn't know. About Lucia trying to do something to me ... Have you any idea what he was talking about?' she asked her father. 'I thought I was adopted when I was only a couple of weeks old.'

Please don't say that was a lie too. Had they all been lying to her about Lucia wanting to keep her? Was it possible that she had been taken away from her mother for her own safety? Her mind conjured up a disturbingly realistic image of a pillow being placed over the face of a tiny baby, hands pushing down.

Her father took a deep breath. 'We do know what he's talking about and it's something we did think of when you found out about Lucia. Myself and Paul felt we should tell you but ...'

'I was supposed to tell you that day I called into you at the paper,' Paul explained, 'but you were already so upset. I was afraid it would be too much on top of everything else that was going on.'

'I don't believe this! What the hell is wrong with you all? You knew how upset I was at being kept in the dark for so long about Lucia. How did you think it would be a good idea to keep more bloody secrets from me? Surely that would have been the right time to bring everything out into the open.'

'Because we were trying to protect you, Cara.' Paul had raised his voice, his frustrated tone taking her aback. 'All we've ever done is love you, watch out for you and try to bloody well protect you. You have no idea of what Mum and Dad have gone through over the years – that we all have. No idea at all.'

'Shush, Paul, it's not her fault,' her father said, then turned back to her. 'We did what we thought was right, love, but it's time now for everything to come out. Jesus, where do I even start?'

He looked at his hands, then back up at her. 'OK so. You know what that girl Sandra said about Lucia being pregnant before she went missing? Well, Lucia told Victoria the same thing. It wasn't true. God only knows why she made it up but she was never right after … Anyway, we didn't know at the time that it wasn't true. The day that Lucia told Victoria she was pregnant, she also told her she had a plan. That after she gave birth to her new baby, she was going to try to get you back. She said she'd been forced to give you up against her will and she was going to try to prove the adoption wasn't legal.'

'But surely she couldn't have …' Bridie had mentioned something about this too. Had Lucia been delusional?

235

'No, of course not. She signed the adoption papers, it was all above board, but that wasn't what we were worried about.' He took another deep breath.

'When you were about four weeks old, Mum left you alone in the front garden one day ... It was different back then. You wouldn't dream of doing it now, but back then, people used to go into shops and leave the pram outside with the baby in it. Nobody saw any danger, not like nowadays. It was a fine day. I'll never forget it for as long as I live. You were in your pram, asleep in the shade. The phone rang inside and Mum ran in to get it. She was expecting a call from the public health nurse, and she said she was literally gone for about two minutes ... Anyway, *Lucia* must have been watching because when Mum went back out ...' He swallowed hard. 'When she went back out, you were gone. The pram was empty. Mum ran in next door to Mrs Carroll hoping that maybe you'd started to cry and she'd taken you inside but she said, no, she'd been out the back pegging clothes on the line. They ran into all the neighbours' then. By the time I came up the road from school a few minutes later, she was in an awful state. She came flying down the street, roaring like a lunatic. I couldn't even make out what she was saying but Maura Carroll said you were gone, that somebody had taken you.'

Her father told her how he had run straight home and rung the guards, who were up in a squad car within minutes. Babies didn't just disappear from outside their homes. Not in Galway. Not anywhere in Ireland. The gardaí took the matter very seriously.

Cara held her breath as her father went on. The guards put out an alert and started searching straight away, the neighbours helping, checking back gardens and sheds. Her parents were told to stay at home in case whoever had taken her brought her back. Her father had explained the circumstances of her adoption to the guards: the baby's birth-mother had wanted to keep her, but her parents had talked her into going ahead with the adoption.

They found Lucia up to her waist in the sea at Blackrock, a naked baby Cara in her arms, screaming and shivering.

'She was ranting about cleansing you of all sin, was seen holding you under the water for a few seconds before lifting you up in the air. She was about to do it again when a woman who was walking her dog along the shore ran into the water and managed to distract her. You were blue with the cold. The woman tried to get Lucia to hand you to her, told her you could die from the cold, but she wouldn't let go of you. She said she needed to cleanse you of sin before she could take you back.'

That woman, a nurse, had saved her life, her father explained. She had called a man digging castles with his son in the sand, and told him very calmly to get the guards. She kept talking to Lucia until the gardaí came, telling her what a beautiful baby she had, asking her name and how old she was. Lucia told her the baby's name was Maeve.

Her parents got a call to go down and meet the ambulance at Blackrock. Cara and Lucia were taken off in separate ambulances. Cara was treated for mild hypothermia and kept in overnight for monitoring before her parents were allowed to take her home. Lucia was taken to Casualty and admitted to the psychiatric unit in Galway before her parents had her transferred to a private facility in Dublin.

'She was diagnosed with post-partum psychosis. She spent months in hospital. If that woman hadn't been out walking her dog ...' Her father shook his head. 'It doesn't bear thinking about.'

So that was what Kitty had been ranting about in the hospice. It had been a real memory, not the morphine. No wonder she had worked herself into such a state.

'Mum and Dad could never rest easy after that. None of us could,' Paul said. 'Even after Lucia came out of hospital and went back to Kylemore, there was always the worry that she could come after you again.'

'It wasn't her fault, God help her,' her father said. 'She couldn't cope with having to give you up, and we couldn't cope with the possibility of losing you. So when she disappeared, that whole never-ending eighteen months, we barely slept a wink. We couldn't let you out of our sight, terrified that she'd have another breakdown and might try to take you again.

'We had to warn the school to keep a close eye on you. We couldn't let you out to play with your friends without one of us there minding you. And when her body was discovered, it was terrible but ... Don't get me wrong, we'd never have wished that on the poor girl, but at the same time, it was if a tonne weight had been lifted off us because finally, after so many years of worry, we knew you were safe.'

45

She had spent the rest of the weekend wrecking her head, going over all that she now knew. Talking to Kian, her father and Paul. Wrecking their heads too, probably.

She had been aware of post-partum psychosis. There had been that awful case in Belfast a few years ago, a young mother who had taken her own life in a maternity hospital when medical staff failed to recognise that she was suffering from the rare but serious mental-health emergency. Cara had looked it up on Friday night after she'd got home, stayed up for hours reading horrifying cases of mothers killing themselves and sometimes their children. So many tragedies.

Kian had tried to get her to go to bed, to stop tormenting herself, but she was too wired to sleep.

Post-partum psychosis, or PPP as it was known, affected a woman's sense of reality, causing hallucinations, delusions and paranoia. People with the illness had a much higher risk of dying by suicide or harming their children. The condition was dangerous but early treatment increased the odds of a good outcome. One article she'd read suggested that some people with PPP went on to develop bipolar disorder.

Was it possible that this had happened to Lucia? Cara had written about the illness in the past, had interviewed people who lived with it, and knew that those going through a manic episode sometimes suffered from delusions, hallucinations and disturbed thinking. And she also knew that it ran in families.

As the night darkened, so too did her thoughts, inevitably bringing her to the terrifying realisation that if her mother had been suffering from a serious mental illness, she herself might be at an increased risk of developing the same thing. Maybe she already had it. She had googled the symptoms and realised, to her horror, that she had quite a few of them. In the past weeks, she had been cycling between sadness, hopelessness and irritability to feeling elated, full of plans to get justice for her birth-mother and being easily distracted. All symptoms of bipolar disorder. She had lain in bed most of the night in a complete panic, her heart racing, wondering how to tell Kian she was a manic depressive.

She had woken on Saturday to a horrible feeling of impending doom, as if the world was about to end, but this had passed once she got up and showered. With the lucid light of day came the realisation that she had allowed her irrational night fears to hijack her brain. A far more likely scenario was that her mood swings were a normal reaction to the emotional shit-storm she had been living through over the past weeks and months, not symptoms of a serious mental disorder.

She went for a walk on the Prom to clear her head while Kian called over to visit his parents with Maisie. It was a dreary October day, with a breeze that would cut you in two, but at least it was dry. She sat in her mother's spot on the steps at Blackrock for a long time, breathing in the briny air and staring out over the choppy sea as the wind tossed her hair about.

She realised that from this spot she could see the beach where Lucia had carried her as a newborn baby into the water. How lucky she was to be alive. How often must her mother have sat here and thought the same thing?

Her father was in the kitchen, sitting in the same spot at the table, with another cup of tea, a toasted ham and cheese sandwich, and the radio on in the background. The sink was full of unwashed dishes, the counter covered with Weetabix crumbs, and the milk carton had been left out without a lid. There was nobody to nag him to put things away after him. It looked tidier than it had yesterday, though, and she suspected Paul must have cleaned up last night after she'd left.

He looked delighted to see her. 'Cara, love! I wasn't expecting you.'

The dog came hurtling through the open patio doors at the sound of her name, launching himself at her.

'Look who's here, Ralphie. Isn't this a nice surprise now?'

She lifted the little terrier in her arms and went over to put the kettle on. Her father started to get to his feet. 'Stay there, Dad. I'll make myself a cup and sit down with you. I'm in no rush.'

She sat opposite him, his face so fond, this man who had taken her into his home and his heart and loved her so much. 'I'm sorry, Dad.'

'What? No, love. I'm the one who's sorry.'

'You have nothing to be sorry for, you and Mum. All you did for me ...' Her voice broke. 'All you've ever done ... I had no idea what you must have gone through, how hard it must have been … If I could be half the parent for Maisie that you've been for me …'

He came round the table then, sat beside her and put his arms around her and they cried together. The pressure of her grief had been building inside her and it was a relief to raise the sluice gate now and release a stream before slamming it shut again.

She had expected Kian to be delighted to hear about her visit to her father, but while he was glad to hear they had patched things up, he seemed unusually subdued all weekend. Quiet and distracted. Not himself at all. Probably exhausted after all the drama of the past weeks. He had been going through it with her.

She suggested getting a babysitter and going out for a few drinks on Saturday evening – it had been ages since they'd gone out – but he had no interest. He would usually have jumped at the suggestion, would have been the one to make it. She picked up some bottles of beer for him instead, a bottle of wine for herself, and ordered a Thai takeaway after they'd put Maisie down. She told Kian to pick a movie to watch while she went down Salthill to collect the food.

When she came back half an hour later, he was still sitting on the sofa staring into space.

'Did you find anything?'

'Hmm?'

'To watch? You were supposed to be picking a movie for us.'

'Oh, shit, sorry, love. I totally forgot. I'm easy really, whatever you want.'

She decanted their food onto plates and brought it into the sitting room on trays to eat in front of the TV. Kian popped the lid on a bottle of beer and took a deep slug.

'Are you OK, love?'

'Me? Yeah, of course I am.'

'You just don't seem yourself at all.'

'I'm tired. This job is fuckin' stressful and, well, there's been a lot going on.'

'I know. And I know I've been distracted but we all need things to go back to normal now. As normal as they can be anyway, without Mum. I've decided to forget about the cold-case review. I've no idea what was going on in Lucia's head, whether she was mentally ill and genuinely believed she was pregnant or ... what the hell was going on with her. She might have had another breakdown and thumbed a lift from the wrong person. I think I need to let it go. To accept, like the Caseys have, that we'll never know what happened to her.'

'Yeah. It might be for the best, love,' Kian said, turning to his food. He half-heartedly pushed it around his plate. He normally attacked a beef massaman curry like a starving mongrel.

'There's something else going on, Kian. What is it?'

He pushed the tray to one side, pressed his head against the back of the sofa and sighed. 'I didn't want to stress you out even more with all the shit you've been going through ...'

Her heart plummeted. *What now? What else? Work. It had to be.* She'd known going out on his own had been a bad idea. 'Is it the business?'

He nodded. 'I priced the school job low to get the contract – that's what you have to do when you're starting out and building a name for yourself – but with the cost of everything gone sky high ... I'm probably going to lose money. Best-case scenario I break even on it.'

Oh, God, no. 'How bad is it?'

'I don't have enough in the account to cover the lads' wages this month but I'll sort it. I'm going into the credit union on Monday to try to get a loan, just to tide me over until I get paid for this job.'

Jesus Christ!

This was all they bloody needed.

46

'Cara, can you come in to me for a minute?' Fitzie stuck his head around the newsroom door.

It was mid-morning and she had just put on her coat to go out for coffee with Orla and another couple of colleagues. She was in desperate need of a caffeine hit.

'Sure. Go on ahead of me, guys,' she said. 'I'll see ye over there.'

She stood in front of Fitzie's desk. Something repulsive that might have been a banana skin had welded itself to a pile of yellowing newsprint, and a half-drunk mug of coffee was incubating blue mould spores.

'Sit down for a minute.'

Sit down? This must be serious.

She lifted a pile of old *Champions* from a chair, and threw them onto the floor beside her.

'We've had a letter about one of your court cases from Friday's paper.' He held up a headed letter. 'Dave Hughes wants to meet us this afternoon about it. I just wanted to give you the heads-up and have a quick chat before we meet him.'

Cara felt the heat rise inside her. She was an experienced court reporter, usually meticulous about double- and treble-checking her copy, but she had written her city court reports in such a rush last week, had been so very tired. And still was. All the broken nights had left her brain fuzzy and sluggish. The worry about Kian's business had kept her awake the last two nights and the falling dreams were back.

It wasn't the first time she had been the recipient of a legal letter during her career, but the previous one had been a minor issue resolved with a short clarification in the following week's edition. This was the first time she had ever been called into a meeting with the paper's solicitor.

Christ.

'What case is it?'

'The Burke case. Johnny Burke's son. Drugs.'

'Oh. What's the issue with it? He pleaded not guilty. It was a simple remand on continuing bail.'

'What's the son's name?'

'Em ... Michael. A right little shit by all accounts. The guards have had their eye on him for a while.'

'The problem is you don't mention Michael in your report.'

What was he on about?

Her editor handed her a copy of last Friday's paper, open to page five, two words circled in red.

Johnny Burke.

Her stomach lurched. How could she have made such a stupid mistake? A potentially very expensive one. 'Shit, Fitzie, I don't ... Oh, fuck, fuck, fuck!'

She had basically accused one of the city's most prominent property developers – a man who hadn't got where he was by being Mr Nice Guy – of dealing coke. In print. 'How bad is it?'

'We'll have to wait and see what Dave says. Johnny is bulling over, as *he* puts it, being *falsely accused* of drug dealing. His line all along has been that his son got in with a bad crowd and was framed. A hard one to stand over really, considering the coke was found in the boot of the young lad's X5, but that's not what's at issue here for us.'

Cara leaned forward on his desk, head in her hands. 'It's my fault, rushing ...' Just one incorrect word, more than enough for a major defamation case.

'Listen, don't panic. The story about the young lad hasn't been picked up by the nationals, and I very much doubt Johnny's going to want to draw any more attention to it. It'll turn into a much bigger story if he decides to sue us. He's a shrewd operator, he'll see that himself. He'll need us again down the line and won't want to burn his bridges. If I was him, I'd settle for a clarification in Friday's paper, and leave it at that.'

Fitzie had been in this business a long time. Cara hoped he was right.

She felt a strong urge to get out of the building, to suck in some fresh air, but it was a miserable day, the heavy grey sky pressing down on the city and spitting drizzle, so she went to the Ladies instead, locked herself into one of the cubicles and sat on the toilet seat. The stench of chlorine stung her nostrils. Her bowel clenched and spasmed, and she grimaced. Her stomach was empty – she hadn't eaten a proper meal in days. There was no point: everything she ate came straight out the other end. It had been bad enough while her mother was sick, the condition exacerbated by stress, but since she'd found out about Lucia, her IBS seemed to be in a constant flare-up.

She really didn't need this on top of everything else. Her brain had felt at bursting point when she'd got into work that morning. She had contemplated calling in sick, which she never did, but figured she'd probably drive herself insane at home alone. She was better off trying to keep busy.

Now she couldn't even trust herself to do her job properly. She had made a stupid, stupid mistake that could seriously damage the paper's reputation, not to mention her own, and cost the *Champion* a lot of money.

47

Another call came from Marcus on Thursday, this time to tell her that Annette was dying. Only days now, the doctors had told him. He was bringing her home to die in her own bed.

Would Cara like to come out to see her over the next day or two?

He didn't need to spell it out. She would be going to say goodbye.

Kian offered to go with her, but she said she wanted to go out to Kylemore on her own after work on Friday afternoon. He needed to stay on top of the school job, and she wanted him to collect Maisie from crèche so she wouldn't be under pressure to rush back.

The paper still hadn't heard back from Johnny Burke's solicitor. She had been praying he would have accepted an apology and clarification in this week's edition, but it hadn't happened. It wasn't looking good.

The day was dull but dry. She drove out to Kylemore on autopilot, barely taking in her surroundings.

A soft-spoken woman, who introduced herself as Phillip's wife, Grainne, met her at the front door. She took her jacket and brought her into the sitting room where she had met the family before. The house was hushed, people speaking in quiet voices. Hugh came forward to greet her with a warm hug as if he had known her for years, not met her just once before. Phillip, more restrained, gave her arm a light squeeze. Denis, they explained, was en route from America. There was no sign of Marcus.

Cara met Hugh's wife, an attractive Italian woman called Cecilia – she took to her instantly – and Phillip's sons, James and Matthew, back from London and Dublin respectively for the occasion. Grainne had just handed her a cup of coffee when Marcus senior arrived into the room, and made a beeline for her. He looked tired and drawn, but was dressed smartly in a navy sports jacket and highly polished dark brown brogues. 'Cara, my dear. So glad you came. I'll bring you up to see your grandmother now. Father Moran has just left. He calls every day to see her, God bless him. Her faith has always given her great comfort, no more so than now.'

He led her up the elegant curved staircase and along a carpeted hallway to the front of the house. She had expected a dark room, the sour tang of sickness, but the room was softly bathed in lamplight, and there was a gorgeous smell; ginger and something else, fig, maybe. A little altar had been set up in one corner with a crystal vase of freshly cut garden flowers, and three fat flickering church candles on a starched white lace runner, watched over by an extended family of holy figurines.

Marcus gestured to a chair beside the bed where Annette lay, her skin a delicate tissue laid over bony scaffolding. Her eyes were closed, sunken in their sockets, and she was so still that, for a moment, Cara feared she might have died in the time since the priest had left. But, no, her chest was still rising and falling, barely perceptible. She heard a whirring sound she recognised: a syringe pump driver. Her mother had had one, delivering morphine subcutaneously over a twenty-four-hour period to keep the pain at bay.

'Two days, they reckon,' Marcus said. 'At most.' He sighed wearily. 'At least she's not in pain.'

'And she's at home in her own bed. I wish we could have done that for my mother, but the cancer ... it was too complex. We couldn't have given her the care she needed at home.'

'Well, Annette was a formidable woman.' Marcus smiled. 'She point blank refused to go into hospital unless I promised I wouldn't let her die in there. And she meant it. I thought they might have been able to do something for her to give her a bit more time but sadly, it wasn't to be. Her faith never wavered despite everything she went through. A lot of people would have given up on God after losing a child the way we lost Lucia. I certainly did for a long while, but Annette never did.'

They sat there in companionable silence for some time. A sheep bleated from somewhere in the distance, muted voices trailed up the stairs, and a clock ticked somniferously on the bedside locker. Cara felt her eyelids grow heavy.

Marcus cleared his throat.

'Myself and Annette had been talking ... before she took a turn for the worse ... We had been discussing you and, well, I wanted you to know that it's my intention to amend my will. To include you in it, Maisie too.'

'There's no need ... really ... That's not why ...'

She was mortified at the idea that the Caseys might have thought she had contacted them with a begging bowl in her hand.

Marcus put up a hand. 'I know it's not something you expected, but Lucia was our daughter. She sadly didn't live to inherit her share of our estate, and as her daughter and granddaughter, we want to look after you now. Just as we are doing for the rest of our family. I'm not getting any younger, and Annette and I want you all to be taken care of, financially at least, after we're gone.'

That was the last thing she had been expecting.

48

She called Kian from the end of the main hotel driveway. As usual, he didn't answer, so she left a message telling him to ring her ASAP as she had some good news.

Marcus had hinted that he was talking about a significant sum of money. This could be life-changing for them. She felt like punching the air. She was acutely conscious that it was highly inappropriate to be feeling so elated when she had just left the deathbed of her grandmother, who the next time she saw her would probably be laid out in her coffin, but she couldn't help it.

It would never have occurred to her that her birth-mother's family would look after her financially, that she, the outsider, would be treated like the Casey grandchildren who had grown up within the flock. The money aside, she felt as if Marcus had opened his arms and folded her into the midst of them all. And she hadn't even told him that she had decided not to pursue the cold-case review. She hoped he lived for many years to come, that she had a chance to build a relationship with him at least, and with the rest of the family while he was still alive.

It was enough comfort to know that the money was coming down the line. That Kian could take out a loan if he wanted and invest in the business, safe in the knowledge that he would be able to repay it if he couldn't make a go of it. They might be able to pay a chunk of their mortgage, replace the car with a newer model, go on a sun holiday.

As she drove back towards Galway, she couldn't resist spending their unexpected future windfall in her head.

Her phone rang. It must be Kian. She glanced at her hands-free screen.

Sandra, returning Cara's call from a few days ago.

'How'ya, loveen? Sorry I keep missing ya.'

'No problem at all. I was only ringing because I realised after I left you and Bridie the last day that I forgot to ask you about the man who was seen hanging around the house in Canal Road before Lucia went missing. I'm sure you'd have told the guards at the time if you had any idea who he was ...'

There was silence at the other end of the line. She must be driving through a bad patch.

'Hello? Sandra.'

'I'm still here,' she said, her voice small and odd-sounding. 'That man. I know who he was. And he had nothing to do with what happened to Lucia.'

49

'I just can't believe it. I mean, to say nothing when she knew the guards were trying to trace him because she was afraid of what her feckin' mammy would say ...'

'Well, there was the small matter of his wife too,' Kian pointed out.

'That's no bloody excuse. The amount of time they must have wasted trying to chase that false lead. Just to cover her own arse.'

'Yeah, it's not great alright. Did Marcus give any indication of how *significant* a sum he's talking about?'

'Jesus, Kian, is that all you can think about? The man has more on his mind at the moment. Like picking out a coffin for his wife!'

'I know, I know, sorry. I'm just so bloody relieved.'

'And so am I. I just can't get over how Sandra could have kept quiet all these years. I'm livid.'

Cara had narrowly avoided hitting a sheep that had decided to take a nap in the middle of the road when Sandra had revealed the identity of the mystery man during their call: a Malaysian cardiologist she had been having 'a bit of a thing' with. He had apparently told her he was separated and living under the same roof as his wife but when she found out he had two kids, one only six months old, Sandra had finished it straight away. Casanova hadn't taken it well, though, had taken to lurking near the house until he found himself the prime suspect in the case of a missing woman.

'I'm not proud of it, Cara,' Sandra had said, 'but I was very young and I was terrified. Mammy would have murdered me if she'd found out, and if it had got out at work, I'd never have been able to show me face in the hospital again. It's not as if I didn't think about it over the years, of getting in touch with the guards, but I never told my husband about Umar and it had gone on so long. It wouldn't have made any difference anyway. He wasn't even in the country when Lucia went missing. He'd gone back to Malaysia for his father-in-law's funeral. With the wife and kids.'

Sandra was willing to go to the gardaí now if Cara wanted her to, but she would have to talk to Eric first. Cara had told her not to do anything until she'd had a chat with Donal McGann to find out if there was some way Sandra could discreetly give this information to the gardaí. She was probably right that it wouldn't make any difference now, and even though Cara was sick and tired of the mess of secrets and lies, she didn't see any point in needlessly upsetting Sandra's elderly mother.

50

When she looked back, today would be the day from which there was no turning back. It was the day on which events began to coalesce, forming a forward motion that took on a momentum of their own. The day the distant butterfly flapped her wings and the tornado started to build.

Annette had died the day before, Sunday, passing away peacefully in her sleep, according to Phillip, who had called Cara to break the news. She felt numb when the call ended. Her grief for her mother was backing up inside her, the pressure of keeping it contained wearing her down. She didn't have anything left in her to feel much for a woman she had never known, blood relative or not.

While she hoped Marcus would be around for another while, she had to face the fact that she couldn't use her birth-mother's family to stuff the chasm left by her mother.

She stuck her head around Fitzie's door as soon as she arrived into work. 'Any news?'

'Nothing yet. I'll let you know as soon as I hear anything.'

She wished Johnny Burke would put her out of her misery. Let her know if he was going to sue or not. If he was, she'd have to deal with it. The not knowing was hell. Please God Fitzie would be right and he'd be happy not to make a bigger deal out of it than it already was. It would still be a black mark against her, though, and the board certainly wouldn't be impressed by her carelessness. She had to put her head down now, battle through the fog of fatigue and inertia and make amends for her fuck-up.

She was at her desk writing a to-do list for the coming week when her landline rang.

'There's a woman down here looking for you, Cara. An Olive ... Sorry, what did you say your surname was? Hernon. An Olive Hernon. She doesn't have an appointment.'

'Could you tell her I'm in the middle of something, Caroline, and ask her to leave her number?'

'No problem at all ... Hold on a sec. Sorry?'

Cara could hear a woman's voice in the background.

'Yes, I'll tell her that. She's just about to go into a meeting so she's asked me to take your number and she'll call you back.'

Good old Caroline.

The other woman was speaking again. *Fucksake!* Probably some old crank complaining about a pothole outside her house. Or a spelling error in one of her reports.

'She asked me to tell you she's Colman Ryan's mother,' said Caroline. 'She's around until about twelve and said she needs to talk to you, but doesn't want to do it over the phone.'

What the ...?

'Tell her I'll be right down.'

Cara grabbed her phone and trotted down the stairs, pressing the release button at the bottom for the door that led to Reception. There was only one person there besides the receptionist. A small woman, bundled up in a grey puffer jacket, a woolly hat and scarf, was standing beside the counter, leafing through a copy of last week's paper.

'Olive?'

She turned, striking blue eyes set in a face etched with the shadows and lines of a hard life. Beautiful bone structure. She must have been a stunner in her youth, Cara thought. Hard to put an age on her, early to mid seventies maybe.

'Thanks for coming down to me. I've been ditherin' over whether to come in to you for weeks, ever since Colman told me he'd spoken to you.' She glanced over at Caroline. 'Is there somewhere we could maybe speak in private?'

The little woman was as twitchy as a feeding bird, her fingers gripped tightly together. She turned back towards the counter when the main door opened to admit a couple of the lads from Advertising, with an icy breeze.

'Of course. Come upstairs with me and I'll see if there's somewhere quiet for us to chat.'

The interview room at the top of the stairs was free, so Cara ushered her in there. It was a stuffy, windowless affair, with a few wonky chairs, a battered desk and a dusty wall clock salvaged from the newsroom during its modernisation. She asked Olive if she'd like tea or coffee, and was relieved when she said no because that meant she didn't have to go downstairs to cadge milk from the tea room. Cara apologised for the state of the place while the other woman shed a few layers. She sat with her arms wrapped about her middle as if trying to protect herself from something.

'Thanks for seeing me at such short notice. I'm sure you're very busy,' Olive said. 'I don't really know where to start.'

'There's no rush, Olive. Take your time,' Cara said. 'Can I get you a glass of water?'

'No. Thank you.' Olive took a deep breath and then she started to talk.

'The reason I got in touch was that Colman mentioned to me that you were going to try to get Lucia's case reopened.' Cara had sent Colman a voicemail telling him about her plan to call for a cold-case review to keep him in the loop in case he heard it elsewhere.

'Well …' She was about to tell the woman she had changed her mind, but something made her pause.

'I met your mother once,' Olive continued, her voice tremulous. 'A lovely girl, pretty. Gentle. Very different from the rest of them.'

How did Colie's mother know the Caseys?

'I blame myself … Jesus, how do I explain it to you?' She covered her face with her hands.

Cara moved from her side of the table to sit beside her. She rested a hand lightly on her arm. 'It's OK, Olive. Just take your time.'

'I've never told anybody, you see … all these years.'

Jesus. She knew something.

They sat there in silence, Cara's hand on the other woman's arm, the wool of her jumper itchy beneath her fingers, but she didn't dare move a muscle.

'I only met her the once.'

Her voice was clearer now, as if she had drawn strength from somewhere inside.

'They were going out together about six months and Colman brought her to the house to meet me. They got the bus out to Moycullen and she brought me a cake from Lydon's. The white-iced one with chocolate whirls on top. Colman had obviously told her it was my favourite. I remember thinking how thoughtful it was of her and that maybe she might be the girl for him. She had this lovely way about her.

'I had sandwiches made for them, so we sat down at the table and started chatting, the way you do when you meet somebody for the first time. Me trying to be friendly without interrogating her. My daughter Ellen was there too. I assumed Lucia was from Galway because she was working in the hospital – I didn't even know her surname yet. When she mentioned she was from Connemara, I was a bit surprised that Colman hadn't said anything, seeing as I'm from Tully Cross myself, but that's men for you. I asked her where she was from and she said, "Kylemore, from the hotel." I nearly died. The colour must have drained from my face but they didn't seem to notice. They were all chatting away around me, Ellen saying how I was from near Kylemore and what a small world it was and how I had moved away when I was young, and Lucia saying, yes, Colman had told her that alright. He had no idea, of course, the poor young fella. No idea at all.'

She sighed, looked down at her hands. Cara waited, barely breathing.

'Let me go back a bit,' Olive said, looking at Cara again. 'I grew up in Tully Cross, and went to the secondary in Clifden, but I had no interest in school. I got a part-time job waitressing at the Kylemore Manor at the weekend. Old Mr Casey, Neilus, was running the place at the time, and Marcus was duty manager. I enjoyed the work, and when they offered me a full-time job, I jumped at it. My parents didn't try too hard to encourage me to stay in school. There were five of us, and only my father working, so the few bob I was making came in handy at home.'

Olive told her how Marcus had singled her out from the very start, always complimenting her appearance and sitting beside her in the staff room.

'Of course I was flattered. He was so handsome. Tall and dark. A look of James Dean about him. The other girls all fancied the arse off him. We'd all seen *Rebel Without A Cause* when it came to the cinema in Clifden. He knew it too. He was a right flirt, but I was the one he paid the most attention to. He was ten years older than me, and seemed so grown-up and cool compared to the clowns my age. And, of course, I fell head over heels for him.'

As the black minute hand ticked round the white clock face, Olive's story unfolded. A tale as old as time. Of a powerful older man preying on a younger, vulnerable girl, reeling her in with the lightest of touches on her hand or waist as she passed him. Small gestures, huge to her. Then the day he had waited for her in the corridor by the back kitchen and pulled her into a storage pantry. Told her he couldn't stop thinking about her.

'And, sure, you know yourself. He threw every trick in the book at me, told me I was the most beautiful woman he'd ever seen. Woman!' she scoffed. 'I was just seventeen and so feckin' innocent, a child really. Growing up out there. Back then. Sure I'd barely even been kissed. To be kissed by a man like Marcus Casey, well, I felt like I was in the movies.'

Olive explained that she had lost her virginity to Marcus a few weeks later, in one of the bedrooms where they had started to meet after her shifts. She had known he was *doing a line* with Annette Lynch, whose family owned a knitwear factory in Clifden. They'd been together for a while at that stage, but Olive had believed Marcus when he told her he was just waiting for the right time to break it off. There was no mention of contraception, and while Olive did worry about it, she believed him when he promised he was going to break it off with Annette and marry her.

The newsroom door opened, releasing a babble of conversation and a burst of laughter before closing again. Olive shrugged.

'You can probably put two and two together and figure out where this story is going. I got pregnant. I told Marcus and that was the end of our big romance. He wanted nothing to do with me, said he had no idea who the father of my baby was, that I was so quick to open my legs for him it could be any number of possibilities. I was devastated. His father rang me that night, told me never to set foot near his hotel again. He warned me that if I repeated my lies about the bastard in my belly – his exact words – he'd make sure no member of my family ever worked in Connemara again.'

Cara sat in stunned silence as she listened to the rest of Olive's story, while trying to get her head around the repercussions of what she was saying.

Lucia and Colman were half-brother and -sister!

Olive explained that she was sent to her mother's sister in Birmingham to have the baby, and by the time he was born, Marcus and Annette were married. Her parents told her the only way she could come home was if she gave up her baby for adoption, but her auntie Ka, a nurse and closet feminist, who had no kids, supported her to keep her child. Even in a big city in England, the stigma around an illegitimate baby in the 1960s was huge, especially among the Irish community, but Olive kept Colman, and she and her aunt reared him between them. Olive met her husband Brian Hernon over there, a decent, kind man, and they moved back to Galway, settling in Moycullen, when Colman was around ten. They had two daughters, Katherine, after Aunty Ka, who moved back to Ireland with them when she retired, and Ellen.

'Jesus, Olive! You must have got an awful shock when you realised who Lucia was. I mean the chances ...'

'It wasn't something I'd ever even thought about. I mean, why would I? I rarely went back home, apart from family funerals. Too many bad memories, and I'd drifted from my own family after what happened. I never told Marcus I'd kept the baby – he couldn't have cared less either way. I knew Annette had given birth to a son not that long after Colman was born, only months between them. My friend Mags, back home, had told me in a letter. She was the only one who knew I was pregnant and she never told a soul. I was in bits over it at the time.'

Olive said she knew for a fact that Colman wasn't Marcus Casey's only love child. A young receptionist had left suddenly a few years after Olive, but not before threatening to tell the whole place that she was pregnant with his baby.

'The next thing anyone knew she was living above in a swanky apartment in Dublin telling everyone the baby's father was an American tourist. You can be sure she wasn't the only one either, and there was Holy Mary Annette turning a blind eye to it all, too busy licking Father Kenny's arse.'

'What did you tell Colman? Did he not ask about his father?'

'We put a false name on the birth cert. Seamus Ryan. So common he wouldn't have been easy to find even if he'd existed. We told Colman he'd died in an accident on a building site, fallen through a roof. And that his grandparents on that side were dead. He never questioned it. He was a happy child, reared by two mothers who adored him, and then Brian, far better off than a lot of kids who had a mother and father.'

'So what happened when you realised who Lucia was? Did you have to tell him that Marcus was his father?'

Surely she had told her son about his relationship to his girlfriend but then, why had Colman not mentioned it? Or Donal McGann for that matter.

51

Cara waited, every nerve tingling.

'I don't know how I got through that lunch with Lucia and Colman that day. Sitting there looking at them. Knowing what I knew about them. You couldn't tell by looking at them. He's like the Caseys, dark and blue-eyed. Not as tall as them, though, or as broad. She was more like her mother's side.'

Olive explained how she had rung her friend Mags as soon as her son and his girlfriend left. She had stayed in touch with Mags all the years she was away, and she was the only one outside her family who knew the identity of Colman's father. Mags told her to come straight over to her in Oughterard. Olive said she was in an awful state by the time she got there.

'The thought of having to tell him they were half-siblings ... How would he cope with knowing they'd been committing incest? And that I had been lying to him for years?'

'So what did you do?'

'Mags made me drink a brandy. That settled me a bit. We talked about it for hours and, in the end, I made a decision that I fear led to, well, a decision I've had to live with ever since.'

Olive told of how she had phoned Marcus Casey and said she needed to meet him urgently, threatening to show up at the hotel if he didn't come to her. Mags drove her out to Kylemore and he met them in the Abbey car park. She asked him straight out if he was aware that his daughter was going out with her son. *His son*. He went the colour of buttermilk, Olive said. For all his talk about the baby not being his, he knew bloody well. He pulled himself together pretty sharpish, though. Said he didn't know what she thought it had to do with him who her bastard son went out with. He told her to stay away from him and Kylemore. He all but spat in her face.

Cara found it hard to picture the polite, genial man she had met behaving in such a way.

'Mags was shocked. She'd only ever seen charming Marcus. I knew he'd have to do something about it, now that he knew. I thought he might try to force Lucia to move home or send her away or something ...'

'What did he do?'

'Well, that's the thing, you see. I don't know. Poor Colman didn't know what was going on, because any time he mentioned Lucia's name, I'd change the subject. I started encouraging him to move to Boston to Brian's nephew, telling him he could make a fortune on the Big Dig there. He was so confused – I could see it in his eyes. He asked me did I not like her. I had to lie and say I thought she was a lovely girl, but I wanted him to see a bit of the world while he was still young. Anyway, a few weeks later, the poor girl went missing ...'

Cara let out a long breath. 'Jesus.'

'I had absolutely no proof that Marcus or the Caseys had anything to do with Lucia's death, Cara, but I knew it. Deep in my gut. You probably think I'm a terrible person, not going to the guards about this, but I couldn't risk Colman finding out.

He was in such a bad way after Lucia went missing and then after they found her body. I was terrified I'd get a call saying he'd been pulled out of the river. There was no way I could tell him he'd been sleeping with his own sister on top of everything else. Or that his father was very much alive but wanted nothing to do with him. You must understand, I was afraid of the Caseys too. If they'd done something to their own daughter, what might they do to me, or to Colman? I was so relieved when he moved to Boston, got away from here. It wasn't until after Lucia was found that he told me she might have been pregnant. If Marcus had somehow found that out ...'

'So you just kept quiet. All these years.'

Cara could barely comprehend what she was hearing. Yet another person burying the truth. How many more secrets were festering away? She imagined layer upon layer of them, like bodies thrown carelessly in on top of each other in a communal grave.

'I did. And I'd do the same all over again. If you have children yourself, Cara, you'll understand. If Colman found out what I've just told you, it would kill him. And even if you did go to the guards with it, what evidence do you have? Marcus Casey would deny the conversation between us ever took place, deny all knowledge of Colman's existence. The last thing I want is to drag all this stuff up again. The only reason I'm here today is that I couldn't forgive myself if something happened to you and I hadn't told you. If history repeated itself. I had to meet you and warn you that you need to be very careful.'

52

Lucia
Galway city
1990

*I*ncompatible with life.
    Anensomething. A serious birth defect.

Some of the words she couldn't understand. Most of it went over her head as she lay on the examination table, her belly slick with the gloopy gel Uncle Luke had smeared across her. There was nobody there to assist him: he had come in on Saturday especially for her.

Parts of the brain and skull missing.

A birth defect so severe her baby had no chance of survival.

'No, it can't be ...' Panic tightened her chest. 'Please no.'

She looked up at her uncle, begging him to assure her this wasn't happening.

'I'm so sorry, Lucia.'

He did look sorry. She had never been close to Uncle Luke – she found him a bit intimidating – but he was different today. Warmer.

'No, there has to be a mistake.'

She thought of the drawer in her bedroom she had already filled with soft Babygros, pretty cotton dresses and tiny hats.

All carefully washed in Fairy non-bio. Too early, of course. Tempting Fate.

This was her fault. She couldn't do anything right.

Uncle Luke shook his head sadly. 'See here.' He pointed to a dark amorphous blob on the scan. 'This is where the front part of the brain should be. I really am sorry, Lucia.'

She needed to get out of there. She sat up quickly, and got to her feet. A sickening rush of dizziness forced her to grab the bed to steady herself.

'Just sit down for a few minutes, Lucia. You've had a terrible shock.'

'No.'

She didn't want to be anywhere near that awful image on the screen. That alien baby.

'Sit here so.' He pulled a chair behind her, eased her into it. 'Put your head between your knees for a few minutes.'

She leaned forward, her head hanging limply. Her uncle put his hand on her shoulder, squeezed gently. Poor Uncle Luke: this must be his worst nightmare, having to break such news to a family member. After he had been so good to come in on his day off.

She stood again, needed to get out of this airless box and talk to Sandra. She would know what to do.

But, oh, God! Sandra and Bridie were in Manchester at a family wedding and weren't due back until tomorrow night. Lucia had no way of contacting her.

And what could her friend do anyway? What could anybody do? Nobody could fix her broken baby. Not with that kind of damage to her poor brain.

It was hopeless.

She wished now she had told Victoria she was busy, that she couldn't make the scan her uncle had so generously arranged for her outside his clinic hours at such short notice. She had been so upset with Victoria for not keeping her pregnancy a secret, as she had promised, but she knew her cousin had been coming from a good place, and was anxious that Lucia and the baby get proper maternity care.

'Is there any hope?' She stood with her fingers on the door handle.

'I'm afraid not. Your baby is unlikely to survive much longer, given the severity of its condition ... and, Lucia, much as it pains me to tell you, continuing with this pregnancy could seriously hamper your chances of ever having another baby.'

'What do you mean?' She turned her head to look at him, leaning against the door as another wave of dizziness crashed over her.

'My recommendation is that we perform a procedure to end this pregnancy as soon as possible.'

'You mean ... kill my baby?' Horror clawed its way up her throat. 'No, no ... that's not even legal.'

'Lucia dear, you must understand that the foetus is barely alive. It's going to die but this way, difficult as it is, would be a much more merciful death.'

She's not an it, she's a her, she roared, inside her head. He had told her it was too early to tell the baby's sex, but she didn't need a scan to confirm it. She knew.

'It's also the only way of guaranteeing that you will be able to have another baby. If you continue with this pregnancy, you have an extremely high chance of being left infertile.'

'I have to go.'

'Are you sure you don't want to sit down for a few more minutes? You've had an awful shock.'

'No. I have to get out of here.'

'I have the car outside, I'll drop you home.'

She had to get out of that windowless room, out of the hospital. She needed fresh air, didn't want to get into a car with her uncle after what he had just told her, but she didn't think her legs were capable of carrying her the whole way home. The walk to his car, parked in his reserved space at the front of the maternity department, was a blur, as was the short drive out of the main gates and down towards Canal Road. The pungent smell of air freshener, a masculine musk, stoked her nausea, and she asked him to drop her at the top of the road.

'I'll tell Victoria to call into you. She mentioned that your flatmate is away. You shouldn't be on your own after such a shock.'

'Thank you.'

She didn't want to be on her own. She needed to talk to somebody, to get some advice, and she couldn't talk to Colie. Not now. How could she tell him she was expecting their baby but the poor little mite was horribly deformed? She couldn't think about that right now. This was all her fault. Her fault for not going to a doctor sooner, for sometimes forgetting to take the folic acid Bridie had given her every day, for drinking before she realised she was pregnant. Her fault for being so stupid.

'Talk things through with Victoria and get some rest. If you do decide to do the best by your baby, I'll help you, Lucia. I can't do the procedure in the hospital. You're right, it would be illegal so it would have to be done somewhere else. And

I'd make sure you're not in any pain. You don't need to worry about that. Your parents are aware of your pregnancy. I had to tell them when Victoria told me. I'm sure you understand.'

She couldn't care less that her parents knew. It didn't matter now.

'Their only concern was that you and your baby were being properly monitored. I'm going to have to tell them about the baby's ... condition now, and my recommendation. If you decide to opt for the procedure, and I hope you do as it really is for the best for you and ...' He nodded towards her stomach. 'But nobody else can ever know about it. If it got out that I did this for you, it would mean the end of my career and possible criminal charges. I understand the father of the baby doesn't know about the pregnancy, and you can tell anybody who does know that you had a miscarriage. It wouldn't really be a lie.'

53

After she had walked Olive out to the street and said goodbye, Cara went back to her desk, picked up her jacket and her bag and left the building without saying a word to anybody. She felt as though she had been shunted into an alternative reality to the newsroom where her colleagues were focused on the mundane news of a small city. A recent spate of burglaries in Salthill, the seizure of mistreated dogs from a farm near Gort, twenty new jobs at a technology start-up in Newcastle. It all seemed so remote from her, so trivial.

She fired off a quick text to Fitzie saying she wasn't feeling well and was going to work from home for the afternoon. Then she got into her car and drove out of town with no direction in mind, ending up on the Prom. It was too miserable to get out and walk so she sat there, rain splattering against the windscreen, the car swaying slightly in the wind.

She picked up her phone to ring her mother and dropped it again, her heart sinking, as it did every time this happened. It was just so hard to fathom that somebody who had always been there had been so entirely erased from the world.

She contemplated driving up the hill to her father but didn't have the energy. She needed time to fully absorb what Olive had just told her before she could begin to try to put it into words herself. The whole thing was just so messed up. If it was even true.

Was it possible that she was surrounded by fantasists, that they were all mad? Lucia, Sandra, Olive. All these women with their crazy stories.

She was beginning to feel as if she was living in an episode of *Black Mirror*. According to Olive, Lucia had been involved in a sexual relationship with her half-brother, unknown to either of them. And she had gone missing just weeks after Marcus Casey, the father they shared, had become aware of this. If it was true, that could not have been coincidence. And if it wasn't, Olive Hernon had missed her calling in life with her Oscar-worthy performance.

If she *was* telling the truth, though, the implications were huge. Marcus couldn't have let the relationship continue if he was aware of it. And what if Lucia had been telling the truth about her pregnancy? Had Marcus somehow found out? Victoria knew, according to Sandra. Victoria, who, Cara realised, had still not called her back. Had she told her father or Marcus? And if so, what had he done about it? And why had nothing shown up in the post-mortem?

Christ Almighty. Her head was ready to explode. There had been an article in one of the nationals last week about a man knocked out in a one-punch attack. He had been unconscious before he hit the ground. The surgeons had had to remove part of his skull to relieve pressure and he had been in a coma for weeks afterwards. She had imagined the surgeon replacing the section of bone after the swelling had subsided, carefully matching up the edges, like a piece of Kintsugi pottery. If only she could open a little door in her own skull and release the pressure building inside. She couldn't take any more.

She wished to God she had never found out about Lucia. Wished she could go back in time and get delayed in traffic, even for a minute or two, enough to stop her arriving at the hospice at the right moment to overhear that conversation. She'd have been so much better off not knowing.

And what could she even do with any of this? If she went to the guards and told them what Olive had said, what would they do? Would they think she was crazy, too, or would they track down Colie in Boston and do a DNA test? The result might destroy him, if what his mother was saying was true. For what? Maybe it would prove Marcus had a motive to end the relationship with her half-brother, but that wasn't the same as a motive to murder his daughter. There was no evidence whatsoever of that.

She understood Olive was trying to protect her child, no matter that he was now a man in his mid-fifties. Olive, who, like Lucia, had been impregnated as a teenager by a man who had walked away without a second thought, while the girls were forced to pay such a high price. One banished from her community and family, the other separated from her baby. And Marcus Casey, Cara's grandfather, the common denominator.

54

She had just got to sleep sometime after two when she was jolted out of it by Maisie's caterwauling. The stench hit her from the hallway. She raced into her daughter's room. *Jesus Christ!* Maisie was sitting up in the bed howling. There was vomit everywhere, on her face and her bedcovers, in her hair, down her neck. And all over Pookie, the beloved velvet bunny she couldn't sleep without.

Cara felt like crying herself. She could barely keep her eyes open and now she had to tackle this horror show in the middle of the night.

'It's OK, baba. Mommy's here. Ssh, it's OK now, pet. I've got you.'

'KIAN!' she roared. How the hell could anybody sleep through this racket?

She lifted the child from her bed, her own stomach convulsing. Maisie started to retch and Cara ran for the bathroom, making it halfway across the landing before the child vomited again.

Kian emerged from their bedroom, rubbing his eyes blearily. 'What's—?'

'Towels,' she snapped.

She ran warm water into the bath, while she sat on the toilet seat and stripped the slimy pyjamas off her daughter. Maisie's forehead was hot, and her cheeks were flushed.

'No, nooo. Me no want bath.' The child tried to wriggle off her lap as Cara tested the water with her hand.

'Just a quick one, pet, to get rid of that yucky smell.'

'Noooo. Me want Pookie.'

Kian came in with the towels. 'You hop into the bath, Maisie, and Dada will get Pookie,' he said.

'No,' Cara said, making eyes at him. 'You take over here while I sort out her bed and grab the Calpol.'

The puke-covered rabbit would have to go into the washing-machine with the bedclothes. Her father had brought the soft toy into the hospital when Maisie was born. It had been pale pink then, but it was a weird beige now, the fabric worn to the nub from Maisie's constant rubbing. Pookie had turned out to be the bane of their lives because the child couldn't settle without it. Cara lived in fear of ever losing it, and their daughter never sleeping another night.

It took them ages to settle her. She had vomited again in the bath, so Cara had had to drain the water and shower her. She was inconsolable when she heard Pookie had gone for a swim in the washing-machine, and it was nearly an hour before Cara eventually got her off to sleep in their bed, having sent Kian to the spare room to get some rest.

It was after four when Cara finally got to sleep, and less than two hours later when she was woken by Kian's alarm going off on his bedside locker. There was no sound of him getting up, so she had to go in to wake him. There was still a strong smell of vomit on the landing even though she had scrubbed the carpet on her hands and knees. She'd have to give the place a good airing today. She went downstairs to hang Pookie on the clothes horse by his long ears to dry, and threw the bedclothes into the tumble dryer. Then she went back to bed and drifted into an exhausted half-sleep. What felt like seconds later but turned out to be two hours, she was awoken by the sound of a car door slamming outside. Kian was long gone to work so it must have been one of their neighbours. She wished she could just stay in bed and pull the covers over her head.

Maisie, who was usually bouncing around full of beans by this time, was still out like a light. Cara hoped she was over the worst of it, that it wasn't the dreaded vomiting bug. She didn't want to wake her from the deep sleep she obviously needed, or chance sending her into crèche sick so she rang to tell them she was keeping Maisie at home for the day, then called Fitzie to say she had to take the next couple of days off. No way could she function at her job with everything that was going on. Fitzie told her to mind herself, and to ring him any time if she needed to talk.

Annette was being waked at home that evening. Phillip had been in touch again yesterday with the arrangements. Family and close friends only. Anybody travelling to Kylemore would be put up in the hotel. The plan had been for Cara and Kian to go out and stay the night while Maisie went for a sleepover at Kian's parents' house, but Cara wasn't happy for them both to leave Maisie when she was sick so they agreed that Kian would stay behind with her again.

He hadn't been keen on her going out alone, although he was incredulous at Olive's story, so he had roped her father in to accompany her, instead of driving over with Paul the next day as planned.

55

Annette was laid out in a large formal room to the left of the front door. Most of the furniture had been moved to make way for the coffin, which took centre stage, the chairs pushed back against the walls. A vast antique cabinet that housed china and glassware suggested that this was the dining room. Despite the wake being private, there seemed to be people everywhere.

Hugh left his spot on the receiving line to greet Cara and her father and introduce them to Annette's two younger, albeit equally creaky, sisters, who sat facing the coffin, and to a number of cousins and in-laws whose names and connections to Annette they hadn't a hope of remembering.

As she passed the corpse, Cara blessed herself and stood beside her deceased grandmother looking suitably solemn. She looked better in death than she had in life, her hollow cheeks plumped out by the undertaker, taking years off her. Cara's mind flashed up a screenshot of her own mother lying in her coffin. She had borne little resemblance to the jolly, vibrant woman she had been before the cancer consumed her. She pushed the memory away and moved on.

Hugh introduced her to his brother Denis, home from the States for the funeral. Shorter and portlier than his two siblings, he was the most overtly upset at his mother's passing, his eyes swollen. Maybe because, as Hugh had whispered discreetly in her ear, he hadn't made it back in time. His mother had taken her last breath an hour before his plane touched down in Shannon. Cara reached out her hand to shake his in sympathy. For one long, awkward moment, he just stared at her without moving to take it. Then he grabbed her in a bear-hug that went on for far too long before he finally released her.

By the time she got to her grandfather at the top of the line, a tight band of tension had bolted itself to her skull and she was feeling slightly nauseous. She hoped she hadn't picked up anything from Maisie, but thought it more likely that her symptoms were caused by simply being in the presence of this man after everything Olive had told her. And having to let on that nothing was wrong. It certainly wasn't the time or the place to bring up the topic.

'Cara, my dear,' he said, holding her hands, the epitome of polished gentility. 'I'm so glad she had the chance to meet you before she left us. You have no idea how much it meant to her. She left this world at peace.'

She nodded and smiled, trying to act normally. He was so convincing. Was it possible that it was all an act? That he was an entitled cad at best? Some kind of monster at worst?

It was later that evening, when most of the mourners had gathered in Lorenzo's, the hotel bar named after one of Mitchell Henry's sons, that Cara caught sight of Andrew. He was sitting at the bar with an older man and a slight, dark-haired woman, who looked like Victoria from the back. She left her father with Phillip's wife and sons, telling him she'd be back in a few minutes, and made a beeline for Andrew.

She was conscious that the drink was going to her head. Although waiters were doing the rounds with trays of delicious canapés, she had only nibbled at a couple of gourmet cocktail sausages. Three glasses of white wine on an empty stomach probably hadn't been a good idea, especially not when she was meeting so many members of the Casey family for the first time. She had needed something, though, to loosen the valve a little. And at least she didn't have to worry about driving home tomorrow. Her father, who had finally gone for a haircut and was looking more like his old self, had insisted on driving to take the pressure off her. She was glad he was with her.

'Andrew, hi,' she said. He turned to her, immaculate in a pressed white shirt, with a lightly striped black tie, a coordinating black jacket hanging on the back of his chair. The Casey men liked their style.

'Cara. Hello. How are you doing? A sad day. I'm so sorry for your loss.' He took her hand, squeezing it lightly.

He was the first person who had actually sympathised with her today, she thought. She had only just met Annette but she had still lost a grandmother. How kind of Andrew to acknowledge that. Especially after their last fraught conversation at Glenlo Abbey.

'You know Victoria, of course,' he said, nodding to his sister, 'and Dad.'

She hadn't seen Luke Casey since she was a child but she would have recognised the man on Andrew's left as her grandfather's brother a mile away. The same straight back, the arresting blue eyes that his son had inherited, the height.

'You won't remember me. You were only a baby the last time I saw you,' Luke said. 'Marcus has been telling me all about you, though. And your little girl. I heard she's the image of Lucia. Is she here with you?'

'No. She's sick, I'm afraid. My husband had to stay at home with her. Dad came out with me instead.'

Luke was in the middle of making an innocuous comment about it being 'such a pity' that Maisie and Kian hadn't been able to come when a man with a bad case of halitosis and an even worse case of dandruff that speckled his black sports jacket pushed past Cara, clapped Luke on the back and rudely interrupted their conversation.

Ignorant pig. Another drink or two and she would have said it to his face.

She turned to Victoria, taking her in properly for the first time.

Oh my God!

She hoped her shock didn't show on her face. The woman was practically skin and bone. Her head was perched incongruously on a neck that looked far too frail to support it, the bony ridges of her shoulder bones protruding from beneath her beautifully tailored three-quarter-sleeved black dress. Victoria had always been thin, unhealthily so, but she seemed to have lost even more weight since Cara had seen her at her mother's funeral. She had passed the stage of skinniness that other women would envy and was clearly either suffering from or balancing on the edge of an eating disorder. Her skin looked as if it had never been exposed to a ray of light. Her dark cocoa hair was chopped into a sleek bob that framed her face. She would have been stunning if she wasn't so painfully thin. Cara wondered how she could do her job when she was clearly unwell herself.

'I'm sorry to meet you again under such sad circumstances, Cara,' she said. 'It's a pity you had so little time to get to know Annette.'

'Yes, it is, but I'm glad I met her before ...'

Victoria nodded sympathetically.

'Actually, Victoria, I've been trying to contact you.' Emboldened by the alcohol, she continued, 'I was wondering ... did you get my messages?'

'Em, messages?' The other woman's eyes darted around. 'No, I didn't, but my old phone was acting up. I got water into it and I had to replace it. You're not the only one who had trouble contacting me. I'm sorry about that.'

Cara hadn't intended to reach out to Victoria again. But that was before she had met Olive Hernon. 'No problem. The reason I was calling was to ask you if it's true that Lucia told you she was pregnant before she went missing?'

Cara had never seen anybody blanch so visibly before. Victoria would have made a terrible poker player.

'Pregnant? God, no. A friend of hers did spread a nasty rumour at the time, it was all very upsetting, but there was no truth in it. If Lucia was pregnant, she would have told me first, not some work colleague she had only known a wet week. We were always close.' Victoria lifted her glass and drained it. 'Now I must apologise but I'm desperate for the bathroom.'

285

Cara watched her scurry through the bar as if she was really bursting to go and wondered why she had lied to her about Lucia's relationship with Sandra. And if she had lied about that, what else was she lying about?

If she had gone to bed a few minutes earlier, she would have missed all the commotion. The irony didn't escape her. How mere moments could have such life-changing consequences. You could step on to the road at the wrong time and be hit by a bus, or leave the house a few seconds late and just miss a head-on collision. Or you could stand outside a hospice chapel or a five-star hotel and hear something that could flip reality as you knew it.

She had been heading for the stairs with her father when she was stopped in the foyer by Hugh's wife, Cecilia. Her father had gone up ahead of her to bed while she stood for a quick chat. They were saying their goodnights, Cecilia kissing her on both cheeks, when she noticed a scruffy-looking man coming across the foyer towards them. In a pair of dirty jeans crying out for a belt and a cheap puffer jacket, with a jagged rip on one shoulder exposing its synthetic white filling, he was completely out of place among the smartly dressed mourners. A local, maybe, who hadn't got the *family and close friends only* message or had chosen to ignore it.

He walked straight up to Cara, and stopped in front of her. The reek of booze nearly knocked her. Probably the local weirdo. She tended to attract them.

'Lucia?'

Definitely the local nutter. This was all she needed.

'Tommy,' Cecilia warned, as Cara shook her head.

'No, sorry, I know you're not her,' he slurred. 'What I meant is you're her daughter, aren't you? I heard you were here and I jus' wanted to come in and see you. She was my best friend, you know, Lucia. A lovely girl.'

Tommy. She had never got his number, had been put off contacting him by Marcus. She had met his father, Simon, and his three brothers earlier. A couple of them were big-deal property developers in Dublin – she'd read about them from time to time in the nationals. The complete opposite of the inebriated man with the stained teeth standing too close to her now.

'Tommy, I got your message but I had no number to call you back.' She took a step away from him.

He grinned at her. 'Amn't I some eejit? Tell you the truth, I was after a few jars when I rang you. Needed a bit of Dutch courage.'

'Well, never mind, you're here now. It's lovely to meet you. I've heard so much about you.' Her mind flashed to the smiling brown-eyed boy in the photos, full of mischief. A happy child. How had he ended up like this? 'The two of you were great friends, weren't you? I've seen lots of photos of you both when you were younger ...'

'Whatever you've heard about me, it's not true,' he said, moving closer than was comfortable, especially when he didn't seem that steady on his feet. 'Don't believe them. Well, OK maybe some of it is true but ...'

'Tommy, what are you rawmaishing on about now? Would you leave the poor girl in peace?' Hugh had materialised beside them. Cecilia had disappeared from Cara's side – she must have gone to get her husband, Cara thought.

'Fuck off away from me, you,' Tommy said, raising his voice and jabbing a finger in Hugh's chest. 'I'm talking to Lucia's girl.'

He turned back to her. 'I never knew a thing about you ... They never told me. That time she went away to have you, they told us she was after having a breakdown. And then she really did because *they* drove her to it, the fuckers. The first I heard about you was down the pub a couple of months ago because none of my own fuckin' family bothered to tell me ...'

'OK, that's enough now, Tommy. Will you show a bit of respect, for God's sake, the day that's in it?' Phillip had come out to join them, with one of Tommy's brothers, whose name she couldn't recall, at his heels. Unlike Hugh's softer approach, his furious tone brooked no argument. 'Cara, I'm very sorry about this. Tommy's had a bit too much to drink. As usual,' Phillip said as he threw a look of disdain in Tommy's direction. 'He's going to leave now and allow us to mourn our mother in peace.'

'What's wrong, Phillip? Are you afraid I'll say something to her?' Tommy's voice rose in volume, attracting the attention of everybody in the foyer. Phillip's cheeks flushed an apoplectic shade of purple as his cousin continued to rant. 'Are you? Are you afraid I'll tell her—'

'Shut up, Tommy! You're a bloody disgrace,' Phillip said, grabbing him by one arm while Tommy's brother took the other and they proceeded to drag him across the lobby as Cara watched in horror. Hugh put a hand on her back, apologising profusely, and tried to guide her towards the bar, but she pulled away, said she was tired and needed to go to bed. She headed for the stairs and went up halfway, turning back as soon as she saw Hugh disappear out the front door after his brother and cousins.

She slipped silently after them into the darkness. She was afraid Tommy was going to get hurt, and he had only wanted to talk to her. She felt sorry for the poor man who was clearly troubled. She could still hear him, roaring like a bull.

She followed the sound of his voice into the parking area at the side of the hotel, staying in the shadows close to the wall.

'Get into the car, Tommy.'

'Oh, I'm not welcome here, is that it? Persona non grata at my own aunt's funeral.'

'You're drunk, Tommy, and you're making a show of yourself. As usual. Get into the fucking car.' Phillip hissed the words out through gritted teeth.

'You just don't want me talking to Lucia's girl in case I tell her. I'm not fuckin' stupid, you know. I'd say she'd be very interested in hearing that Lucia was here the night she disappeared.'

'Shut up, Tommy! You're only looking for attention.'

'I saw her going in the front door of the house with my own two eyes. You know it's true, Philly boy, because you were there too, ya dirty cunt. What did ye do to the poor— Ow! Get off me, ya fucker. You're hurtin' me.'

'Shut your mouth, you waste of fucking space!'

Cara's heart felt as if it was going to pound out of her chest. Phillip sounded vicious.

'As if anyone would listen to a word that came out of your mouth! You're a bloody disgrace.'

Tommy let out one last roar before he was shoved into the back seat, Phillip slamming the car door behind him. Then

Tommy's brother jumped into the driver's seat, the engine roared to life, the tyres spun on the gravel and the car took off down the driveway. She suspected he was well over the limit, but the law didn't seem to apply to the Caseys the way it did to everybody else.

56

They were gone from the hotel before any of the other guests began to stir the following morning. Cara left a message at Reception for Marcus, apologising for being unable to make Annette's funeral: Maisie had got worse overnight and she needed to go home to her. Her daughter was actually back to full health, but there was no way she could continue to act normally around her grandfather now.

It was a bleak morning. The mountains loomed ominously over the landscape as Cara and her father drove away, the peaks shrouded in a pale grey mist. Her head was pounding so hard it hurt to turn it, and she felt as if she had swallowed battery acid, her stomach roiling. Her father had to pull into the side of the road after the marble quarry in Recess for her to throw up, the bitter bile burning her throat. She retched and retched until all that was left was foam.

Her whole body hummed with an agitated energy that made her long to climb out of her skin. She might have to see her doctor to get something to calm her down. She had always been wary of going down that road, aware of how addictive those drugs could be, but she had never felt like this before. She would take anything to escape this sensation. It was as if every fibre of her nervous system was being stretched between the impulses of fight and flight.

Her father hadn't known what to think when she'd rung his room at seven this morning and said they needed to leave. She told him she'd meet him at the car in fifteen minutes and would explain everything then. As they left Kylemore and her mother's family behind them, she had filled him in on the events that had unfolded after he'd gone to bed.

'I really don't know what to think, Dad. I mean, it could have been just the ravings of a drunk. But what if it's true? If Lucia really was there that night? That would mean they were all lying. They all said they hadn't seen her in the days before she disappeared. Why would they lie about that? And if she was out at Kylemore that night, how did she get there? What was she doing there? And how the hell did she get from there to being dead and buried in that bog?'

'I really don't know, but that Tommy lad has been bad with the drink for years. A bit of a black sheep. All the brothers moved away and did very well for themselves, as far as I know. He's the only one who stayed at home. I don't think he ever held down a job. Even if you manage to get him to give a statement to the guards, I'm not sure how much credit they'd give to anything he has to say.'

'It's not just that, though. There's all the other stuff as well. Sandra has pretty much ruled out that man seen hanging around the Canal, and if Marcus really is Colie's father ... There's too many arrows now all pointing in the direction of the Caseys and Marcus in particular to ignore them. I need to get a contact number for Tommy to find out, first of all, if he's OK after practically being abducted from the hotel last night, and also to talk to him when he's a bit more sober if possible.'

Her father had dropped her home and advised her not to make any rash decisions. 'That man is burying his wife today, love. What if you're wrong and he had nothing whatsoever to do with Lucia's death? Just promise me you won't rush into anything. That poor girl is dead thirty years now. Another few days or even weeks won't make any difference either way.'

He was right, she knew that. Just as she knew that if she went to the guards with all of this, whether she was right or wrong, she could kiss goodbye to any kind of a relationship with her birth-mother's family, along with her inheritance and any chance of financial freedom for herself and Kian. This was not the time for any knee-jerk reactions.

When she went in, the house was empty, Maisie at crèche and Kian at work. She switched on the kettle and switched it off again. She should be at her desk in the newsroom right now, not sitting at home drinking tea, but even work, her usual refuge, had become a source of stress with the threat of the legal action hanging over her. The detritus of her husband's and daughter's breakfast had been abandoned on the kitchen table and the wash she had put on yesterday was still sitting in the machine, but she couldn't muster up the energy to be annoyed with Kian and she couldn't face sorting it out either. The walls seemed to be closing in around her. She had to get out.

She got into the car and drove down the Prom. She pulled in just before Blackrock and debated going for a walk to clear her head. The Clare hills were invisible today, swallowed into the mist. A heavy stretch of pregnant grey cloud drifted low over the bay. Rain was on the way. A few hardy swimmers were braving the cold and the choppy waves, tiny heads bobbing up and down, pale arms slicing in and out of the water, like leaping salmon. The best cure for a stressed head, no doubt about it, but Cara had never been one of the all-year-round swimming brigade, which had swelled in numbers since lockdown. Staring at the deep green water now, though, she felt an urge as physical as thirst drawing her towards the sea.

She hopped out of the car and opened the boot she had been threatening to clear out for weeks. It was nothing short of a disgrace – sand everywhere, buckets and spades and wellies and raincoats and God only knew what else all shoved to the back to make room for her weekly grocery shop. She rummaged around in the mess until she found what she was looking for: a pair of togs and a musty-smelling towel. She jogged down to the changing shelter in Blackrock before she changed her demented mind, and wriggled into her togs, the chill seeping through the cold stone into her feet, which had already turned pink.

She must be mad. All she needed now was to get pneumonia on top of everything else.

An elderly man, bald as a coot, emerged from the water and shook his lanky limbs like a dog. 'Aaah, that's the tonic.' He noticed her standing there, teeth chattering. 'Get in quick, love, before you get sense,' he advised, smiling at her.

She stepped out from under the shelter and the bitter breeze lashed her, raising crops of goose pimples all over her body. *Jesus, this is insane.* She was frozen and she hadn't put as much as a toe into the water yet. It had been years since she had jumped off the diving tower, but even if she had been tempted, the tide wasn't in far enough. There was nothing for it but to inch her way through the icy shallows. Apart from a woman walking her dog across the rocks, and the old man, who was now vigorously towelling his private bits, there wasn't a soul around.

She slipped and nearly landed on her arse going down the slimy algae-coated steps into the water, where she clambered over the uneven stones, wincing as the arch of her foot came down awkwardly on a sharp edge. Her body felt like one giant shuddering goose bump, sea spray stinging her eyes and nostrils. She was the only lunatic in the water now.

Imagine if Kian happened to stroll by, improbable as that was. He'd probably think she was trying to top herself. She sniggered. *Yes, I'm definitely losing it.* She kept moving, one foot in front of the other. The water was at her thighs now, her jaw chattering so hard it hurt. This was pure and utter torture.

What if I have a heart attack? Like those people in the lakes during the hot weather.

The water was creeping around her crotch now, then her stomach, the worst bit.

Christ Almighty. I can't go any further. I'm going back.

But something drew her on. The water reached around her waist like a pair of icy arms, and as she kicked away a clump of bubbly brown seaweed that had attached itself to her leg, she stumbled on the stones. One of her legs went from under her and she was down.

Gasping. Baltic. Shuddering. *Jesus fucking Christ!*

She found her footing again, plunged in and swam out until she could no longer feel the seabed beneath her feet. Until she could no longer feel the cold, feel her limbs, feel anything. She lay back, her neck extended, and drifted. Then the skies above her opened and there was water everywhere. Above and below and all around her.

She emerged from the water with not a single less worry than she had gone in with, but somehow feeling lighter, calmer. As if the salt water and sea breeze had performed some kind of reboot, had tuned her nervous system to a less frenetic channel.

She would take her father's advice. She wouldn't rush into anything, but she was clearer in her mind now about what she had to do.

57

Out of respect for the bereaved family, she left it a week after the funeral before she reached out to Andrew. He had acted as go-between from the start of all this. Now she was going to ask him to do it again for what was likely to be the last time.

They met in her father's house this time, her dad and Paul both present. It wasn't the kind of conversation they could have had anywhere public, that was for sure, and they had insisted they wanted to be there when she spoke to Andrew.

He had stared at her, aghast, after she laid it all out in front of him in the sitting room of her childhood home. Everything she had been told or overheard or discovered. She left nothing out.

'But ... this is just absurd, Cara. You can't seriously think ...' He looked to Paul and her father as if hoping they might be able to talk some sense into her. 'You can't seriously think Marcus murdered his own daughter or the boys their sister. Tommy is a raging alcoholic, has been for years now. You can't take anything he says seriously. And I wouldn't believe a word that comes out of that Sandra's mouth. The post-mortem proved *her* a liar. As for that other woman, Colman Ryan's mother, I mean come on ... That's just ridiculous. I wouldn't be surprised if the two of them are in cahoots.'

'I know it sounds crazy, but I've thought long and hard about this over the past week and I believe I have a duty to go to the guards with it all. It'll be up to them what they do with it after that.'

'This is just insane.' He looked utterly appalled. 'They'll laugh you out the door, Cara.'

'If they do, they do, but at least I'll know I've done the right thing. I wouldn't be able to live with myself if I did nothing.'

After Andrew left, she waited for the inevitable call from Marcus, but when her phone rang later that same evening, it wasn't her grandfather asking her to meet him urgently before she spoke to the gardaí. It was somebody else. Somebody she would never have expected.

58

Lucia
Kylemore
1990

She can feel herself getting weaker. No energy to cry for help. There's a horrible smell. Wee. And something else. Gross.

The spasms have stopped, thank God. She'd thought the pain would never end. That it would split her wide open. Waves of it slamming into her over and over. No room to catch her breath between them. It had seemed to go on for ever. Hours, days, she couldn't tell. Time had stopped making sense. How long had it been since Victoria had sat with her and helped her to see that she really had no choice? That it would be cruel to leave her baby in pain. That, monstrous as it felt, it was the kindest thing to do.

Kind. There's a statue of Our Lady on the chest of drawers opposite the bed, her hands clasped in prayer. She looks kind. Her mouth is smiling, but her eyes are sad. So sad. She seems to be staring directly into Lucia's eyes.

How long had it been since Andrew had driven her out to Kylemore, collecting her from the top of Canal Road in his bashed-up old Fiat? The drive out a blur. Flashes of memory drift in and out. Her father standing at the front door. Tommy's pale face in the back of his father's car.

She had thought the pain would kill her at one point, but it hadn't. She's still afraid she might die, though. If somebody doesn't come soon.

Surely somebody will come soon.

Her nightdress is soaked through, the sheets beneath her rumpled and soggy. She's shivering and sweating at the same time.

She needs to change the bed. Doesn't want to ruin the mattress.

She hopes Sandra has called in sick to work for her.

Sandra. She'll be worried.

She's so thirsty. She needs a drink.

She has been dreaming about water. In her dream, she's wandering through a forest searching for a river and her throat is so dry. It's dark and she's frightened. The trees are so tall they seem to go up for ever. There's somebody with her, a small girl, her little hand hot in hers, holding on tightly. A magical white horse emerges from the trees. They follow her and she leads them to a stream. They shout for joy. They get to their knees, her and the child, and they scoop up the delicious cold water, and they drink and drink until their bellies are fit to burst. They wade further into the stream to cool down because they're so very hot and they sit with only their heads sticking out so their clothes are soaked, and she wakes up and her clothes really are soaked, but she's still thirsty, so thirsty, and her throat hurts really bad.

She thinks she might have wet the bed, but she doesn't care any more. Too weak. Her legs feel sticky. She touches the sheets under her bottom. Feels something squelchy under her fingers. Like jelly. Her fingers are sticky now. She tries to lift her hand to see what's on them, but her arm's not working. She's so tired. So very, very tired.

Mary is still smiling down.

Why is she not doing anything to help her?

59

The day had started off well. Fitzie called her into his office as soon as she arrived into work.

'Good news. I said I'd let you know straight away. We just got a letter in from Johnny Burke's solicitor. He's agreed to settle for a clarification in this week's paper. He won't be taking it any further, as I predicted.'

'Oh thank God.'

Muscles released that she hadn't realised she'd been clenching. That was one big worry off her plate at least.

'I knew if his advisers were any good at all, they'd tell him he'd want to be off his head even to think about suing and drawing the national media down on him. Still, you never know with these big egos. This is the same man who was on to Jim Brennan a few weeks ago, threatening to pull all future advertising from the paper unless we agreed not to cover his son's case.'

'You never told me that.'

'I didn't want to stress you any more than you already were. Anyway, he was told in no uncertain terms that his son's case would be covered the same as any other drug dealer's, whether or not his father ever took out an ad with us again. And that was the end of that.'

She was so relieved it was all over. Now she needed to focus on her work and not allow herself to be distracted by trying to figure out what the hell Maryanne wanted to talk to her about.

Her aunt had sounded so odd on the phone last night, her voice strained. Not at all her usual self. She had asked if Cara could meet her this morning, said she needed to talk to her about her conversation with Andrew. Cara had explained that she had to work all day, and couldn't afford to take any more time off, but she could meet her that evening. She offered to call into Maryanne's house if that was easier, but her aunt was adamant she didn't want to see her there so they arranged to meet in her parent's house.

Then she made Cara swear to her that she wouldn't contact the gardaí before she spoke to her.

It was all very odd indeed.

60

Maryanne had nearly puked all over the hand-tufted Alexander McQueen rug Graham had spent a small fortune on last year, when Andrew rang and told her what Cara had found out. And what she was planning to do about it.

This rotten thing they had interred so deep for decades was exhuming itself, as if Lucia herself was clawing her way out of the ground, coming for them. Maryanne had gone upstairs to take the call, anxious that Graham didn't hear her side of the conversation. He knew nothing about the hell her ex-husband had plunged them into all those years ago. It hadn't been hard to keep it from her second husband. It had always felt like a particularly vivid nightmare, not something that had actually happened. Too awful to be real.

She would never forget that morning that Luke had come hammering on her front door. It had been early on a Monday in December. Andrew, a fourth-year medical student at the time, had been out late the night before clubbing, or so she had thought, and was still in bed. Victoria, too, was still asleep. It had been a couple of years since her ex-husband had dragged her through the courts, loath to give her what she and, happily, the judge believed was her just reward for being married to an arrogant prick like him. Her sister had been right about him all along, but Maryanne had allowed herself to be blinded by his wealth and false charm. She regarded herself well rid of him, and had been enjoying the freedom of her new single life, yet to meet her beloved Graham.

It was totally out of the ordinary for Luke to show up at her front door. Even more so for a man who was the epitome of cool control to arrive in such consternation, and at such an ungodly hour.

Lucia.

Dead.

Found in her bed at home in Kylemore that morning.

Shocking and awful indeed, but his frantic reaction seemed over the top. As if it had been Victoria who had been found dead, not a niece to whom he had never been especially close.

'How? What happened to …?'

She heard a strangled moan and turned to find Andrew and Victoria on the stairs, both staring at their father, their faces matching white masks of horror.

Victoria's eyes rolled back in her head and she slumped onto the stairs, Andrew catching her before she walloped her head off the wall.

Oh, God, poor Victoria. She had been close to her cousin, the only two girls among all the Casey boys. This was going to hit her hard. Lucia was so young, what on earth had happened?

Could it have been suicide? The girl had a history of mental-health problems.

Maryanne turned to attend to her daughter but Luke pushed past her, heading down the hallway towards the kitchen. 'I need to talk to you all.'

'What the hell is wrong with you?' she shouted after him. 'Your daughter has just fainted, for Christ's sake.' Not for the first time, she asked herself how she had stayed married to him for so long.

Victoria was coming round. Andrew helped her into a seated position, her head between her legs.

'Deep breaths, Tor.' He looked like he was about to burst into tears.

Victoria pushed away his hand and got to her feet, holding onto the banister. 'Where's Dad gone? We need to talk to him.' Her eyes were wild, panicked.

They trailed into the kitchen where Luke was sitting on a tall stool at the island, his head in his hands, breathing heavily.

'Dad. What happened?' Victoria asked, in a weird, reedy little-girl voice.

'It's a fucking nightmare. It should have been straight-forward. Everything went well ... There was no sign ... Jesus Christ.'

'What's going on, Luke? What are you talking about? No sign of what?' Maryanne was utterly perplexed now.

He raised his head. 'Do you have any brandy?'

She was about to point out that it was just gone eight in the morning, but she had never seen him like this before. She went into the front room to get the bottle of Courvoisier from the drinks cabinet and a crystal brandy glass. She placed them in front of him on the marble island. He poured a generous measure, knocked it back in one go and turned to face Maryanne.

'Lucia was pregnant. She told Victoria a couple of weeks ago. Victoria came to me, rightly so, and I told Marcus. He was extremely concerned, understandably, after what happened last time ... the psychosis ...'

Had she done something to herself? Surely not.

'You have to understand, Maryanne,' he said. 'The whole thing was a total fucking mess. Marcus had found out, you see, that ...'

Andrew jumped in, his speech rapid, jittery. 'Her boyfriend, the father of the baby ... Marcus was his father ...'

'Marcus was the father of her baby. Jesus Christ Almighty.' She had to sit before the legs went from under her.

'No,' Luke said. 'Christ, no. It's fucked up but not that. Marcus was the father of the guy who got her pregnant. Lucia's boyfriend. Marcus had a fling with his mother years before when she worked at the hotel and she got pregnant. The stupid bitch never told him, just went off to England and had the baby. He had no idea he had a son out there. He was working at the Regional as a porter – that was where he met Lucia. I mean, what are the fucking odds of that happening?'

'I don't understand. So what are you telling me? How did she die?'

'Marcus couldn't let the pregnancy go ahead. You have to see that. The risk of the baby being ... damaged in some way ... I mean, it was incest. And he couldn't tell her the truth because she was already unstable. He was afraid it would push her over the edge altogether so he came up with a plan.'

'Please tell me it's not what I'm thinking.' It couldn't be. They couldn't have.

'It should have been straightforward. I did hundreds of these procedures when I was working in the UK ...'

'*Procedures?* You mean abortions.'

'Whatever you want to call it, Maryanne. This is not the time for pedantry. I did it in the house in Kylemore, and everything went according to plan. She wasn't that far along. There were no complications, no sign whatsoever that anything was wrong ... but when Annette went in to check on her this morning ... she was gone.'

'How could she be gone, if it all went *according to plan* as you say?'

'She must have started bleeding during the night and ...'

Jesus Christ. The poor girl had bled to death. All alone.

'But how did nobody notice? Were they not checking on her?' Andrew asked.

'They were. Annette went in twice during the night and she seemed fine, asleep both times. It wasn't until this morning when she tried to wake her ... and then she lifted the bed covers ... She's in an awful way over it. They all are.'

'Jesus Christ, Luke. You killed that girl, you and Marcus between you. Annette must be distraught ...'

She looked at Andrew, whose hand was clamped over his mouth, eyes wide. Victoria was breathing rapidly, and her lips had gone a funny shade of grey.

'Annette came up with the *solution to the problem*, as she described it. I shouldn't have agreed to help them but Marcus was beside himself with worry when he came to me.'

Annette. Holy Mary Annette. No way.

'I don't believe that for one second. Annette of all people. Sure she's the staunchest pro-lifer you could meet. Wasn't she out campaigning against abortion during the referendum? She wouldn't ...'

'Well, she did. I know it sounds insane but it's true and—'

'So what happens now? Are the guards there? Are you going to be arrested?'

Andrew rushed from the room. Sounds of retching followed by the splash of stomach contents hitting porcelain came from the downstairs bathroom. Victoria appeared on the verge of passing out again.

Her poor children. What a nightmare for them. Their father, an esteemed professor and consultant, arrested in connection with the death of their cousin. How would they ever be able to show their faces in college after this?

'Marcus is calling the guards as we speak to report her missing,' Luke said, once the sound of their son emptying his stomach mercifully eased off.

'What are you ... Missing? But she's not missing sure.'

'They had to report her missing because her drama queen of a flatmate has been calling the house since yesterday evening saying there's no sign of her and she never came home last night, which is obviously out of character for Lucia. But we can't tell them what happened, Maryanne, because if we do, we're all fucked. I was on to Simon earlier. He said we could be charged with manslaughter. Even though we didn't deliberately—'

'I couldn't care less what you and your disgusting excuse for a human being of a brother are charged with. Annette too. To do that to their own daughter! Do you think you deserve to just get away with this? With taking the life of an innocent young girl? And her poor baby? I'm going to call the guards myself, right this minute.'

She moved to the phone on the kitchen wall, picked up the receiver.

'Put it down, Maryanne,' Luke said, a warning note in his voice.

She ignored him. There was no way she'd have any part in protecting him, any of them.

'I mean it, Maryanne. Put the phone down right now. Unless you want your own son and possibly even your daughter to face charges as well.'

She turned. 'What are you talking about?'

Andrew was standing at the kitchen door, eyes filled with fear. The same fear that blazed in her daughter's enlarged pupils.

'WHAT THE HELL ARE YOU TALKING ABOUT, LUKE?'

61

'If you call the guards, Andrew could face charges of manslaughter, too, or at the very least aiding and abetting. He drove her out to Kylemore last night, Maryanne. And he assisted me.'

Jesus Christ Almighty!

The phone fell from her hand, hanging from its cord like a bungee jumper.

'But you asked me to, Dad. You said you needed me ...' Andrew covered his face with his hands but not before she saw the tears on his cheeks.

'I know that, son, and I'm not trying to blame you for this mess. None of this is your fault. Or Victoria's, but she helped talk Lucia into going ahead with the abor– procedure. If this comes out, she could be implicated too.' Victoria began to sob, gripping her hair in her hands and twisting it. 'None of us could have foreseen this. It was just a tragic—'

'You bastard – you stupid, arrogant fucking bastard,' Maryanne said, her voice tight with loathing. 'Dragging our kids into it. I'll never forgive you for this.'

'You can call me whatever names you want, Maryanne,' he said, speaking to her as if she was the difficult family member of one of his patients. 'I just hope you understand that if you don't keep your mouth shut, it won't be just myself and Marcus who will have to pay the price for what happened.'

Maryanne had stared at her children's father, revolted. 'I actually didn't think it was possible to hate you any more than I already did.'

'This is all my fault,' Victoria howled. 'Lucia should be in work now.'

'Of course it's not your fault, Victoria,' Luke said. 'Marcus and Annette would have found out she was pregnant anyway, once she started to show. They'd have heard it from somebody. You need to keep it together. You can't fall apart. If the guards come to us asking about Lucia, when we saw her last, we all need to stick to the same story, OK? None of us knew she was pregnant.'

Was the man deranged? How could he possibly think they could get away with this?

'But the scan – there'll be a record of that and surely somebody saw her in the hospital,' Victoria said.

'There's no record. There was no official file on her. I did it on the QT. The scan was done outside clinic hours and there was nobody in the scanning suite over the weekend.'

'But the sonographer ...'

'There was no sonographer. I did the scan myself. I told you we wanted to keep it all hush-hush. The bottom line is that, as far as we are aware, Lucia was happy and healthy and we didn't have very much contact with her, which is all true,' Luke said.

'Oh, my God, the scan,' Victoria said, looking at her father in horror. 'Please tell me that wasn't a lie, that the baby did have anencephaly. I'd never have tried to talk her into it if I hadn't believed the baby wasn't going to survive, and Andrew would never have helped ...'

Jesus Christ, this just kept getting worse.

'That foetus was damaged. It was the product of incest. We were only doing what we felt was best for Lucia. It's done now and there's no going back. We all just need to keep it together ...'

'Where is she?' Andrew asked shakily. 'Is she still at home or has she been taken to the morgue?'

Luke cleared his throat. 'You're not listening to me, Andrew. How could she have been taken to the morgue? They'd do a post-mortem and find out how she died.'

'But ...' Maryanne raised her hands in confusion '... where is she, then? A doctor will have to pronounce her dead and it will be obvious she didn't die of natural causes. There'll have to be a post-mortem.'

Luke proceeded to outline for them the full horror of what Lucia's father and oldest brother Phillip were planning to do with her body under cover of darkness later that night.

Her children's lives had been destroyed by their involvement in the events of that night. The guilt would haunt them for ever. They had thrown themselves into their studies, and graduated with distinction, but each was messed up in their own way by what had happened.

Victoria tormented herself with thoughts of what Lucia would be doing now, whether she would be married with her own children if Victoria hadn't 'signed her death warrant', as she described it. If she hadn't betrayed her – hadn't blurted out the news of her pregnancy to her father, thriving on the drama of it all, knowing full well that Luke would tell Marcus – Lucia would probably be alive today. She might have lived happily ever after. And even if she hadn't, she'd still be alive.

They would have found out about the pregnancy eventually, of course, but Lucia hadn't planned on telling them until she was much further along and if, as Maryanne and her children strongly suspected, the scan had been fake and the foetal abnormality a lie, it would have been too late by then for anyone to stop it. The poor girl would probably have found out at some point that the father of her child was her half-brother, but people had got over worse and the baby might have been born healthy.

Victoria had fallen asleep on the night of Lucia's 'procedure' safe and sound in her own bed in her mother's house, hoping that everything had gone smoothly and that Lucia wasn't in any pain. It had tormented her ever since, the realisation that her sweet, innocent cousin, who had wanted a baby so badly, had been bleeding to death in her bed while Victoria had slept without a care in the world. She had been contacted by the gardaí when Lucia had gone missing. When had she seen her cousin last? they asked. What had her mood been like? A few days later, they were back to ask Victoria if Lucia had ever mentioned anything about being pregnant.

She had somehow managed to stick to the script her father had given her, her hysteria flattened by Xanax. She was still visibly upset, but that was only to be expected, given that her cousin had disappeared.

Victoria had gone down to six and a half stone, starvation her hair shirt of preference. She had been starving herself again since Cara had found out about Lucia and started digging, picking at the scab. She ate just about enough to function. Her diet was one of the only things in life that Maryanne's daughter could control. That and her career. Her marriage had been a disaster, which was not surprising, really, when she had married a man with an even smaller heart and bigger ego than her father, and her two sons walked all over her. It was clear she was in desperate need of psychological help, but that wasn't an option: she could never open up to a therapist about the root cause of her suffering.

Andrew's life had been ruined too. His first marriage had ended in a divorce so bitter it made Maryanne and Luke's break-up seem like a friendly spat, and it was looking likely that his second could be heading down the same road. He refused point blank to speak about what had happened to Lucia, or their role in it. It was as if he had packed it into a box, sealed it and stowed it away. He, too, used work as a distraction. Devoting himself to improving obstetric outcomes for the women of Ireland was his preferred form of penance.

And now Maryanne would have to tell Cara the truth about what had happened to Lucia that night. And to beg her niece not to go to the guards with what she knew. To beg her not to tell anybody outside the family. She had to get her to see that

Andrew and Victoria had paid dearly over the past thirty years for the consequences of actions they had taken when they were young, but their intent had never been to cause harm to their cousin. Her children had been pawns in a sickening plot concocted by trusted adults playing God that had gone horrifyingly wrong.

62

This year marks thirty years since the body of Lucia Casey was found buried in a bog in Connemara eighteen months after she went missing without a trace from her home in Galway city. What happened to the tragic twenty-two-year-old nurse's aide has remained a mystery ever since. Now amid calls for a cold-case review of the investigation, gardaí have received new information that suggests Lucia may have met her death on the day she disappeared, or in the early hours of the following morning.

With me in the studio today is Lucia's daughter, local journalist Cara Joyce, who, in a truth that really is stranger than fiction, only discovered the identity of her birth-mother earlier this year. Understandably stunned, she embarked on a mission to try to find out what had happened to Lucia Casey. She has provided gardaí with shocking new information, including the names of those she believes were involved in the murder of her mother, and she is calling on them now to bring the alleged perpetrators to justice. It is believed that three men, two in their eighties and one in his sixties, are currently helping gardaí with their enquiries.

Cara didn't bother to correct Paddy Tiernan, the presenter of the local radio morning show. It was unlikely that anybody would face a murder charge. As Donal McGann had explained to her, if charges were preferred – and there was no guarantee of this, given that no actual evidence linked anybody to Lucia's death – it would likely be involuntary manslaughter. You never knew who might be listening to the show, though, who might hear something that sparked a memory that could further strengthen the case she had presented to the gardaí.

She had met Tommy a number of times since Maryanne's shocking confession. He had brought her to visit the grave where Lucia was buried in Ballinakill cemetery. He was still living at home with his father, although they barely spoke to each other, these days. He told her he suspected he'd probably have been thrown out long ago if his father wasn't afraid he'd blab what he knew around the village, but he was happy to give a statement to the guards now if she wanted him to.

'I don't care any more what happens,' he had said to her. 'My life is a fuckin' mess and has been for as long as I can remember. I've tried more times than I can count to give up the drink, but I can't cope with life sober. It's shit enough when I'm pissed drunk. My father can throw me out and cut me off, I don't care. If I do this for Lucia, and for you, at least my life mightn't have been a total waste.'

Cara had weighed up the situation, the options open to her, going over and over it with Kian, her father and Paul. Closing the door on an inheritance that would change their lives was not a decision to be taken lightly, and she gave thought to a scenario in which she stayed quiet about what she knew, allowing Marcus to live out his remaining years an innocent man and doing nothing to scupper her chances of being included in his will. Would she be able to live with that? To sleep at night without being haunted by her dead mother?

In the end, the decision was quite easy.

The only way of getting justice for Lucia was for the people responsible for her death to be made to pay for it. It was as simple as that. Those people were Lucia's parents, her uncle Luke and her brother Phillip. Annette should currently be burning in the fires of eternal damnation if there was any substance to her religious beliefs. Cara still couldn't believe that the woman who had spent her life shoving her Christian values down other people's throats was the one who had come up with the idea to kill her own daughter's baby, but she certainly wouldn't be the first zealot to display an abysmal disregard for the values she preached so loudly. She had thrown the miraculous medal Annette had given her into the bin, then taken it out, washed it and put it into the bag for the charity shop. She mightn't be religious, but she wasn't sacrilegious either.

As far as Andrew and Victoria were concerned, she felt they had already paid for their involvement in the events that had led to their cousin's death. She had spoken to them both, had believed Andrew when he bowed his head and told her how often he regretted not being strong enough to say no to his father and his uncle, for allowing them to bully him into taking part in a back-room abortion and keep it from his mother. He hadn't stood a chance against such powerful, controlling men. And Victoria, those haunted eyes staring from her gaunt face, her poor starved body, how could she possibly have known the depths to which Lucia's family would sink? She hadn't been responsible for what had happened to her cousin even though she had clearly held herself so ever since.

As a mother, Cara had tried to put herself into Maryanne's shoes. If Victoria was Maisie, could she say she wouldn't have done exactly the same thing to protect her child? No, she could not. In fact, she knew without a doubt she would have done exactly the same thing.

So she had come up with a proposition she had brought to Maryanne, and Maryanne had brought to Luke to present to his brother and nephew. They were to be told that Cara knew what they had done. And she was going to the guards with it. Apart from the involvement of Andrew and Victoria. It would be tough enough on them if, as she hoped, their father, his brother and nephew were charged, and the truth of what had happened to Lucia was made public. Marcus, Luke and Phillip all needed to pay for what they had done. They, too, had been devastated by what had happened to Lucia, according to Maryanne, but they had caused her death, then callously dressed her body, thrown it into the boot of a car and driven to the remote bog where they had dumped it. They couldn't be allowed to get away with that.

Marcus had requested a meeting with her before she went to the guards with what she knew. She was prepared for it, knew he wouldn't go down without a fight.

She couldn't stomach seeing him face to face but agreed to a Zoom call, set up at his end by Phillip, who, she was sure, was lurking in the background of the sitting room at the house in

Kylemore where they had all played happy families not so long ago. Marcus was a crumpled, faded version of his usual dapper self.

'I'm willing to go along with your plan, Cara,' he said. 'I'll never forgive myself for what happened to Lucia and I know I deserve to be punished, but it's Luke, I'm afraid. He's refusing to agree to your proposal. I've tried talking to him, and I really can't understand how he could do it to his own children,' his voice hitched, 'but he said that if one of us pays, we all have to pay for what we did.'

'I see. Well, that is a pity, then.'

'Believe me, Cara, we've paid for our sins. We've lived with the guilt of this for thirty years now, every moment of every day. And we deserve to pay for what we did, Luke and I, but not Andrew and Victoria. Or Phillip. They were only doing what Luke made them do. My brother has never been an easy man, I'm afraid. We should never have agreed to go along with his insane plan.'

'We? Are you saying it was all Luke's idea?'

'Yes. We should have said no, Annette and I, of course we should, but we were under such pressure at the time, the pregnancy was advancing and, as you are now aware, Lucia's mental health was very fragile. She was at high risk of psychosis again after the birth. It really was a Catch-22 situation. If we told her the truth about the baby's father, she would have fallen apart but we couldn't not tell her because they might have stayed together and gone on to have more babies.'

She tutted faux-sympathetically. 'That's dreadful, but the thing I don't understand is why Luke would put pressure on you and Annette to get rid of his niece's baby. It's not like she was his daughter.'

She could picture the cogs turning in his brain, still running smoothly despite his age.

'Well, if Lucia had had that baby, it was bound to come out. That boy's mother would never have kept her mouth shut. It would have been a huge scandal. People love to see wealthy, successful families like ours brought down. It would have affected all of us, including Luke, and his reputation mattered to him more than anything.'

He was so convincing and there were probably elements of truth among all the lies that slid off his tongue so slickly, but in trying to pass the blame for the death of his daughter to his brother, Marcus Casey had only strengthened Cara's conviction that she was doing the right thing. He and Annette had had far more to gain by getting rid of her baby than Luke had. And far more to lose, too. Phillip might have been a pawn, like his cousins, but he had helped his father to dig a hole and bury his innocent sister in a bog. For that, he had to pay.

'The problem, Marcus,' she said, 'is that I don't believe a word that comes out of your mouth. You've been lying to me since the first day I met you and you're still lying to me. I fully intend going to the gardaí with all the information I have about Lucia's death, apart from anything to do with Andrew or Victoria. I'll leave that ball in your court, yours, your brother's and your son's. Maybe for once in your lives you'll do the right thing. Maybe you won't but I don't really care as long as I get justice for my mother.'

She wasn't sure what she would have done if they called her bluff. She had no plan B worked out. They didn't, though. Maryanne rang her that evening to tell her. In the event that the gardaí did press charges against them, Marcus and Luke had agreed that they would cooperate with the investigation, leaving out any mention of Andrew and Victoria. That way, the full sordid truth about Colman Ryan's parentage would never have to come out. The story would be that they were concerned for Lucia's mental health and the scan had shown up a serious congenital abnormality. It was a compromise Cara had agreed to accept, not to save the Caseys any face, but to protect Colman Ryan and his mother, two decent people who didn't deserve their whole world to be turned upside-down again.

She struggled a little with the idea of two elderly men spending their last years in prison and with the impact of this on Phillip's wife and children – also on Hugh, who had been kept totally in the dark about everything, and his family – but she reminded herself that, thanks to them, Lucia would never see old age. Had never even seen middle age. Never became the mother she had dreamed of being, never got married. Never had a life beyond twenty-two. There wasn't a day that went by that Cara didn't thank God that the Caseys had given her up for adoption, that her parents had adopted her and she hadn't grown up as Maeve Casey, an illegitimate child in the heart of that vile family.

She had made an appointment to see a bereavement counsellor in the new year. She couldn't keep the grief over the loss of her mother – the only one she had ever known –

at bay any longer. With the first Christmas without her fast approaching, the riptides of emotion that swept in out of nowhere, threatening to pull her under, were becoming more frequent and powerful. She knew she couldn't face alone the deluge that was heading her way, and needed professional help. Hers was a complicated grief as she also had the loss of her birth-mother to deal with.

As well as deferring the search for Lucia when her mother got sick, she and Kian had put off trying for a new baby, and she didn't want to put it off for much longer. They wanted a little sister or brother for Maisie, didn't want too big an age gap and there was no guarantee it would happen as quickly as it had the first time. No guarantee it would happen at all. She needed to face her grief and sort herself out before she got pregnant again, though.

She had arranged to meet Maryanne for lunch on Saturday, felt a closeness to her aunt that hadn't been there in years. Maryanne had admitted to pulling away from Kitty and Helena after Lucia's death, the stress of hiding what she knew from her sisters too much. Helena would be joining them, too. Cara was looking forward to seeing them.

On another positive note, Paul was helping them to get Kian's business off the ground. Cara had confided in her father about the shortfall on the school contract and he had mentioned it to Paul who, having paid off the mortgage on his apartment a few years ago, had 'a couple of bob to spare and only meself to worry about'. He had insisted he didn't want them to pay him back, but they had insisted just as vehemently that it was a loan they would be repaying in full. They would make it work somehow, without her grandfather's blood money, just like everybody else did, but her brother had taken the pressure off them in the short term.

Her original birth cert had finally arrived in the post that morning and, as expected, the space for her father's name was blank. And she was fine with that, having even less desire to find him after all the drama with her birth-mother. It was time now to move forward, to leave Lucia to rest in peace and to leave the past in the past.

EPILOGUE

Paul

It was such a relief to have it out in the open. After so many years. As painful as it had been for Cara, for them all.

They needed to start moving on with their own lives again now. To learn how to live in a world without their mother in it.

Of course, Cara didn't know the full truth. The only two people alive who knew it, now that his mother was gone, were his father and Paul.

Or PJ, as he had been known back then. One of three Pauls on the Salthill Devon soccer team: Paul Joyce (PJ), Paul Keady (PK) and Paul McCarthy (Paul Mack).

The only reason he had been in Kylemore that summer was that his mother had been laid up after her operation and Maryanne had come up with the idea of sending him to Connemara with Andrew for a couple of weeks. It had been such an awful time, the house so dull and lifeless without Clodagh in it, his mother mired in her grief while he and his father tiptoed around the edges of her. The hysterectomy had been another devastating blow, the loss of her womb an assault on her very identity.

Paul hadn't been keen on the prospect of spending a couple of weeks out in the sticks, and his parents certainly hadn't expected him to get on so well with Andrew's cousin Tommy or to enjoy himself so much that he wanted to stay longer. They had no idea at that point, of course, or for a long time afterwards, that the real attraction was Marcus Casey's daughter.

It was clear that Lucia had fallen for him: her shy smile, the sideways glances, the traitorous blushes that coloured her cheeks when he looked at her. She was so different from the girls at home, flirty, confident girls like Rachel Power, whom he had been shifting off and on for months. Lucia seemed so much younger than those girls even though she was the same age. He knew she fancied him, and that she didn't know how to play the hard-to-get games the other girls were so good at. He hadn't seen it as taking advantage of her: he had been genuinely attracted to her, loved the way her pretty little face lit up when she saw him.

He should never have let things get so serious so quickly but there was something about the magic of that place, himself, Tommy, Lucia and, the odd time, Andrew and the other younger Casey lads, left pretty much to their own devices to roam the mountain, lakes and bog. An escape for him from a home that felt at times like it might be sucked into the ground with the weight of the sadness inside it.

He had written back to her a couple of times after he had gone home, but the longer he was away from Kylemore, the more unreal that summer felt. Like a dream, a kind of Brigadoon that had disappeared back into the enchanted mist at the end of the summer. He had started his Leaving Cert year, and life was busy. He felt some fleeting pangs of guilt when her letters continued to arrive telling him how much she loved and missed him, but not enough to keep replying to them. He felt only relief when they stopped coming.

The first he knew of Lucia being pregnant was when Maryanne told them. He knew he had been Lucia's first, that there was nobody else, and that she hadn't named the father. He had been a terrified seventeen-year-old at the time, scared witless of the wrath of her father and his own. Of what people would think and say. He waited in dread for the axe to fall on him, for Marcus Casey to come banging on their door, but it never happened. Tommy was the only one who knew how close Paul and Lucia had been, but he knew nothing about his cousin's pregnancy.

Paul was so sure Lucia would eventually tell somebody, especially when she had the breakdown, but she never said a word.

So he, too, had said nothing.

And he continued to say nothing after his parents adopted his daughter and Lucia tried to steal her back, and for another seven years after that. He devoted himself to being the best big brother a little girl could ask for, the kind of brother Cara deserved, and for a long time he managed to convince himself that he could keep the truth hidden for ever.

He would say nothing when his mother made remarks like 'It's the oddest thing, but sometimes she really reminds me of Clodagh. It's like a weird kind of déjà vu ...'

And he said nothing all those times people observed that Cara was the image of her big brother. He and his parents just smiled politely, his parents saying that people saw what they wanted to see, blind to what was staring them in their own faces.

But then Lucia had gone missing. And her body was found in that bog, and about a week after the funeral, he heard his parents wondering if Cara's birth-father might have had anything to do with it.

It had all come spilling out then.

And everything had clicked into place for his parents.

Those times when Cara had looked at them in a certain way or did something that was so uncannily familiar. It would never in a million years have occurred to them that Cara was their grandchild if Paul hadn't told them. They would have carried on thinking how funny it was that their daughter had taken on so many of the mannerisms of her adopted family.

It was too late at that stage to try to explain to Cara and everybody else that the big brother she adored was, in fact, her father. They would have had to tell her about her mother too, open that whole can of worms, and how, his parents asked, in the name of God, could any child cope with that? As they said to Paul, they certainly weren't the first Irish family to rear a grandchild as their own child, and they wouldn't be the last. They assured him that the right thing to do for her was to try to protect her from the truth of her birth-parents for as long as they could, for ever if possible. And, as with any suppression of dark truths, the more years that went by, the more unthinkable the notion that they could ever bring it out into the light of day. Nobody would understand, least of all Cara.

Keeping the truth hidden for all these years had erected a barrier for Paul in maintaining any long-term relationships. There had been a couple of girls, one in particular, Laura, whom he had loved deeply, but the fact that he had secretly parented a child who had been reared as his sister created an invisible wedge between them. How could he tell Laura without telling Cara first? Easier to pull away, to break both their hearts.

When Maisie was born and Paul, now in his early fifties, found himself playing the role of uncle to his own granddaughter, he had gone through a crisis. He began to question whether continuing to conceal the truth from his daughter, now a mother herself, was really in her best interests. Was it the right thing to do? Or was it, in fact, the opposite? He had been bracing himself for a difficult conversation with his parents when his mother got sick and the conversation never happened.

When they had been forced to tell Cara the truth about her birth-mother, Paul tried to convince his father that it was time to bring everything into the open. He felt she deserved to know the full truth, but his father had thought it would be too much for her so soon after losing her mother and then Lucia. Paul was torn. Cara had been devastated that they had kept the truth about Lucia from her, had felt so betrayed, but what if his father was right? What if it was too much for her, if he pushed her over the edge? She had been through so much already over the past few months.

He decided to listen to his father. Now was not the right time. He would wait to tell her.

ACKNOWLEDGEMENTS

Growing up in Ireland in the eighties, it was impossible not to have heard the name Ann Lovett even if as a child myself I didn't fully understand what had happened to her. I just knew it was something bad. I remember being in my granny's kitchen and hearing Gay Byrne read out letters from girls like Ann, who like Lucia and Olive in this book, and so many others had 'got themselves into trouble'. I was well aware, even at the age of twelve as I was when Ann died in 1984, of the shame that surrounded the topic.

As I wrote this book, Ann and her heartbroken sister Patricia, who took her own life less than three months after Ann's death, and Joanne Hayes and all the girls and women who wrote to Gay Byrne and the many others who didn't, were at the forefront of my mind.

I had started writing Lucia's story when I came across Paula Meehan's beautiful and moving poem 'The Statue of the Virgin at Granard Speaks'. I highly recommend that you seek out and read the full poem along with the poet's other work. I am immensely grateful to Paula Meehan and Dedalus Press for giving us permission to publish the last four lines of her poem at the beginning of this book.

To my agent Faith O'Grady of the Lisa Richards Agency, who has believed in my writing from the very beginning, thanks so much for always having my back!

It has been such a pleasure to work with the Hachette Ireland team; a more encouraging, supportive group of people you'd be hard-pressed to meet. To my editor Ciara Considine, thank you for being such a joy to work with and for so gently steering me back on course when I'm heading off in the wrong direction. Thanks for all your support and for helping me to bring my work to a level I could never achieve on my own.

Heartfelt thanks to Breda Purdue, Publishing MD, and Elaine Egan, Publicity Director, for championing my writing with such passion and enthusiasm, and to Joanna Smyth, Marketing and Publishing Operations Director, for being so amazing at what you do. Thanks to Clare Stacey, Head of Design, for your fabulous cover designs. And thanks to everybody else at Hachette Ireland who has worked so hard to get my books out into the world including Jim Binchy, Sales MD, Ruth Shern and Siobhan Tierney, Sales Directors, Stephen Riordan, Publishing Assistant, and Shauna O'Regan, Operations Executive.

To copy editor Hazel Orme, I'm in awe of your talent. Thank you for helping to tighten and tweak my manuscript into shape. To actor Michele Moran, who did such a fantastic job on the audio book for my debut novel, you were the perfect fit.

To the authors who so generously blurbed this book and my debut, thank you so much. To see the names of writers of your calibre on my book covers is truly the stuff of dreams. To all the lovely authors I've met since the launch of my debut in

April 2023, thank you for being so welcoming, supportive and such great fun!

To Vanessa Fox O'Loughlin of writing.ie (aka author Sam Blake), thanks for all your support and for inviting me to be part of the Murder One International Crime Writing Festival 2023, one of many highlights of the past year. And to author Michelle Dunne for inviting me to be part of Spike Island Literary Festival 2023.

To all of the reviewers, bloggers, booksellers (especially the incredibly dedicated John Breen of Waterstones in Cork), librarians and book clubs out there, thank you for being so incredibly positive and supportive. Special mention to Mairead Hearne who gave me my first ever blog review on Swirl and Thread, and who is a great supporter of Irish writers. And to the members of the Rick O'Shea Book Club who really got behind my debut and helped spread word of mouth, you have no idea what a difference your positive comments make to us fragile-egoed writers.

To the amazing human dynamo that is Kate Durrant, I can't thank you enough for everything and I look forward to celebrating your own writing successes in the future. And on this topic, thank you to the pal who has accompanied me on every step of this journey since we did the Faber Academy course together, via email and DMs as we have yet to meet in person, Michele Howarth Rashman. You've written an incredible book and I can't wait to see *Glitterballs* hit the world.

To Ryan Tubridy, gifted broadcaster, champion of Irish authors and complete gentleman, I'll never forget the boost you gave me at the start of my writing career, and thank you for your kindness and empathy.

To Assistant State Pathologist Margot Bolster for again giving so generously of your time and expertise and for all your support.

To beautiful Connemara, thanks for the inspiration, and I hope you don't mind me taking some liberties with the setting. Thanks to the man in the bog who practically drew me a map of the best place to bury a body when I stopped to ask him for advice during a research trip, and who didn't bat an eyelid when I told him I had my husband's body in the boot as I drove off.

While the characters in my books are very much alive in my head, none of them exist in real life. However, anybody who worked for the late *Connacht Tribune* editor John Cunningham (JC) in Galway might recognise elements of him in Fitzie. Much-loved mentor, boss and great pal, JC was one of the good ones and his photo still keeps me company in my office at home.

As I wrote the scenes where Kitty was dying, it brought up memories of my own lovely mother Lucy's final days. We were fortunate to have been able to care for Mum at home until the end thanks to the support of the Galway Hospice homecare team and her great friend and neighbour Mary Costello who inspired Mary C.

This book is dedicated to my father Seamus, a proud Galwegian, who nurtured my love of reading and writing as a child. A man with a big heart that he proudly wore on his sleeve, Dad never tired of telling my siblings and me, and his grandkids, how much he loved us.

To my family and friends, including the four-legged ones, I'm incredibly grateful to have you all in my life. Thanks (again) to Sam, the three-legged Yorkie, who inspired Ralph, and to Daisy, the beautiful Connemara pony, who inspired Misty. And to my very special boy, Brody, the world's cutest cavapoo (IMO).

To Greg and our beautiful children, Lucy, Jake and Kiana, I love you so much.

And most of all, to you, the reader, thank you from the bottom of my heart.